"You're welcome to stay with us as long as you like…"

Remembering Kate's words, Jay linked his hands behind his head and despite the throbbing in his knee, smiled. She'd just invited him into her home.

It was perfect. Jay needed to work in the bookstore for only four weeks to get the inheritance. The sprawling one-story farmhouse was within city limits, fulfilling the residency requirement. He could stay out here for a week or so and discover everything he needed to know about Ms. McMann. He could talk to her, invite her confidences, snoop into her computer accounts. He'd simply follow his instincts to find out exactly what Kate McMann had done to make an old man want to leave her so much money. A chuckle escaped him. This might even be fun.

On the heels of that unkind thought came the image of her tear-stained face. The woman had been stricken by the events of the morning. But he knew she could be a loving mother and a manipulative gold digger at the same time. He'd known women with more conflicting traits.

This was a wonderful opportunity to unearth the truth—one he couldn't pass up.

Dear Reader,

It was with great pleasure that I accepted the editors' invitation to be part of this continuity series centering on a small town in Indiana. The other authors were a joy to work with, and their books are wonderful. I loved being able to use all their characters and tie up the series with an epilogue, too. But have no fear, all the books stand alone, so if you missed any of them, you can still catch up.

This is the story of a man who lost everything on a dreary Christmas Eve when he was twenty years old. He regains all he lost and much more, fifteen years later. I loved creating the hard-edged Jacob Steele, especially since, in the other four books, the characters speculated as to where he was and what he'd been doing.

This is also the story of a hardworking, trusting woman who gets fooled by Jacob, but the tables turn quickly, and for the rest of the book, Jay, as she knows him, struggles to come to terms with his feelings for her and the hurt he causes her. I've often proposed in my other books that people in love can forgive each other anything. Jay and Kate's story puts that theory to the test, but the power of Christmas and the love of family bring both of them through their difficulties.

I hope you like your visit to Riverbend, Indiana, and coming to know all the people who live there.

Please write and let me know what you think. Send letters to Kathryn Shay, P.O. Box 24288, Rochester, NY, 14624-0288 or e-mail me at kshay1@aol.com. Also visit my websites at http://home.eznet.net/~kshay and http://www.superauthors.com.

Sincerely,

Kathryn Shay

A Christmas Legacy
Kathryn Shay

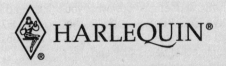

HARLEQUIN®

TORONTO • NEW YORK • LONDON
AMSTERDAM • PARIS • SYDNEY • HAMBURG
STOCKHOLM • ATHENS • TOKYO • MILAN • MADRID
PRAGUE • WARSAW • BUDAPEST • AUCKLAND

ISBN 0-373-70948-X

A CHRISTMAS LEGACY

Copyright © 2000 by Mary Catherine Schaefer.

To Barb Keiler, Pam Muelhbauer, Laura Shoffner,
Carol Wagner and Marian Scharf. It's been wonderful
working with you, ladies. Thanks for all your input, for
answering frantic e-mails and, mostly, for your friendship.

CAST OF CHARACTERS

Jay Lawrence: aka Jacob Steele, estranged son of Abraham Steele, owner of a computer company and River Rat

Kate McMann: Single mother and manager of Steele's Books

Hope and Hannah McMann: Kate's five-year-old twins

Ruth and Rachel Steele: Jay's twin maiden aunts and operators of Steele's Books

Mitch Sterling: Single father, owner/operator of Sterling Hardware and River Rat

Tessa Masterson: Unmarried, seven months pregnant and stranded in Riverbend

Tom Baines: Prize-winning journalist, estranged father and River Rat

Lynn Kendall: Minister and newcomer to Riverbend

Charlie Callahan: Contractor, temporary guardian and River Rat

Beth Pennington: Physician's assistant, athletic trainer and Charlie's ex-wife

Aaron Mazerik: Former bad boy, current basketball coach and counselor at Riverbend High

Lily Bennett Holden: Golden Girl, widow, artist and River Rat

Abraham Steele: Town patriarch and bank president, recently deceased

CHAPTER ONE

JAY LAWRENCE was surprised to discover that he hated Riverbend, Indiana, with a passion. He'd been unaware, after fifteen years of feeling dead inside, that such strong feelings could still pulse within him.

But when he drove past the large rectangular sign proclaiming Riverbend, Home Of The Rivermen, Population 8,793, Jay's heart—inured to most everything—bumped in his chest. He began to sweat, despite the early-November chill that penetrated his light-blue shirt and navy polo sweater. Even his knee ached from his old basketball injury and the recent physical stress from waterskiing.

About twenty yards beyond the sign, he slowed his rented dark green Volvo at a small, unassuming bungalow. The farmhouse. The place he'd spent the happiest days of his life after his mother died, being cared for by his aunts because of his father's busy schedule. Images, imprisoned in his unconscious, rattled the bars. *Oh, Ruthie, come look at Jacob's spelling test. He got another A… That three-pointer, son, from half court? I couldn't believe my eyes… Dad, Aunt Ruth, Aunt Rachel, I've been accepted at the University of Indiana on a full basketball scholarship.*

"All smoke and mirrors," Jay whispered hoarsely into the dim morning light. "Damn it." Hand curled into a fist, he pounded the steering wheel, shooting sharp pain up his arm. *That's it, think about the pain.*

He pressed the accelerator. In about five miles the town proper came into view—an image straight out of a Norman Rockwell painting. Its ornate three-story houses of brick or weathered clapboard nestled on streets lined with maples and elms, providing a stately prelude to the business district. Once he'd loved the quaint roadways with sparse traffic and just a few pedestrians strolling along at a lazy pace. He'd ridden his first two-wheeler down these sidewalks. Now when he left his co-op in New York City, he ran into scores of people. Once he'd loved the wide expanse of land surrounding the river, the woods to the south of town beckoning to eager young boys. He'd relished climbing the big sycamore tree and diving into the muddy water. Now the only open land he saw was Central Park, and the Hudson River was simply something to be crossed, usually in a traffic jam.

Studiously Jay avoided Riverbend High School, the one-story brown-brick building where he'd realized so many of his dreams. He also avoided the Steele house on East Poplar Street, though he had to pass by the bookstore. Sparing it only a quick glimpse, he nonetheless recalled the many wonderful hours he'd spent in the red clapboard building with its three-peaked roof and familiar sign, spelling out in elaborate calligraphy, *Steele Books*.

He turned off River Road, headed down Main Street and was confronted by the town square. Although the three-times-the-size-of-a-man trees were shedding their multicolored leaves onto the grass, he saw, instead, their green foliage, a fitting backdrop for his father, Abraham Steele. A town trustee and president of Steele

Savings and Loan, Abraham had waxed eloquently on the bandstand every Fourth of July. His six-foot military carriage, his wide shoulders, his dark-blond hair showing only hints of gray—to this day Jay resembled him, right down to the unusual dark eyes—Abraham always delivered speeches worthy of Daniel Webster. Jay had watched his father year after year with the innocent pride of a naive schoolboy who had believed the man was a good, honest citizen.

Not the lying bastard he'd later shown himself to be.

Damn, Jay wasn't going to do this. With ruthless self-discipline—his best quality—he pulled into the small parking area a block from the courthouse in front of the law offices of Harrison and James and blanked out the memories. Shutting off the engine, he stared at the storefront. Housed in an old cement-and-glass building that had recently had a facelift, the office was on the first floor. A row of windows dominated the lower level's facade. Once the script on them had read *Smith and Wesson.* It was a joke around town, but the Smiths were a prominent family and Wesson one of the founding fathers, so nobody laughed too loudly. Jay used to tease Sarah Smith about it when they parked by the river in his Ford. That was when he believed in women, too.

Banishing the ghosts, he threw open the door and exited the car. Hell, the town even smelled the same in the fall—the faint scent of the Sycamore River wending its way from the south. The rich loam of the earth. The woodsy smell of the decomposing leaves peppering the lawns.

Determined, Jay strode up to the front door, which opened as he reached it. A tall blue-eyed, dark-haired man dressed in casual black slacks and a light-blue shirt filled the doorway. In high school, his shoulders hadn't been so broad or his chest so muscled. The faint sprinkling of gray at his temples hadn't been there, either, of course. "Jacob, good to see you."

Jay donned his corporate persona, the one he'd honed to perfection. "Nick Harrison. I couldn't believe it when I got your letter."

"Believe it. I'm back." Nick held out his hand.

Jay shook it. "You said you'd never again set foot in this—what did you call it?—narrow-minded hick town."

A flash of regret and remembered pain clouded the man's eyes. Eyes that Riverbend girls had mooned over ever since he'd moved here in junior high. Nick had been accepted into the River Rats—the clique of kids who'd grown up in Riverbend and spent their childhood on the Sycamore River—though he hadn't been a member of the original group. "Yeah, and you planned to move back to town after playing pro ball and raise enough kids for a basketball team."

Noting that Nick didn't divulge why he'd returned, Jay didn't acknowledge his change in plans, either. He didn't really care why Nick Harrison had come back to Riverbend; he was only concerned with his own return to the town.

"Thanks for meeting me so early. I planned to get here yesterday afternoon, but my negotiations in Chicago ran over."

"No problem. Come inside."

Jay followed Harrison into a waiting area. A potted shrub sat in one corner and a set of windows faced the street; plush carpet covered the floor and grass-cloth wallpaper lined the walls. Nick led him into a spacious office that was perfectly appointed with a massive cherry desk, matching floor-to-ceiling bookcases with the requisite impressive law books. Ample lighting was provided by more big windows and chic recessed bulbs. Like Jay, Harrison had gone for the best.

Settling into a black upholstered chair, Jay watched as Nick took a seat behind the desk. "How shall we do this, Jacob?"

"Let's start with my name. I've legally changed it to Jay Lawrence."

Only the slight arch of a brow indicated the lawyer's surprise. And why not? For years Jay had actually believed his father. *You're a Steele, son. That comes with responsibility. You have to set an example.*

"Fine. I'll make a note on the inheritance papers." Nick eased back in his chair. "Quite frankly, I was shocked to hear from you after last July's letter." From a folder, he fished out the terse missive Jay had dashed off when Nick had finally tracked him down to notify him of his father's death and that he'd been bequeathed a considerable inheritance. Jay's response read only, "I decline all claim to any money or property associated with the Steele family."

Straightening his shoulders like the good little soldier he'd been taught to be, Jay made his voice intentionally low—and cold. "My circumstances have changed."

That was an understatement. His circumstances had nosedived after he'd rejected on principle a seven-figure bequest. Instead of having enough cash to buy into a software company, ComputerConcepts, and become a partner, as he'd planned, he'd come up short. He'd ended up needing something from Abraham Steele, after all.

"So you said when you called."

"Is there a problem with that? Legally, I mean?"

"No. As I indicated in my response—" Nick held up another letter "—not fulfilling the terms of the bequest is the only way to nullify the inheritance."

"And those terms are that I come back to Riverbend for eight weeks to live before the end of the year. And to work at Steele Books for half of that." Though outwardly calm, inwardly Jay fumed; even from the grave, his old man was controlling him. But he had little choice, as Mallory had succinctly put it.

I had no idea ComputerConcepts was so strapped for cash. Originally Daddy said your investment of 250K would do it. Now we need three times that. But you'd be half owner, darling, if you bought in with that much money, and combined with my voting stock, we'll control the company.

"Would you like to hear the rest of the terms?"

Unnerved, Jay stiffened. "The rest of them? Are you telling me I have to do something else?"

Brows knitted, Nick shook his head. "No. Actually, it deals with what happens if you don't fulfill the terms."

"I don't particularly care about that."

"You might. If you leave Riverbend before the stipulated time, or if you fail to work at the bookstore for half of that, the Steele assets revert to someone else."

"Ruth and Rachel, I presume." Though he fought it, saying their names for the first time in fifteen years made his insides ache. He experienced again the yawning, cavernous sadness at what he'd left behind.

"No, not your aunts."

"Then who?"

"A woman. Mary Katherine McMann."

Jay gripped the arms of the chair. "A love interest

of my father's?'' he asked nastily. "After him to get the store?''

Despite his professional demeanor, Nick chuckled. "I doubt it, though Abraham did spend a lot of time at the bookstore the last five years of his life.''

"Then why doubt it?''

"For one thing, she's younger than you.''

"So?'' He wouldn't put it past Abraham.

"Second, everybody in town, including Kate— which she goes by—believes the bookstore belongs to your aunts. Abraham told me Kate knew nothing about his finances or the inheritance terms.'' Harrison smiled fondly. "Besides, she's a single mother with five-year-old twin girls and total responsibility for the bookstore. She wouldn't have time to be involved with your father.''

"Every woman has time for a sugar daddy.''

"Kate has a stellar reputation in town as a hard worker. She goes to church, is a great mother. And she looks like the freckle-faced girl-next-door. She's more the Girl Scout type than a femme fatale.''

Though he wondered why the lawyer felt the need to defend this woman—a love interest of his own, perhaps?—Jay held up his hand, where a Rolex peeked out from his cuff. "Spare me. I know for a fact appearances can be deceiving.''

Shrugging, Nick said, "Fine. For the record, I think Abraham wanted her to have the store because she's been running it for Ruth and Rachel for so long. He included the farmhouse in the deal, too—again only if you fail to meet the terms—probably because Kate and her children moved out there when your aunts bought the house next to the bookstore so they could live in town. I think Kate rents the farmhouse from them...well, technically from Abraham.''

''The farmhouse is included in this little game? I thought Abraham signed it over to Ruth and Rachel.''

''Not legally. Just like the bookstore, it's always been in your father's name, though he settled into the brick house on East Poplar Street after he married your mother. You spent most of your time out at the farmhouse, though, didn't you?''

Jay just stared at him.

Nick shifted in his seat. ''Why did you call this a game?''

''Because that's what it is, making me do penance by returning to Riverbend.''

''I'm not sure of his motives, Jac—Jay. In any case, Kate will get everything—the bookstore and its rare books, the farmhouse and all the surrounding land—if you give up your claim by leaving Riverbend.''

Over my dead body, Jay thought viciously. He hadn't wanted the inheritance, but since he'd been backed into a corner, he'd take what was his. Selfishly and without guilt. Just like dear old Dad.

Jay shook his head. ''She won't get anything. I'm prepared to live in this godforsaken town for two months.''

''There's an apartment over the bookstore you could stay in. It's been rented off and on, but it's empty now. I lived there myself when I first came back.''

''Maybe.''

''What will you do with the property after the first of the year?''

Wanting to end this discussion, Jay's tone was purposely curt. ''Is that any of your concern?''

"No, of course not. Just idle curiously. And we used to be pretty good friends."

"If you're interested, I'll let you know my plans." Jay thought for a minute. "As a matter of fact, I'd like to hire you as my lawyer right now to represent my interests here."

"I'd be glad to."

They shook hands on it.

"Fine," Jay said. "Meanwhile, I'd appreciate your not informing anyone I'm back yet. I want to tell Ruth and Rachel myself." He scowled. "But first, I'm going to check out this Kate McMann. See what's really going on." He glanced at his watch. "What time does the bookstore open?"

"It's closed on Sunday."

Jay shook his head. "Small towns."

"Jay, I really don't think she knows the terms of the will."

"The hell she doesn't. Just because Abraham told you that doesn't mean she didn't know. I'll bet my new Jag she cooked up this creative little scheme. Actually, it's a perfect ploy. They had to expect I wouldn't come back, so this way she doesn't look like the gold-digging mistress she obviously is and still gets everything." Jay nodded toward the desk. "Are there papers to sign?"

Nick produced the required documents. When Jay was done he stood, pasted on a phony smile and extended his hand for a shake, then headed for the exit. When he reached the door, he heard behind him, "Jay," and halted. "If you hadn't been in Europe when your father died...if you'd found out in time, would you have come back for the funeral?"

In truth, Jay couldn't answer that. Didn't want to

answer that. Looking back over his shoulder, he said, "Of course not. Why would I?"

RACHEL STEELE sat bolt upright in her antique brass bed and slapped her hand over her wildly beating heart. Disoriented, she scanned her surroundings and took in the faded pink-flowered wallpaper, the Tiffany lamps and the wooden dressers. The clock on the Duncan Phyfe nightstand winked 7:30 a.m. She'd slept in. It was Sunday and she needed to be at church in an hour.

There was a soft knock on the door. "Rachel, dear, are you awake?"

"Come in, Ruthie."

Her twin opened the door. Still in her long purple bathrobe, fuzzy slippers and the net she wore to bed to keep the curl in her short white hair, Ruth bustled in like a cheerful maid carrying tea. "I brought you some— What's wrong?"

Rachel smiled. Twin intuition was on red alert. "I overslept."

Ruth's eyes dissected her, as they had when Ruth had searched for a way to talk Rachel into skinny-dipping in the river with the Mercer boys, or when she'd tried to convince Rachel to go to college in Chicago, or when Ruth wanted to open a day-care center before they'd taken over the bookstore. "Did you have another dream?"

Weary, Rachel sank back into the pillows and nodded.

Setting the tea on the bureau, Ruth crossed to the bed and perched on the edge. She gave Rachel her glasses, then grasped her hand. Rachel took comfort in the contact. Ruth said, "You're as cold as a cadaver, and it's warm in here."

Rachel just stared at her sister.

"You dreamed about him again, didn't you."

"Yes." Rachel picked at the knitted afghan covering her bed.

"It's because Abraham's gone, dear."

Valiantly Rachel battled back the tears for the brother she'd never get used to losing. "I know, but this one was so real. Jacob was back in town."

Ruth's dark eyes flared angrily. "It's because you expected him for the funeral, and in the months since, you kept thinking he'd walk through the door."

"I can't believe he didn't come."

"I can. Something terrible happened between Jacob and Abraham all those years ago. We'll never see him again." She puffed out her chest. "You have to accept that."

"I won't. We'll see Jacob, and soon. I know it." Rachel patted her heart, still keeping up its rapid tattoo under her light flannel gown. "Here."

"Yes, well, maybe he'll come to *our* funerals."

Rachel straightened her shoulders. "That remark is un-Christian and beneath you." Though everybody in town believed Ruth ran roughshod over her, no one except maybe Lynn Kendall, their young minister, and Katie understood the real dynamics of their relationship. "I know he'll be back, Ruth. Just like I knew when he and Sarah got stranded up the river that time. Just like I knew when he hurt his leg in practice at Indiana his sophomore year. Just like I knew when he and Abraham had it out the last time we saw him."

Ruth stood and held herself erect like the prim schoolteacher she used to be. "All right, dear. Your psychic powers with Jacob are duly noted." Then more softly, "I just hate to see you get your hopes up and then be disappointed.'' Ruth crossed to the tea service and poured the Earl Grey, its sweet fragrance filling Rachel's nostrils. Adding just a dab of cream and sugar, she returned to the bed, handed Rachel the tea and plumped the pillows. Though Ruth was a ''tough old bird,'' as Abraham used to call her—in return Ruthie had labeled him Big Brother—she had a tender, nurturing side to her, too. ''Now, drink your tea and haul your—''

''Ruthie!''

''—butt and hit the shower. You need to practice the organ before the service to get your old bones warmed up.''

''My bones are just fine,'' Rachel muttered around the Wedgwood teacup from the set their mother left them.

And so was her heart. Though it still ached for the boy she'd lost, the boy she and Ruth had practically raised when Mary Steele died, Rachel firmly believed they would see Jacob again.

But to help things along, she'd discuss it with God at services today.

HER SHOULDERS ACHING, Kate raised the ax over her head and brought it down hard into the wood. The log split neatly in the center, drawing a satisfied grin from her. She was getting as good as Paul Bunyan at this. A slight breeze teased a lock of her shoulder-length hair from its ponytail and cooled her sweaty brow. Tucking back the wayward strands, she made a second chop, then a third until the big log was in several pieces. Bending over, she tossed each one into the wheelbarrow. That filled it, so she hid the ax behind the pile Mitch Sterling, a friend in town who was like a brother to her, had delivered just yesterday. *I got a cord of uncut wood, Katie. You can have half dirt cheap. I'll even deliver it.* Though she never accepted charity, she was a world-class bargain hunter and never passed up an opportunity to save money. Just to be safe, she'd drop by Mitch's hardware store tomorrow with some of those brownies he loved. Mentally she added, *Bake brownies* to her Kitchen to-do list.

As Kate grasped the handles of the wheelbarrow, wincing at the blister that had formed beneath her worn gloves, Hannah yelled, "My turn to ride." Kate groaned inwardly, wondering how she'd gotten into *this* game. Her five-year-old daughter raced toward her, blond hair flopping wildly in the wind that had just picked up, her jacket open, her denim overalls already dirty. Hope, Hannah's twin, dressed in pretty pink sweats that could be featured in a detergent commercial for the "after" shot, was rooted to the spot, two fingers stuck in her mouth.

Kate released the wheelbarrow and neatly intercepted Hannah as she drew near it. Encircling her waist firmly with her hands, she chided, "Hold on, baby." Kneeling to be face-to-face, she stared straight into slate-blue eyes exactly like her ex-husband Billy's. "Is it really your turn, Hannah?"

The devil danced in and out of her wild child's expression as she nodded. Kate continued to give her the stern-mother look that women miraculously inherited in the delivery room. Finally Hannah shook her head.

"It's not nice to lie, Hannah, or to hurt Hope by cheating her out of a turn. Mommy's told you many times it's a sin to lie and cheat." *Too bad nobody told your daddy.*

Sheer horror brought a quiver to the little girl's lips,

as if the Headless Horseman had spoken to her. "I
don't wanna hurt Hope."

"I know you don't, honey. But you *know* Hope
would give you anything you asked for." *And do anything you want, unfortunately.*

"I'm sorry, Mommy."

Kate kissed Hannah's forehead. "Now go tie up the
kites. The wind's stirring and we don't want to lose
them."

"Mine's the best," she said proudly.

Kate angled her head.

"Mine and Hope's," Hannah added quickly. "I
can't wait to show Allison." Allison Pennington was
the twins' best friend. Her parents, Grace and Ed were
older than Kate, as was Allison's aunt Beth. Kate had
gotten to know her better when she'd come back to
town this fall and become engaged for the second time
to Charlie Callahan, another Riverbender who watched
out for Kate.

She glanced at the kites they'd stayed up too late last
night making. After they'd finished, she done her
chores, spending the hour a day she allotted to fix up
the spare room, doing the laundry and putting the last
touches on the new dresses she'd sewn for the girls to
wear to church today. She'd fallen into bed at one, long
after the house was quiet.

Hannah scooted away and Hope skipped to the
wheelbarrow. She stopped, gave Kate a hug of thanks,
though not a peep of complaint escaped her lips, and
climbed onto the pile. Kate's back ached at the added
weight, but she pushed the wood to the enclosed porch
off the back of the house, which had been winterized
to hold things like the washer and dryer, and also
served as a shed to store the wood. She sang "Sixteen

Tons,'' all the way. Hope giggled and sang along like the happy camper she always was.

After the girls helped her stack the wood in the shed, they returned to their kites with her admonishment, "Zip up your jackets, ladies, it's getting cold." Kate checked her watch. She could spend another half hour on the wood before she showered and dressed for church. Facing the twins, who were trying unsuccessfully to get the kites in the air, she amended her timetable to fifteen minutes for wood, fifteen for flying. It was unusually windy for this early in the morning, so she'd take advantage of it.

Chopping wood again, Kate smiled at how even the decorations they'd chosen for their kites illustrated the differences between her two girls. Rachel had ordered blank kites for the store, three of which she gave to the McManns. On hers, Hope had meticulously colored a peaceful, sun-drenched day complete with a pastel sky and green, green grass. Hannah's sported hungry fire, dragonlike monsters and dark colors.

And what did you draw, Katie girl? Abraham would have asked.

She groaned at her choices. She'd created a happy family: two girls, two grandma-types, a grandpa, a mom and dad, and a dog. She'd thought about adding a baby boy, but Kate didn't want to tempt the fates. She'd be happy with just a little more than she had now.

A squeal from Hannah made Kate's head jerk up; the ax missed its mark, the wind gusted and a spray of sawdust hit her in the face. Some of it lodged in her eye and stung mercilessly. She yelped, which drew the attention of the girls. Abandoning the kites, they raced to her.

"Should've bought those goggles in the hardware store last week," she groused, slapping her hand over her eye. But Mitch had told her they were going on sale tomorrow, so she'd decided to wait.

"Mommy, you okay?" Hannah asked.

Hope stared, wide-eyed, and stuck her fingers in her mouth again.

"I got something in my eye. Head into the house."

Hannah said, "But I want—"

Gently Kate interrupted. "Hannah, Mommy's hurt. Get into the house *now*."

Small hands crept toward each other. Their fingers locked, the girls pivoted as one and marched into the porch.

Like the Cyclops from Homer's *Odyssey,* Kate tracked their progress with her one good eye. Inside, she secured the hook on the screen door—placed as high as her arms could stretch—and turned to the twins. "Sit down on the bench next to the washer and dryer. I'll be right back."

"What about our kites?" Hannah whined.

"They'll be fine for a few minutes. You can watch them from the window."

Hope knelt on the bench and faced outward. Hannah pouted. Kate's patience frayed. "Hannah, show some consideration." The girl nodded and repeated her sister's actions.

Shaking her head, Kate hurried to the kitchen sink to wash out her eye. The process stung even more than the grit. As she doused it, she bemoaned the mistakes she'd made raising her kids. She'd spoiled them rotten, because it had taken seven long years to conceive them. Then, after she'd left Billy, and the twins were born, they became the center of her universe. Ruth and Rachel's doting made the situation worse, but Kate knew they did it because they missed their nephew so, the mysterious Jacob Steele, who'd broken their hearts by abandoning his family when he was twenty. Kate allowed the aunts to spoil her twins, partly to ease that loss and partly because it made Kate feel as though *she* had a real family. All told, Hannah had turned into an imp of *The Ransom of Red Chief* proportions, and Hope, though sweet-natured, always went along with her antics.

As she finished up at the sink, Kate decided to put *Pray for better guidance* on her Spiritual to-do list.

INSTEAD OF PULLING into the driveway—he didn't want to alert Ms. Mary Katherine McMann to his arrival— Jay swung his car to the opposite side of River Road and parked on the street. He waited as a few cars whizzed by, carelessly fast even for this far out of town, then opened the door, wincing as he wrenched his knee sliding out. Damn good thing he'd brought his brace. He'd need to wear it if his knee got any worse. Ironically, it was a reminder of the halcyon days that had begun and ended in Riverbend. He stood for a minute by the Volvo, staring at the farmhouse. It had not worn well. The white clapboard needed a paint job, though the roof looked new. The porch appeared rickety. Concrete steps leading to the road had been added, as well as a path to the backyard.

He was about to push away from the car when he saw a kite float up and out from the side of the house. Then everything happened at once.

First, one towheaded child popped out of nowhere and ran toward the road. Another followed.

The kite sailed higher.

Jay straightened and cupped his hands to warn the kids about running into the road.

A pickup truck came over the slight rise and barreled down the road at about forty miles an hour, windows open, some god-awful heavy-metal rock blaring from the radio. Its engine grumbled noisily from a front end hefted off the ground.

As if guided by an invisible hand, the kite sailed over the road and the kids darted out after it.

Jay lunged toward them. Seeing him—at six-four *he* was visible over the raised hood of the car, though the children were not—the teenager in the truck hit the horn and braked. Jay scooped up a girl in each arm and swept them across the pavement, right into the concrete steps. Unable to stop the momentum, he lifted his leg to take the brunt of the impact.

A roar erupted from his chest as his injured knee connected with the solid stone of the step. Pain splintered his leg, but he angled his body and held on tight to cushion the kids' fall as he crashed to the ground.

CHAPTER TWO

WITH EVERY OUNCE of strength she had, Kate willed back the stark panic that bubbled inside her. Summoning false bravado, like Jane Eyre facing down Mr. Rochester, she straightened the covers on the old sleigh bed and plumped the pillow behind the man who had saved the lives of her children. Nightmarish images tried to surface in her mind, but she fought them back. There'd be time enough later to deal with the demons. Right now, she was grateful for the angel she'd been sent.

"Are you comfortable?" *That's stupid, Kate. His face is pale with pain.*

He watched her through thick lashes, his brown eyes, undiluted by flecks of green or gold, looking somehow familiar. "Not exactly."

"Now that we have you in the house, I'll call the doctor."

"I don't need a doctor."

"I can understand why you wouldn't want an ambulance to take you to the hospital, but a doctor will be glad to pay a visit out here. It's a small town. People do those kinds of things here." She nodded at his knee, which she'd propped higher than his heart and immediately iced after she and Jesse Carmichael—the kid driving the truck—had practically carried the man into her house.

"As I told you, it's an old injury." His voice was hoarse, probably from pain. He raked back his dark-blond hair and shrugged mile-wide shoulders. He was a big man with the build of an athlete. "I know how to take care of it." Angling his head to the door, he asked, "Are the boy and Chief Staver gone?"

"Yes. And the police chief called Jesse's parents about the accident. They'll talk to him about driving safety." She smiled weakly. "Now I can just take care of you."

The man stiffened. "You don't have to take care of me."

"Of course I do." Again the emotion in her throat tried to get out. "You saved my daughters' lives." She clenched her hands behind her until they hurt so she wouldn't cry. "And I don't even know your name."

"Jay Lawrence."

"I'm Kate McMann. The twins are Hope and Hannah."

He stared at her.

"I suppose you're wondering how this happened," she said.

"How did it?"

"I was chopping wood before church, and the girls were playing with the kites we made last night. Some sawdust flew into my eye. I came in to wash it out."

"You left five-year-olds alone outside when you live on such a busy road?"

She knew she deserved the censure in his voice, though his reasoning was wrong. "No, I brought the girls in with me. I sat them down in the back porch and told them to stay put. I locked the hook at the top of the screen, way above their heads. Apparently Hannah dragged over a stool, stood on it and managed to unlock it.'' Kate shook her head, horrified by what had almost happened. ''I never imagined she'd disobey me so blatantly.'' Tears misted her eyes, but she didn't let them fall. ''Thank God you were there.''

''God had nothing to do with it.'' He seemed to say the words by rote, as if to himself, not to her.

In any case, it was an odd remark. But she was too shaken to discuss theology with him. If she could just keep it together for a few more minutes... ''I saw it happen from the side of the house.''

His quick intake of breath told her he understood, on some level at least, the significance of witnessing the two most important people in your life almost lose theirs. It was the only emotion he'd shown in the past hour.

''It was like watching a movie. I saw Hannah run out there first, then Hope follow. Then the truck came over the rise.''

''Ms. McMann, you don't—''

She shook her head. ''You ran right in front of that souped-up clunker.'' Her voice caught, but he said nothing. ''If Jesse hadn't been able to stop, you would have been killed.'' Again Jay Lawrence presented an almost perfectly blank face. His cheeks were pinched with pain and his lips thinned, but the average person would have had *some* reaction to a near-death experience and to saving the lives of two little girls. ''Why did you do it?'' she asked him.

At first it seemed as if he might not answer. Then he said reluctantly, ''I knew the driver couldn't see the girls. He could see me, though.''

Sitting on the edge of the bed, she took his hand. Sprinkled with dark-blond hair, it dwarfed hers. She squeezed it gently. "You risked your life for my children. I...don't know how... I can't thank..."

Oh, no, the tears were coming. She'd held them at bay during the crisis, helped Jay into her house, put the girls into separate rooms, called the police and dealt with the careless teenage driver. But now, in front of this stranger, she was going to lose it, like the whiny little victims in the fairy tales she told Hope and Hannah never to imitate. Digging her fingernails into the palm of her free hand, she tried to quell her response.

But it was all too much. When she'd seen the girls run out into the street, Kate thought her life was over, really over, this time. She'd been through a lot in the past—catching her husband in bed with another woman, having the twins come two months early and dealing with their birth alone, then the continued anxiety around being their sole provider. But she rarely let herself cry. Now she was powerless to stop. The emotional flood erupted like water held behind a weak dam, and it came despite her embarrassment. She bowed her head as the tears fell.

Jay gripped the hand that held his. Through a whirlpool of terror and disbelief, she heard him say, "Shh. It's over. It's all right."

Tears became sobs. Tugging her hand away, she braced her elbows on her knees, buried her face in her hands and wept.

After a moment, Kate felt something in her hair. His hand. It rested lightly on her crown, then stroked downward tentatively. His touch was comforting and she leaned into it. Accepting solace from anybody was rare for her, and to take it from this stranger was crazy, but she couldn't help herself.

He continued the motion and the soothing words until she quieted, removed her hands from her face and straightened. He let his arm drop to the mattress.

Grabbing a tissue from the side table, she averted her eyes, blew her nose and raked the hair off her face. "I'm sorry. I can't remember the last time... It's just that..." She shrugged helplessly.

"I understand."

"No, really, I'm not a weeping willow. I'm—" She stood abruptly. "Look, I'm not the important one. You are. You're obviously in a lot of pain. Please let me call a doctor, or at least the physician's assistant, Beth Pennington, to come out and look at you."

His eyes flared at the mention of Beth's name. She could have sworn it was with a spark of recognition. "No." More quietly he said, "This is a chronic injury. I first got it when I was in college. It'll swell and be sore for a few weeks. All I need is the ice, some pain pills and rest."

"Do you carry the medicine with you?"

"Yes, along with my brace. My knee's been bothering me since I—" He stopped as if he'd said too much. "In any case, the pills are in my car—in my shaving kit."

"I'll get it for you."

He tried to get up. "No..." Then he fell back into the pillows. "I guess I'm fairly immobilized." Under his breath he said, "Damn."

"I'm sorry." She gazed down at him. "Could this keep you laid up for a while?"

"Yes."

"Will your family need to be contacted to come and get you?"

"I have no family," he said tightly.

"Friends, then."

He shook his head.

"Are you from around here?"

"I used to be."

"Oh. Of course, you're welcome to stay with us as long as you like." She glanced at his knee. "Until you're better or someone can come for you."

"No, I—" He cut off his response.

"Let me go get the medicine. We can talk about this when you aren't in so much pain."

Bending over, she adjusted the ice on his knee, smiled weakly at him and held out her hand. "The keys?"

He tossed them to her. "The small traveling case has my shaving kit. So bring that in." Then he added, "Please."

"Be right back."

She sensed his eyes on her as she left, as if he was analyzing her. The feeling was odd, and she wondered if she was missing something.

YOU'RE WELCOME to stay with us as long as you like...until you're better or someone can come for you.

Jay linked his hands behind his head and, despite the throbbing in his knee, smiled. What a setup. She'd just invited him into her home.

It was perfect. He needed to work in the bookstore only four weeks to get the inheritance. This sprawling one-story farmhouse was within the city limits, fulfilling the residency requirement. He could stay out here, anonymously, for a week or so, play the injured hero and discover everything he needed to know about Ms. McMann. Had she used his aunts to get control of the store and keep a roof over her head? Maybe she was hoping to get everything once they died. *Hot damn.* He could talk to her, invite her confidences. His gaze rested on the computer across the room. If he was lucky, her business accounts were on that little baby, as well as her personal finances. He could do it while she worked at the bookstore, blissfully ignorant of his machinations. He could even snoop through her personal belongings.

A chuckle escaped him. If he believed in God, he'd thank Him for the golden opportunity. But since Jay Lawrence had learned to believe only in himself after the showdown with his father fifteen years ago, he'd simply follow his instincts to find out exactly what Mary Katherine, aka Kate, McMann had done to cause an old man to make her the possible beneficiary of so much money.

It might even be fun.

On the heels of that unkind thought came the image of her tear-ravaged face. The woman had been stricken by the events of the morning. Harrison was right. She really did look like a hardworking single mom in her faded sweatshirt and jeans, her reddish hair yanked back in a loose ponytail. Her hazel eyes had been filled with such terror it affected even him.

But hell, she could be a loving mother and a manipulative bitch at the same time. He'd known women with more conflicting traits. He'd read somewhere that Marie Antoinette had been a good mother. Anyway, this was the perfect opportunity to discover the truth.

He closed his eyes to stop seeing the room that had been his as a child. He'd slept in this very sleigh bed on the nights and weekends he'd stayed with his aunts. It was no use. The yellow wallpaper had faded, but all the furniture was the same. One wall still sported shelves of his basketball trophies and his Larry Bird posters. The computer and desk were new. But the whimsical lamp with the basketball base was still there. He wondered idly what had happened to his books. He pictured Ruth and Rachel reading to him as a child, or hovering over him when he was sick with flu and they'd nursed him back to health. The irony of recuperating here now didn't escape him.

"Is this it?" a soft voice asked from the doorway.

She was more composed. Her face had a healthy glow, as if she spent a lot of time outside. *I was chopping wood before church...* Her eyes were greener, like the multifaceted marbles he and the other River Rats had stashed in secret hiding places. In those eyes was determination. Very different from the cream puff who, just a few minutes ago, had sobbed at his bedside. He'd think about that discrepancy later.

"Yes, that's the bag."

Crossing the room, she handed him the small Louis Vuitton case Mallory had bought him in Paris. Setting a glass of water on the nightstand, she watched as he unzipped the case, found the pills and gulped them down. Automatically she checked her watch and smiled. "Every four hours?"

He nodded. She indicated his leg. "The ice should come off in a few minutes."

"Twenty minutes on, twenty off," he said. "I know the drill." His voice was cold, as biting as a winter wind.

"I'm sorry for this inconvenience," she said.

"It's not your fault."

Her expression said, *Yes, it is.*

For some reason he felt the need to distract her. Make her feel better. It was as foreign to him as laughing, and he almost didn't recognize it. He glanced out the door. "Where are they?"

Her naturally arched eyebrows knitted. "One is in the room they share, the other is in my room. No books, TV or toys are permitted."

Almost chuckling, he said, "Harsh punishment."

"They ain't seen nothin' yet." She shook her head. "The worst for them is separation. The next worst thing is being cut off from their books."

An opening to get to know this family. "Not their toys?"

"No, although they love the kites Rachel got them."

Jay's heart sped up. *Jacob, I got you this at the store today. It has your favorite character on it—Zorro. If you do all your chores, Ruthie and I will fly it with you.* He said critically, "They love those kites a little too much."

She blanched. "I know." And bit her lip. "So, you'll stay until you can get around better?"

"Ah, yes, I will. I'm on a working vacation for the next few weeks. Scouting out some property, dealing with some people out here." Not exactly a lie. "A lot of it I can do with a computer and my cell phone."

Her eyes darted to the desk. "You can use my computer."

Score one point for the bad guy. This was going to be a piece of cake. He'd be sure to hide his laptop. "That would be great."

"Is the cell phone in your car?"

"Yes. I'll get my gear later."

She studied him with knowing-mother eyes. "You're not used to anybody taking care of you, are you, Mr. Lawrence."

"Shouldn't you call me Jay?" He shot her a full-bodied male smile that Mallory said could charm a snake.

A hint of female interest crossed her face. "Yes, if you'll be staying here. And of course, since you…" She shivered. A few seconds later she seemed to pull herself together. "Call me Kate. I'll introduce you formally to the twins from hell in a few hours. They're in solitary confinement until then."

Again he had to bite back a grin. "Will I meet your husband soon?" he asked, though he knew she was a single mother.

"I'm divorced. Billy rarely even visits."

So there is something wrong with you, sweetheart. Are you too heartless and calculating? Frigid, maybe? Abraham was old…

"I didn't mean to pry." He almost winced at the outright lie. He intended to pry, big time. When he was done with her, he'd know her inside out, right down to what color of underwear she wore. And she wouldn't have a clue what hit her.

"Let me remove that ice pack," she said. When she grabbed it, he noticed her nails were cut short, her skin roughened. He loved long red fingernails on a woman. They were so feminine. She flinched when she picked up the ice.

"Something wrong?" he asked

"Just a blister." She crossed the bedroom to the bathroom that his aunts had had installed for him and dumped the ice. From the doorway she asked, "What shall I get from your car?"

"My cell phone's in the glove compartment." The laptop was stowed under the seat. "The big bag in the trunk is probably too heavy."

She grinned as if he'd said something foolish. "I can

handle it. I'll get your luggage and cell phone. Why don't you just rest? Usually pain pills make people drowsy.''

"I am tired.'' In reality, he needed to plot out his strategy. He closed his eyes so she'd leave. Quietly, she switched off the light and crept to the door. From under half-open lids, he caught her watching him. After a moment, she shook her head and sighed.

She was probably thinking he was a godsend, the savior of her little girls.

Instead, he was going to rip her life apart. But that was all right. Most likely she deserved it. If she didn't, what the hell. He knew for a fact that Riverbend, Indiana, didn't protect its innocent. It was why, after all, he'd left the town.

"I SUSPECTED SOMETHING was wrong when you didn't come to church this morning. Now I know it. You're cooking up a storm.''

Kate started, then turned off the burner under the frying pan before facing her best friend, who was standing just inside the kitchen door. Lynn Kendall's perpetual smile slipped a bit, and her minister mask fell into place as soon as she got a good look at Kate.

"Sorry I surprised you. I knocked, but you didn't hear,'' Lynn said soberly. Drawing closer, she cocked her head. "What's happened?''

Briefly, Kate closed her eyes. "It's been a terrible morning. Let me finish this minestrone and I'll tell you about it. Pour yourself some coffee first and have a seat.''

With the robotic movements she'd employed for the past three hours, Kate stirred the sautéed vegetables, their spicy garlic-and-onion aroma wafting throughout the kitchen, then emptied the pan into her stockpot.

After pouring coffee, Lynn sat silently behind her, waiting, as always, for Kate to open up. It was one of the things that made her such a good minister and friend. Often, on their lunchtime walks, Kate confided in her.

Grabbing a mug for herself, Kate sat down at the scarred hardwood table across from Lynn. Understanding gray eyes peered watchfully over the mug, which read, So Many Books, So Little Time.

Kate said simply, "The twins ran into the road this morning and almost got hit by a truck."

Lynn's eyes widened. "Oh, Lord."

"I thought maybe you heard about it from Ethan Staver."

"No, I came straight here from church." She grasped Kate's hand. People thought she and Kate looked like sisters with their reddish hair, their freckles and their lack of interest in makeup. But Lynn was more fine-boned and slight, very much the way Kate pictured Emma from Jane Austen's novel. "They're all right, though?"

"Uh-huh. Unless I murder them myself."

Lynn smiled.

"They're banished to separate rooms until further notice."

"Can they have visitors?" Lynn asked.

Her wry question eased the tension Kate was feeling. She gave Lynn a wobbly smile. "Only you."

"I'll go in later." She squeezed Kate's hand. "Want to tell me about it?"

Kate bit her lip and nodded. She knew from other experiences that talking to Lynn about things helped.

In halting sentences, battling back the tears—God, she couldn't *believe* she'd broken down in front of Jay Lawrence—Kate related the entire story, putting *Be stronger* on her Emotional to-do list as she did.

"Oh, honey, I'm sorry. But surely you don't blame yourself."

"I shouldn't have left them on the porch."

"The girls are five years old, Kate. You can't keep them in your sight every minute. Hannah was wrong, not you. You're right to punish her."

"Hope, too. She's got to learn not to follow her sister's every command."

"What happened to the guy who saved them?"

Straightening her shoulders, Kate glanced toward the hall. "He's asleep in one of the spare rooms."

"Asleep?"

"He hurt his knee. Actually, it's a chronic injury and he banged it pretty hard on the cement steps."

"That's not good."

Sipping her coffee, Kate said, "I invited him to recover here. He accepted."

"Excuse me?"

Kate repeated herself, filling in details.

Lynn just nodded, and Kate recognized the thoughtful look. She'd seen her friend use it on parishioners and on her husband-to-be, Tom Baines, when she disagreed with him. "Honey, are you sure it's a good idea to invite a complete stranger to stay with you?"

"It wouldn't be if he hadn't risked his life for my girls. Lynn, he could have gotten killed himself. Doesn't that tell you he's a good Samaritan?"

"Yes, of course, but it doesn't mean it's…safe having him here."

"What it means is that he's a good person. I watched

the whole thing. He didn't even hesitate when he jumped in front of that truck. Without a second thought, he was willing to give up his life for somebody else. In my book, that's a good person. I have nothing to fear from him.''

''I guess I can see your reasoning. Still, it's a little scary.''

''It's the right thing to do.'' Kate stood, crossed to the stove and stirred the soup.

Lynn tracked her movements. ''Been cooking all day?''

''Uh-huh.'' Lined up on the counter were Mitch's favorite chocolate-mint brownies, no-bake oatmeal cookies, which were Lynn's weakness, banana bread for Charlie Callahan and snickerdoodles and *biscotti* to take to the bookstore tomorrow. It was well-known around Riverbend that whenever Kate was upset, she cooked. Scanning the counter, she knew her feelings about the morning's events were evident.

''He could stay with Tom,'' Lynn finally said.

Returning to the table with some cookies, Kate sat down again. ''Thanks, but no. This guy isn't going to save the girls' lives, then turn into Hannibal Lecter in the middle of the night.''

''Probably not. But I'll worry.''

''Don't. I'm safe with Jay Lawrence. I know it.''

HE'D SLEPT. The room had been awash with morning sunshine when Kate McMann had left. Now, late-afternoon shadows made crisscross patterns on the wall behind the desk. He'd spent a good deal of his youth watching those patterns change while planning his future, huddled right under this very afghan which Rachel had made. Thinking he could even smell her cooking, he swore. Not one single thing he'd wished for during that time had happened, teaching him the foolishness of childhood dreams.

His knee throbbed. Easing himself to a sitting position, he switched on the basketball lamp and reached for the pain medicine. A still-cool glass of water rested next to the bottle. That Kate had come in while he slept didn't sit well with him. He'd have to find a way to keep her out of here. He glanced at the bathroom, then at his knee. How the hell was he going to—

A light knock sounded at the door.

He geared his voice to neutral. "Come in."

The door creaked as it inched open; Kate stood in the archway holding crutches. "Hello. Feeling any better?"

"I'm fine." In truth, not only did his knee hurt like a son of a bitch, but his shoulders ached and his hand was sore. The fall had battered his thirty-five-year-old body, which didn't bounce back as fast as it used to. He pointed to the crutches. "Where did you get those?"

"The church minister, Lynn Kendall, came out to see why I wasn't at the service this morning. I told her about your injury, and she borrowed these from the 'lending cupboard' they operate."

"Your minister checks up on you when you miss a service?"

Kate chuckled, the mirth lighting up her eyes. She'd showered and changed into simple clingy black pants and a long-sleeved hip-hugging T-shirt, tie-dyed in a swirling autumn rainbow. Her curves were more generous than the baggy sweatshirt and jeans had indicated. She wore no cosmetics and her hair fell in waves to her shoulders, the color straight out of a Titian painting. "Lynn's my best friend, too. She and Tom Baines, her fiancé, came back out with the crutches. They were hoping to meet you."

Tom Baines. His cousin? And a lady minister? It couldn't be the same guy. "They from around here?" he asked casually.

"No. Tom used to visit here. He's from one of Riverbend's oldest families, the Steeles, and although his family moved, he spent the summers with his aunts, uncle and cousin Jacob." Jay detected a distinct chill in her voice when she spoke his name. "I'm surprised you haven't heard of Tom. He's a Pulitzer prize-winning journalist. He came back here when he inherited a piece of property, fell in love and stayed."

"Happily ever after," Jay said sarcastically.

"It *does* happen."

"If you're Snow White." He threw off the afghan and gingerly slid his legs to the floor. "Can I have those? I'd like use the bathroom and shower."

She stumbled back as if he'd physically pushed her. Her expressive face showed a ripple of surprise and a good dose of pity. "I'm sorry. I should have thought. Here." She handed him the crutches.

He checked out their length, grasped them in one hand and stood, holding on to the nightstand for leverage. Kate backed up farther. "You need any help? Getting stuff out of your suitcase or anything?"

"No. I can manage by myself. I've done it often enough."

She bit her lip and the guilt flashed in her eyes again. They were the color of fall leaves now. "I'm sorry."

"It's not your fault," he snapped.

Nodding, she left him alone.

With crutches, it took five times as long to use the

lav, shower and dress in clean clothes. At least he'd brought a couple of sweatsuits and some fleece shorts. Getting into the sweats was complicated enough; there was no way he'd be able to wear the jeans he'd packed. His knee was too swollen.

He'd just climbed back into bed when there was another knock at the door. Damn. "Come in," he said irritably.

Again, Kate appeared. This time she held the ice pack. "It's time for this," she said, entering.

"Fine."

She plumped pillows and he settled his leg onto them. By now he was sweating. Covering his knee with the ice, she asked, "Are you hungry?"

"A bit."

"I made minestrone soup. It's Rachel Steele's recipe. She and her sister own the bookstore where I work."

No, they don't.

Trying not to be a complete oaf, he sniffed appreciatively. "Smells good."

She hesitated.

"Is there something else?" he asked.

"I, um, have two people out here who want to see you."

Baines and the minister. It was going to be a real challenge keeping his true identity from her.

"I really don't want any company, Kate. I don't feel up to meeting people."

She cocked her head.

"Isn't it your friends with the crutches?" he said.

"Oh, no, they're gone, though they did want to meet you. To thank you. A lot of people in town will feel the same. When this gets around."

"Gets around?"

"Everybody'll know about it by tomorrow. We reported it to the police, after all."

Great. "Look, I'm not a very sociable guy. I don't feel comfortable with strangers, which is why I work with computers. I'd appreciate it if you would run interference for me, head off any well-wishers."

"Really?"

"I insist on it."

She shrugged. "All right." She glanced behind her. "Does that include Hope and Hannah?"

"Un, no, of course not. Is that who you meant?"

Smiling, she nodded. He was distracted by the fullness of her lips and their deep pink color.

"I'll bring them in just for a minute. They're out of their rooms only to thank you and eat. Then they're history until school tomorrow."

He held back a grin. The woman before him could be tough when necessary. He watched the gentle sway of her hips in the long T-shirt as she left. In minutes she returned with two contrite, somber little blondes. She waited in the doorway as they approached him.

Docile, the girls took baby steps to the bed. One was dressed in red footed pajamas, her hair damp and pulled back with a simple band. The other was decked out in pink pajamas with pastel clips restraining her hair. They stood before him like criminals before a firing squad. Then each held out a hand.

He accepted the two colored pieces of paper with glue and sparkly stuff and some writing on them.

"Mommy said we could make these for you," the one in red told him.

The other stuck her fingers in her mouth and nodded.

"Is that so?" He studied the handmade card the first

twin had given him. It had "Hannah" in uneven letters, with a picture of a truck and a road on it. Over the road was a big red X, and, again, just recognizable, was "Thanks."

The other card sported a multicolored rainbow and small block letters reading, "Thank you for saving us. Hope."

"These are very nice," he said, his throat tight. "Thanks for making them and coming to visit me."

"We gotta go right back to our room after we eat," Hannah confided softly.

"Why is that?" he asked.

The little girl frowned and stared at the floor.

"We did a bad thing." This from Hope.

Hannah reached out her hand and touched the ice covering his knee. "Does it hurt?"

"A little."

"It's our fault," Hope said. *Just like her mother.*

"Well, it was your fault that you ran into the road and needed saving. It's my fault that I hit the steps on a knee that was already hurt, though." For a minute, he was bombarded by the stark terror that had ripped through him when he'd seen these two dart into the road.

"Mommy was real mad," Hannah said.

He glanced at Kate. The expression on her face pole-axed him. It was the loving look of a parent who valued her child more than anything in the world. Jay had seen it directed at him many times, when he was young.

"And she cried," Hope whispered.

I know.

"You both can do something to make this easier for me," he told them seriously.

Two pairs of big sky-blue eyes stared at him.

"Promise you'll never do anything like that again. Obey your mother and never go near that road without her."

Both girls nodded vigorously.

Kate coughed and this time Jay avoided looking at her. "All right, girls. Let's leave Mr. Lawrence alone to rest now."

Hannah smiled at him, turned and skipped to the door. Hope hesitated, then in a move so quick it startled him, threw her chubby arms around his neck. Jay felt something wet on his cheek. Driven by another totally foreign need, he placed his hand on her back and soothed her. She smelled clean and sweet. Closing his eyes, he fought the warmth that enveloped him because of the innocent gesture.

Hope pulled away and gave him a watery smile. Then she followed her sister out the door. His gaze landed on Kate, poised at the entrance. "Thank you," she said, her own smile shaky. "You're a nice man."

His heart lurched. The reality of what he was doing to her peaceful little existence began to penetrate.

He was anything *but* a nice man.

CHAPTER THREE

BRIGHT AND EARLY Monday morning, Kate unlocked the front door of Steele Books and hurried inside. It was her favorite time of day—when she was alone in the store before Ruth and Rachel, the other employees or any customers arrived.

It was just Kate and her books. Passing the L-shaped checkout desk to the right of the entryway—she still loved the dark green she'd painted it last summer—Kate crossed the polished oak floor heading to the office at the far end of the store. As she wandered through the stacks, she breathed in the unique scent of the books. Here, amid them, was the only place she ever felt she truly belonged. When she was in high school, getting a job at Steele Books had been a godsend. She was able to earn the money for clothes and other necessities, escape from a beleaguered mother who held down two jobs and looked right through Kate when she *was* home, and pretend that the pretty girls who never gave Kate a chance weren't important to her. Here, in the company of Thoreau and Socrates, with George Eliot, Charlotte Brontë and Virginia Woolf as her girlfriends, Kate was at peace.

Depositing the paperwork she'd taken home over the weekend on her huge metal desk, she hung up her coat and made the coffee she provided for customers. As it dripped, she booted up her computer. Number one on her store to-do list was to update her private account, the one nobody knew about. The one that would allow her to buy Steele Books from Ruth and Rachel someday, even if she did have to forgo new shoes for another month, sew all the girls' outfits and purchase her own clothes from L.L. Bean's sale catalogs. Kate bought good-quality—though out-of-date—clothes cheap, because they lasted, and the girls still liked her homemade ensembles. When they were ready for labels, she'd find a way.

Quickly she entered the data: how much she was able to put into her savings for the month of October and what she could deposit into the funds for fixing up the farmhouse. Mitch and Charlie had promised to give her an estimate on rebuilding the front porch this week, and she was hoping to have that task crossed off her Home-Repair list before winter set in.

All told, it didn't amount to a ton of money, but she was making headway in achieving her lifelong dream of owning the bookstore. Even if it did mean scrimping. *You're better off than some,* she chided herself as she finished up at the computer, filled a tray with the coffee and the cookies she'd brought in and went back out to the shop. She smiled as she passed the posters of famous people encouraging others to read. She'd seen the display in a high-school library once and sent for the materials. Edward James Olmos suggested the value of reading in Spanish. Doug Flutie held a book in one hand and a football helmet in the other. Michael J. Fox peered out through studious-looking glasses stressing the importance of learning via the printed word. As a backdrop, she'd hung a subtly striped light-green wallpaper, giving the entire place a warm feeling. Yes, she was better off than many. She had a lot to be thankful for, especially the girls. When the chill started to creep up her spine again, the one that had sent her into the bathtub at 2 a.m. because she couldn't get warm any other way, she battled it back. She simply didn't have time now to allow her fear to consume her.

"All right, Kate," she told herself as she moved through the aisles to her favorite spot in the store. "You had a close call. Count your blessings and forget it. Just be grateful."

She *was* grateful to the stranger who had materialized out of nowhere to save the girls. He was on her mind when she reached the front of the shop—a sitting area, carpeted in green-flecked Berber, with several small, light-oak coffee tables and dark-green padded chairs, two overstuffed chairs and two plushly upholstered couches. She set out the coffee and treats on a sideboard and drew herself a cup from the fancy thermal container Ruth had bought from a gourmet kitchen catalog. Plunking herself down into one of the couches, she sipped her coffee and closed her eyes, thinking about Jay Lawrence. He'd had a restless night, too, moving around. She'd heard him use the bathroom and go to the kitchen, then to the sprawling family room, where he watched a little TV. She'd left her room once to see if she could help. He'd been curt and prickly, and she excused his manner because she sensed he was an independent man, not used to accepting help from others.

He'd looked like a brooding Heathcliff, except for his blond hair. Those dark eyes, accented by the white T-shirt he wore with navy sweatpants, brimmed with cynicism—and some hostility she didn't understand. She'd vowed to give him the space he needed. Although, of course, she'd brought him breakfast, along with more ice this morning for his knee. He'd been begrudgingly grateful, and she could see he was in pain. It had hit her then that he was a man accustomed to being in pain.

The thought made her sad.

The bell over the door tinkled. Kate smiled as she looked up into the kind face of Simon Manchester. At almost seventy, he had a big heart and a lively mind. "Caught you, did I, Katie?"

"Spinning my fairy tales, Simon." She noted his gait as he crossed to the counter to leave his things behind it. "Your leg bothering you again?"

"Being old is bothering me again."

"Come sit for a minute. I've got coffee ready." She rose and went to the sideboard. As she poured him a mug and put two cookies on a plate, she smiled at the paintings on the wall behind the coffee station. Lily Mazerik's art was the perfect addition to the store. She couldn't have asked for better ambience than the impressionistic acrylic paintings of the Indiana landscape provided. The swirling pastel colors and light brush strokes were soothing to the eye. Though she hadn't known Lily well in high school—Lily was older than Kate—she'd come to know and like her since they'd hung the art.

When Kate returned to the couch, Simon was seated opposite her. He studied her face as she placed the food on the table where a huge *Architecture of the Midwest* book of photographs lay. "You look tired, Katie."

"It was a rough weekend."

"So I heard." He took a sip of the coffee, then bit into the *biscotti*. "Those little ones all right?"

"Yes, very demure today for once in their lives."

His gaze was shrewd. "You've done a good job with them, young lady."

"Thanks, Simon. But they're a handful."

"They're spunky and need a father to watch over them, is all."

"Unfortunately Billy doesn't want that role."

"More the fool." He smiled. "Now, what's this I hear about a stranger staying with you?"

"News travels fast." Simon's gaze was implacable, and Kate knew what had made him one of the most popular, but toughest, English professors at the University of Chicago. When he'd retired and moved to Riverbend with his wife of fifty years to be near his daughter, and asked for a part-time job at the store, she'd felt as if she'd been given a gift.

Briefly she told him why she'd asked Jay Lawrence to stay at the farmhouse. Simon listened carefully, then nodded. "Sounds okay. Not too many mass murderers up this way with rented Volvos and cell phones. Just be careful."

"I always am."

He lumbered to his feet. "I'm going to inventory section A in the rare books. Are Ruth and Rachel here?"

"No. I saw them going into the beauty shop when I dropped the girls off at school."

"Gird your loins, girl. They'll have a lot to say about the accident and the stranger staying at your house after a morning of speculation at Clip, Curl and Dye."

She rolled her eyes.

But Simon was right. Just before noon, Ruth and Rachel descended on the store like a couple of tornadoes and demanded to hear the whole story.

RUTH STEELE loved a good mystery, and the stranger who'd swooped out of nowhere, saved Katie's little darlings and was now recuperating at her house provided the perfect stimulant for an otherwise boring day. "Is he handsome?" she asked Kate a half hour after letting the subject drop, so as not to appear pushy. Both she and her sister would love to run Kate's life—she was like the daughter they'd never had—but they were careful not to smother the poor girl.

Kate perused the catalog from Baker and Taylor. "Who?"

Rachel dusted the display case behind the desk and winked at Ruth.

"Zorro and the Three Musketeers all rolled into one, from what Jesse Carmichael's mother said."

"Remember how Jacob loved Zorro, Ruthie?" Rachel asked.

A huge swell of regret and loss engulfed Ruth. She battled it back. "Jacob loved everything he read. He'd memorized the *Adventures of Zorro* by the time he was a few years older than the twins."

Ruth's face took on a faraway expression. "I wonder if he still reads."

They all went silent. From the corner of her eye, Ruth saw Kate's face flush, with anger, no doubt, at the man who'd deserted them. Katie had let it slip more than once that she was furious at their nephew for abandoning them. Sometimes Ruth felt the same way.

"In any case," Ruth finally said, "I want to know what this stranger looks like."

"We should be asking what kind of person he is," Rachel put in.

Glory be, her sister could be such a stick-in-the-mud.

"I *know* what kind of person he is," Ruth said. "He risked his life for our babies. He's a hero."

"I wonder what *he* likes to read," Kate mused.

"Why?"

"I'm going home to fix lunch for him." Kate glanced at her watch. "I thought I'd bring him some books."

"Aren't you and Lynn walking today?"

"No, I canceled. So, what about the books?"

"Handsome men like adventure novels." Ruth knew that for a fact. "Is he good-looking?"

"What *does* he look like?" Rachel finally repeated Ruth's unanswered question.

Kate cocked her head as if she was drawing the guy in her mind. "His eyes are dark and he has thick hair the color of wheat fields in fall. Straight. Square-cut jaw. There are worry lines on his brow and bracketing his mouth."

Ruth exchanged a *Well, this is interesting* look with her sister. "He sounds like the perfect rake out of one of the novels in the romance section." She smiled at her whimsical thought.

"I guess," Kate said. "He's attractive in an almost world-weary way."

"My kind of protagonist."

"Maybe he'd like this one," Rachel said, producing Patricia Cornwall's latest medical thriller.

"And this one," Ruth added, picking up an Elmore Leonard mystery with a good dose of humor in it. She loved men who could laugh easily.

In no time, Ruth and Rachel had assembled a stack of books for the real-life hero staying with Kate and paid for them as a way of saying thank-you.

As Kate headed out of the store to run some errands

and go home to fix him lunch, Ruth called out non-chalantly, "Ask if we can meet him, Katie."

Kate turned at the door. "Oh, Ruth, he's already said he's not up to visitors."

"That's fine, dear. We understand. You run along." Rachel closed the door behind Kate and faced her sister. "Ruth Steele, what are you up to?"

"Honestly, Rachel, did you hear how she described him? Hair the color of wheat fields? I don't think I've ever heard Katie wax poetic like that."

"You're such a romantic."

"Of course I am. And we both know Kate's secret wish is to have a husband, and father to her daughters."

"Still, I don't think you should interfere."

"Who, me?" Ruth said innocently, already calculating how she was going to meet this man and see for herself if he was worthy of their Kate. "I wouldn't dream of it."

THE COMPUTER PURRED beneath his hands, the keys responding easily to the light play of his fingers. Jay was as good with machines as he was with women, though he had to admit his chosen work was often more fulfilling than the women he'd been with. Even Mallory. Especially Mallory.

"Come on, baby," he whispered to Kate's computer. Smart girl, she had a password that had taken him several minutes to figure out. "That's it, almost there." A few more strokes. "Yes!"

The Steele Books icon popped up on the screen. For a minute, he experienced a twinge of guilt. But why? He was only ferreting out the truth. Protecting his aunts. Making sure his store and farmhouse were safe from any takeover plans she might have.

Still, he pushed the chair back, grabbed his crutches and limped out to the kitchen to make coffee. His guilt doubled. A carafe was warming on the burner. Next to it on a flowered plate were different kinds of cookies and some banana bread, already sliced and covered with plastic. The note by it read, "Please help yourself. I'm a regular Julia Child in the kitchen." A little smiley face had been drawn next to the boast. Also on the note were scribbles—"Good luck with your knee...be careful today..." Obviously, from the girls. He wondered if Kate told them how to spell the words. Could five-year-olds read and write?

Really, Abraham, he can *read. Come on Jacob, show Daddy what you can do.* Though she'd died of breast cancer when he was seven, his mother's voice, soft and musical, still rang in his memory sometimes. He'd been the center of her world, and she'd taught him to read and to love life.

He selected a cookie and munched on it, thinking of Kate McMann. What the woman got done was amazing, and it was obvious how she managed. He'd heard her working in the room next to his at 10 p.m. He planned to investigate what she was doing there after he studied the store records. Then she'd been humming in the kitchen at midnight, and when he'd come out at one to get something to eat, she'd joined him. She'd been doing *something* in the bedroom, but he didn't know what yet. He swore he'd heard bathwater running after that.

Why was he out here analyzing her? What the hell was he waiting for? But he couldn't seem to bar her from his thoughts. On the slow trek back to his room, he pictured her the way she'd been when she'd checked in with him before she left that morning. She looked different in her plain black skirt and peach sweater set of good quality, if not high fashion. So she spent some money on clothes. Her shoes were leather but a bit worn. Her only jewelry was gold hoops in her ears and a slim watch.

I brought you breakfast, she'd said. *I don't know what you like, so I made a little of everything.* That was an understatement. Julia Child did indeed have worthy competition in Kate McMann. His mouth watered as he remembered the cinnamon French toast, fluffy eggs and spicy home fries.

Reseated at the computer, he deliberately cleared his mind and clicked on the icon. It was stupid to go soft over some silly breakfast. Hell, even Lizzie Borden could cook.

He'd start with the spreadsheets. As each one came up, he analyzed it thoroughly. He was surprised at the total income generated over twelve months. Manipulating a few keys, he scanned the records from the past seven years. Much of the money came from sales of new books, though the figures from the rare and collectible books were excellent. He wondered when they had started that area of the business. Regardless, it was all very impressive. Ms. McMann was making herself some money.

Making you *some money, Lawrence.*

Well, that was good.

He probed further. What was this? Other funds? A separate account. "Now we're getting somewhere," he said to himself, the thrill of the chase spurting through him. She'd hidden money. Savings. Investments. In *her* name, not the store's, yet it was in the same folder as the business account. He scanned the portfolio. Very nice. She was accumulating a significant nest egg. At his expense?

Who knew? Maybe he'd have Nick Harrison get someone to audit the accounts for the bookstore. If she'd stolen money from the business, he'd be damned if she kept it. And he'd need a financial analysis when he sold the place, anyway. Before he did, though, he'd look at her personal finances. Again a password. Again, he breached it easily. He could teach her a thing or two about security. Of course she didn't expect Benedict Arnold to be living under her roof. She'd given carte blanche with her computer to the man who had saved her children, not some traitor who planned to eat her alive.

Hell, it couldn't be helped.

By noon, he had three strikes against her. First, why wasn't she taking any child support from her ex? Did she not need it, or had she done something to preclude it? Second, there was the mysterious account, and third, nowhere was there a record of her paying rent to his aunts. She was living out here for nothing. He wondered how she'd finagled that.

"Hello."

He was startled by the softly spoken word. His wheeled chair tipped and Kate leaped behind him to keep him from falling. "Why the hell did you do that?" he snapped.

"Do what?" she asked stepping back. Her hands wrapped around her waist as if to ward off a blow.

Cool it, Lawrence. Don't make her suspicious.

Carefully blocking the screen with his body, he favored her with a combined *I'm sorry/what a jerk I am* look. "I apologize. I didn't expect to see you."

She still stared at him warily.

Well, he knew how to get to her. "I must be more shaken by yesterday than I thought," he said somberly.

Her face paled. "Is there anything I can do?"

Something clutched at his heart. Damn it. "No, I'm all right." He angled his head. "Why are you here?"

Her smile was sun-bright, making the gloomy November day ludicrously cheerful. "I came home to make you lunch."

"You don't have to do that. I can manage." He shrugged. "I had a couple of cookies a while ago. They were great."

"I made them for the store."

"The store?"

"Uh-huh. We have a small café of sorts, where we encourage people to read. We provide coffee and pastries."

"For a price, naturally."

"No, they're free. I believe it encourages patronage and that people will buy more books the longer they stay around."

"Anderson Books agrees with you, but they charge."

She frowned at the name of the famous chain store that served a variety of foods and gourmet coffees. "I know. They made that very clear."

"Clear?"

"They've scouted us. They're interested in buying Steele Books."

I know.

"You selling?"

"The Steele sisters don't want to sell out to a chain." Her hazel eyes darkened with worry, then lightened in the next instant. "Speaking of the store, I brought you a present."

He cocked his head in question.

"Come on out. I'll serve your lunch while you look at them." Pivoting, she left without even looking at the computer screen. Her innocence and unsuspecting nature made her an easy mark; the odds were stunningly stacked against her. As he escaped her personal-finances program, he wished the thought wasn't so discomfiting.

There was a bag from the store on the kitchen table. As she worked at the stove, he read the quotes printed on it. Among the ten or so sayings were: "Books are the most quiet and constant of friends—Charles Eliot"; "If you read too fast or too slowly, you'll never understand anything—Pascal"; "At school, we first learn to read, and then we read to learn." "Those who don't read good books have no advantage over those who can't read them." All in all, a very nice touch.

Sitting down, he reached into the bag and drew out several books from various authors. "Are these for me?"

"Yes, of course. I thought you might be bored and need some diversion."

No, I'm too busy spying on you. He felt like a slug. The microwave beeped and as she busied herself there, he read the titles.

"Do you like to read?" she asked as she dished out something with a to-kill-for smell.

"I, um, used to. I haven't read much beside newspapers in years."

"How can anyone not read books? If I don't have a TBR pile of at least a dozen by my bed, I have a panic attack."

"A TBR pile?"

"'To be read,' silly."

He pretended interest in Patricia Cornwall's photograph. "Let me give you some money for these." After all, he knew now what a penny pincher she was.

"Nope. Ruth and Rachel Steele paid for them. They said they're a thank-you for yesterday."

His aunts were still buying him books. The thought caused a thick knot to lodge in his throat. "Thank them for me," he finally got out.

"They'd like to meet you."

He froze. He yearned to see his aunts more than he wanted to take his next breath. But that didn't fit his plans yet. "I'd rather not, Kate."

"I know. I told them that. They're okay with it." She set a plate before him.

Its steaming scent penetrated the haze of his memories. "What's this?"

"Artichoke-and-chicken casserole."

"When did you make this?"

"Last night."

"Isn't it for supper?"

"No. We're having spaghetti tonight. Though I thought twice about it, because it's the twins' favorite meal."

"They're off bread and water?" he asked, picking up his fork.

She smiled and he noticed a little dimple in her cheek. "They were subdued today, though Hannah can do that just for appearances."

"I hope for all our sakes she's sincere."

Kate swallowed hard. "Me, too."

They ate in companionable silence. Afterward, she cleaned up. He sipped hazelnut coffee from the mug she provided and noted her efficient movements at the sink. When she was done, she leaned against the counter and checked her watch. "I need to get back. Simon leaves in an hour and I have to talk to him before tomorrow."

Simon Manchester, sixty-nine-year-old retired professor. He'd been employed at the store seven years. "Simon?" he asked.

"One of my part-time helpers."

"One?"

"Yes, I have two others."

Isabel "Izzy" Jackson, seventeen-year-old cheerleader who worked two to six, three days a week, and Joan Kemp, young mother who put in two nights at the store and Saturdays. Kate had kindly provided a short bio of each in her files.

He pretended idle curiosity. "What time will you be home tonight?" He had some exploring to do.

"About five. The twins come to the store after school and we're usually back here by five, but we're working at the food cupboard today for a while, so we'll be late. The spaghetti sauce just needs to be heated, though, so we can eat at a decent hour."

"What's the food cupboard?"

"A Thanksgiving program Lynn runs over at the church. They provide dinners for needy families at the holidays, and I think it's good for the girls to help out others."

"Are there a lot of needy families in Riverbend?"

A shadow crossed her face as she picked up her purse from the chair and searched for her keys. "Enough. Abraham Steele left some money for the program, but we still solicit man-hours."

Dear old dad had been quite the philanthropist. Jay

couldn't resist commenting, "Abraham Steele seems like a town institution."

When she looked up at him and smiled, her face was full of soft approval. "He was. I miss him. I saw a lot of him, especially around the holidays."

"Why?"

"Ruth and Rachel said that was the hardest time for him. It is for them, too."

"Why?" he asked again.

Her pretty features hardened. Her back straightened. With brisk movements, she found her keys and zipped up the bag. "His son abandoned them all fifteen years ago."

Jay kept his face impassive.

"No one knows why he left, although there are rumors."

Jay's shoulders stiffened.

"Anyway, he didn't even come home for his father's funeral, which broke Ruth and Rachel's hearts all over again." She shook her head.

Jay simply stared at her.

"I can't imagine someone abandoning a family as loving as theirs. Lynn says you shouldn't judge, but Jacob Steele is very low on my list of favorite people."

"Did you know him? You're from here, right?"

"He was five years ahead of me in school, so I don't remember him much. But I know him through stories the Steeles told me. They talk about him as if he was some kind of god."

"They? I thought the old man was dead."

"He is. But he shared a lot with me the last few years of his life."

As good as a signed confession.

"I'm—" A noise from the side of the house interrupted her. She turned to glance out the window. And smiled. She cranked the handle to open the window just as a figure neared the glass. "Hi, Mitch. Did you come about the front porch?"

"No," Jay heard from his seat. He couldn't see the man, nor vice versa. "I came here to ask what the *hell* you think you're doing letting a strange man stay here with you."

"Come around to the porch." She set down her purse and faced Jay. "It's Mitch Sterling. He's like a big brother to me." She rolled her eyes. "He's worse than Charlie Callahan in his protectiveness."

The man appeared at the back porch, which she'd apparently locked, given the knocking. "Katie, open this. I wanna talk to this guy."

Mitch Sterling's voice was lower and deeper than in high school. But Jay recognized it.

After all, Sterling had been his best friend until Jay had *abandoned* Riverbend.

CHAPTER FOUR

KATE HATED grocery shopping with a passion. It ranked right up there with root canals, watching the twins cry when they were hurt and sitting through a bad movie based on a favorite book. "Hannah, put down that candy, please."

"I want chocolate," the child whined. Friday night at six-thirty was wearing on all of them.

"You know the deal. Each of you gets to pick out one thing per week. You chose root beer."

Dropping the candy, Hannah skipped down the snack aisle as fast as her red high-tops would take her to where Hope studied something on the shelf. Probably *her* treat, in which case Hannah would try to wheedle her sister into choosing chocolate. Kate made a mental note on her Morality to-do list to discuss with Hannah the downside of taking advantage of others.

"Stay within sight," Kate called to the girls.

As she selected popcorn—computing unit prices to see what was really on sale—she rolled her shoulders and sighed. She was dead tired tonight, as she usually was at the end of the week. Even her houseguest had noticed. That brought a smile to her lips, followed quickly by a frown. She knew she shouldn't let it, but his solicitousness felt good. It had been a long time, if ever, since a man had worried about her....

"You look exhausted," he'd told her as they finished dinner and the girls took off to wash up before their weekly excursion to the supermarket. As he pushed back from the table, the muscles in his arms, visible beneath the rolled-up sleeves of his sweat jacket, flexed; as he raised his left leg to rest it on a chair—keeping the knee elevated reduced swelling— she noticed the bulge of sinews in his thigh, which the fleece shorts revealed. Briefly, she wondered if he'd played sports when he was younger. "Why are you shopping *tonight?*" he'd asked.

She'd changed into worn-at-the-knees jeans and a Riverbend High sweatshirt, which had seemed to draw his attention. Wiping her hands on her pants, she'd shrugged. "We always go on Friday nights, unless there's a basketball game."

"Basketball?"

"Sure, it's *the* event here. Everybody goes to the games."

He stared at her blankly.

"Anyway, we go grocery shopping on Friday nights because the market isn't as crowded as it is at other times. And Saturday is sacred to me and the girls. I don't do any work, and we spend the whole day together having fun." It was a lie worthy of Pinocchio— she worked on the house and the bookstore accounts Saturday nights after the kids went to bed—but she didn't want to sound as if she was complaining. Her life was full and busy, and she liked it that way.

He'd scowled, in the way that meant displeasure, not confusion, and shaken his head. In the five days he'd been staying with them, she'd begun to figure out how to read him, though he was like one of the old, rare collectibles in the store that took a lot of study. "At least leave the dishes for me to do," he'd said gruffly.

"No, really I—"

"I won't take no for an answer." When she protested further, he practically growled, "Look, my masculine ego's taken a beating here. You've been waiting on me all week. My knee's getting better and I want to help." Then almost to himself he muttered, "You work too damn hard..."

The last had surprised her. He'd avoided making personal comments to her and even ignored some of the questions she'd asked him. Obviously, he steered clear of talking about himself almost as much as he avoided seeing people.

When Mitch had shown up Monday, Jay Lawrence had nearly toppled his chair and twisted his knee, hurrying out of the kitchen as fast as his crutches would carry him. Once inside the house, Mitch had been insistent, but Kate knew how to get around him and had secured Jay's privacy. She'd turned the discussion to Tessa, the woman who was working at Mitch's hardware store, the woman responsible for his obvious distraction. The *pregnant* woman. Kate had befriended the lonely Tessa and offered her some of the baby furniture stowed in the attic. Wistfully Kate remembered her own pregnancy. She'd loved every precious minute of carrying the twins inside her, even if there hadn't been a husband around to share the experience with.

"Oh, excuse me." Because of her musings, she'd bumped into a person in the aisle, the action scattering her coupons over the bottom of her cart.

The tall, strikingly beautiful woman glanced at her. As always, she seemed to dismiss Kate, merely nodding.

"How are you tonight, Sarah?" Kate asked, scooping up the coupons.

Sarah Smith Cole's brows arched, probably in surprise that Kate spoke to her. Born into a wealthy family, Sarah was five years older than Kate and was as enigmatic as Daphne Du Maurier's Rebecca. Her blond hair was impeccably styled and her skin porcelain clear; her blue silk pantsuit contrasted vividly with Kate's jeans, and highlighted her cool slate eyes. A widow with no children, she kept her distance from everyone in town and lived in a lavish house up on Bending Road to the south of the town proper. It seemed a lonely existence, and Kate felt sorry for her, which was why she spoke to her.

"I'm fine." She studied Kate. "Kate McMann from the bookstore, right?"

Nodding, Kate smiled; then her eyes darted over Sarah's pretty head. "Hope, Hannah, don't leave this aisle."

Sarah followed her gaze. "Your children?"

"Uh-huh. Kids can really be a chore sometimes. They need to be watched every minute." The stark pain on Sarah's face caused Kate concern. "Are you all right?"

Coldly, Sarah said, "Fine. I'm in a hurry." She glanced down at her small basket, which held a frozen diet dinner and a bottle of mineral water.

As Kate watched the other woman leave and herded the kids over to the frozen-food section, she remembered that Sarah had been Jacob Steele's high-school sweetheart. They'd gotten engaged in his senior year at college, and he'd abandoned her, too, when he'd vanished without a trace. Just another black mark against the man.

The most interesting thing, though, about Sarah Smith Cole was that Rachel Steele didn't like her.

Sarah had to be the only person in Riverbend that Rachel avoided; the deeply religious and ineffably kind Steele sister would only say that Sarah Cole was not a nice person.

"Mommy." Hope tugged on her sleeve. "I know what I want for my treat."

"What, sweetheart?"

"Some 'stachio ice cream." Hope held up a half gallon of store-brand pistachio.

Bending down, Kate peered into her daughter's face. "Hope, you've never even tasted pistachio ice cream."

"It's not in your Wish Folder," Hannah put in, fingering a box of gooey ice-cream-cone sundaes.

Kate spared Hannah a quick smile at the mention of the secret files they kept in the cabinet near the computer and guarded as if they were newly discovered biblical texts. In them, they stored their dreams—little or big, ranging from the kind of treat they'd buy next and the horse Hannah longed for to Kate's goal of owning the bookstore.

Hope shrugged her small shoulders. When they'd started shopping, both girls had whipped off their pink-and-white jackets and stuffed them into the cart. Hope's light-blue overalls and striped shirt were hardly wrinkled, even after a full day in them, whereas Hannah had had to change out of the shirt she'd spilled gravy on at dinner. She'd donned an old sweater that should go in the Salvation Army bin. Kate put that on her Charity to-do list. "The 'stachio's not for me," Hope whispered.

"I don't understand."

"It's Mr. Lawrence's favorite kind. I wanna get him some 'cause he's sick. I'll pick it as my treat," she said earnestly.

"Oh, honey, what a nice thought." Kate had asked *Mr. Lawrence* if he'd like anything from the grocery store, and he'd, of course, said no. She'd never met anyone who was so incapable of accepting even the smallest kindness.

All week she'd offered, and he'd refused. *I can do my own laundry, if I need to… I'm capable of walking to the table, you don't have to bring a tray… All right, I'll watch TV with you three if you promise not to fuss…*

Staring down into Hope's innocent face and sincere blue eyes, Kate smoothed her hair. "I have an idea. Why don't we buy the ice cream as a present from all of us? That way you can pick out a treat, too."

"It's okay, Mommy. We don't have money to spare." Hope solemnly parroted Kate's phrase and her tone of voice.

"We have enough money to buy our guest some food, honey. I even have a coupon for this brand of ice cream. Do you know what else Mr. Lawrence likes?"

She was shocked to hear the list the kids ticked off and amazed at how plain the food was. She'd pegged him as a New York gourmet, but the kids assured her he favored small-town fare—macaroni-and-cheese, oyster crackers, canned asparagus soup. She should have expected the two little inquisitors would ferret out details about Jay Lawrence that she didn't know; they pestered him every time she turned her back. She'd caught them climbing up next to him on the couch and asking him to read their favorite books to them. They made quite a sight, two tiny blond girls and the tall, broad-shouldered man who spanned a good portion of the sofa. And she could swear he'd gotten choked up when reading Mercer Mayer's *I'll Love You Forever* to them. Though the twins had thawed him a little, he was still a mystery to her. Which was ironic, since she had the impression he knew a lot about her.

Hannah yelled, "I think I see Allison!" and darted out of sight. Hope followed her.

"Hannah!" Kate called, rushing down the aisle, narrowly avoiding an old man and his elderly sister. "Sorry, Mr. Kemp. How's your arthritis tonight?" she asked over her shoulder as she raced after the girls.

Lord, she hated grocery shopping.

"LAWRENCE." JAY'S TONE was clipped as he picked up his cell phone and collapsed into a straight chair. He plucked his sweaty T-shirt away from his body and stretched out his braced leg.

"Hello, darling. What are you doing?" Mallory's voice, naturally husky, was pitched even lower, Jay suspected, to remind him of what he was missing. He allowed himself to picture her short, razor-cut blond hair falling artfully into her face, her tall willowy body, kept slender by daily workouts, and her shrewd gray eyes. She was a beautiful, sophisticated woman, just his type.

"Jay, I asked what you were doing."

He scanned the room, taking in the floor, covered with drop cloths, and the furniture, draped in plastic. "You wouldn't believe me if I told you."

"Of course I would." She hesitated. "You're not with another woman, are you?"

For some reason, huge hazel eyes popped into his mind. "No other woman's here right now, Mallory."

"Then what *are* you up to?"

"I'm spackling a spare room."

"Do you know how to do that?"

"I'm managing." In his bumming-around days, he'd done a lot of odd jobs, but any adult with half a brain could spackle. Sometimes Mallory lived in a different world.

"*Why* are you doing that?"

"Damned if I know." It had something to do with one of the many to-do lists he'd found on a clipboard in this room when he'd searched the house looking for clues to Kate McMann. The woman had scrawled, "Spare room (one hour per day): spackle, paint, replace window screens." *Why,* he had yet to discover.

"How's everything going up there?" Mallory asked, not interested in his current activity.

"Just peachy, Mallory."

"Do you like being back home?"

"This isn't my home." His voice was tight, the way it got when a sales rep displeased him.

She heard the ice in his tone. "Sorry. Do you miss me?"

"Of course," he lied. Truth of it was, Mallory was high maintenance and she often required more than he wanted to give her. The story of his life with women.

After Sarah.

"I'd like to come for a visit, darling." Again, the sexy purr designed to spark his libido.

"That wouldn't be a good idea. The terms of this will are more complicated than I'd realized. I'm trying not to call attention to myself here. Riverbend is small, and if you blew into town, the whole population would know."

"Why, Jay, that's the nicest thing you've ever said to me."

Was it? He shook his head and stood, unwilling to

think about the fact that he wasn't very good at relationships. Limping over to the wall, he said, "I've got to go before this stuff hardens."

"Will you call me?"

"Sure."

"You haven't. Not once since you went to that god-forsaken town."

"I will. I promise. Talk to you soon."

He ended the call and tossed the phone onto a chair before she told him she loved him. He hated dealing with the awkwardness when he didn't say it back. He hadn't said those words in fifteen years, and he never planned to say them again.

As he picked up a piece of sandpaper and began smoothing out the plaster he'd applied to the seams of the drywall, he thought about his refusal to get involved. Hell, his refusal to love anybody. When he'd been a part of this household, both the love and the words were as prevalent as the Indiana rain.

I love you, Jacob, Ruth would say. *Even when you're naughty.* Rachel's vows were spoken frequently, too.

Interestingly, this house was still full of love and declarations; its walls practically burst with affection. "Who do you love?" Kate would say when they washed dishes or folded laundry. "I love you, Mommy," the twins would declare. Though once in a while, the little pistol Hannah would tease, "Hmm, I think I love Brad Pitt."

Jay checked his watch. He wanted to finish this up before they came home. Kate would not be pleased he'd exerted himself. Glancing down at the knee brace he'd donned, he knew even that precaution wouldn't salve her concern. Her solicitousness was driving him crazy.

Liar. The little voice poked out of his unconscious, though he'd tried to quell it. Even after only five days, he was getting used to being spoiled. Meals that rivaled a five-star restaurant's. Finding his bed straightened and his room picked up. The little touches like hot coffee left for him, a phone call to see how he was if she couldn't get away for lunch, though she'd come home three times this week. All of it made his hiding his identity and his plans for the store and the farmhouse not as palatable as they had initially been.

As he finished up the spackling, he admitted to himself why he'd done the task—he couldn't bear the thought of her working after she came home from shopping. Sick of this ruminating, he hobbled out of the spare room and found his way to his bedroom. Damn, he needed to get out of this house. But he wasn't finished with Kate yet. He needed to know more.

Once he'd decided to stay, he had called Nick Harrison about auditing the store accounts and expected that to start next week. Dragging the shirt over his head and yanking off his shorts, he frowned as he remembered Nick's reaction when he'd arrived at the farmhouse Tuesday morning...

"I didn't expect you to come out here," Jay had said after he'd surreptitiously checked to see who the visitor was.

Nick's blue eyes were hard. "I know. I couldn't get last night's conversation out of my head."

"Want to sit down?"

His gaze direct, Harrison straightened. "No. You won't appreciate what I have to say, so I'll just tell you and leave."

"Shoot, then."

"I don't like this." He waved his hand to indicate the house.

Jay felt his body stiffen. "What don't you like?"

"Your ruse of playing the hero."

"I saved the twins. Surely you've heard." Not that he felt much like a hero.

"You were on your way out here to confront Kate about her relationship with your father and aunts. I had the impression you were going to tell her who you are and the terms of the will."

"I changed my mind."

"Why?"

"Because I wasn't sure if she was doing anything wrong and I wanted to know what I was up against." He straightened and threw back his shoulders, accentuating his full height. It was a gesture designed to intimidate. For some reason, it made him feel like a jerk. The whole thing did. "I still don't know what's going on with the will. Since she invited me to stay and recuperate, I decided it was a good chance to find out about her real personality and motives."

"Kate McMann doesn't have a deceptive bone in her body. She's exactly what she appears to be. I don't want to see you hurt her."

"What you want doesn't concern me, Harrison."

"How long are you going to keep this up?"

"Not much longer."

"You're just going to announce that you're here to claim the store and house after she's taken you in this way?"

Jay hadn't liked how that sounded, though it was pretty much true. "Yes, I am."

"I don't approve," the lawyer had reiterated.

"As I said, that means nothing to me. And I hope I

don't need to remind you of lawyer/client confidentiality. If you reveal who I am to Kate McMann or anyone in this town before I'm ready, I'll report you to the Indiana Bar.''

"When did you get to be such a bastard?" Nick had asked as he turned to leave.

Fifteen years ago when my whole life fell apart.

"None of your business. Just remember what I said…"

In the shower, as he recalled Nick's angry words and excessive displeasure, Jay wondered again if maybe there was something going on between Kate and Harrison. Were they sleeping together? Was that why he'd defended her so vehemently?

"I wouldn't care if Harrison wasn't my lawyer," Jay said aloud. "She can have as many bed partners as she wants. I'm only interested if my father was one." Which, he was coming to realize, was highly improbable.

He was in a sour mood when he left the shower, dressed in a navy-blue sweatsuit and grabbed his crutches. His knee hurt a little more from the strain of searching the house and doing the stupid spackling. It was more swollen today than yesterday, so he needed some ice.

Hobbling out to the kitchen, he noticed a light on the answering machine. Who had called? Without a qualm, he pressed the button to listen to Kate's messages.

And froze. "Katie dear, it's Rachel. I wanted to ask you about a call we got after you left. Concerning an unpaid bill. Phone me when you get back." Hearing his aunt's voice unnerved Jay, and he gripped the countertop for support. She sounded older and a little frail.

For the first time, he let himself consider the fact of Ruth and Rachel's mortality; his gut twisted at the thought of all he'd missed in their lives.

Viciously suppressing the reality of what he'd done, he zeroed in on the message. Kate was defaulting on bills? He'd have to look into that.

Another voice broke the silence. "Katie, doll. It's me, Billy. I won't be able to see the girls on Sunday. Something's come up. Tell them I'm sorry. I'll call them later."

That must be the erstwhile husband. Jay didn't know much about her marriage and wondered how he could find out more.

A third message—another male voice. "Kate, it's Paul. Are we still on for Sunday afternoon? I'm anxious to see you."

"You're out of luck, buddy," Jay told the speaker on the phone. "Her ex isn't taking the girls."

Jay was glad, though he wouldn't let himself ponder why.

After retrieving the ice, he left the kitchen and made his way into the family room. He debated making a fire in the big fieldstone fireplace. Deciding his leg hurt too much for the effort, he sank onto the couch and elevated his knee.

He scanned the room, his gaze eventually falling on the chest that contained his old board games. He'd dealt with discovering these better than finding his old books, which he'd come across one afternoon when everyone was gone, arranged on several shelves in the twins' room. He hadn't been able to look at those carefully chosen books with their inscriptions from his aunts, his mother and even some from Abraham. He'd left the room immediately. He was more composed, maybe even more prepared to face the pieces of his past, when he'd happened upon the games...

"Wanna play Uncle Wiggly with us?" Hannah had asked Wednesday night when Kate was on the porch doing the laundry.

"Uncle Wiggly?" He'd been drawn to the chest the little girl had just opened. Sure enough, all his childhood games were there—Sorry, Monopoly, Chutes and Ladders, and several others. The sight of them, and their smell, stole his breath. It was like finding a box full of old photographs.

"Mr. Lawrence, you okay?" Hope had asked.

He'd nodded.

"You wanna play?" Hannah's face lit up.

It just slipped out. "I used to love these games."

"Don't tell them that. They'll hound you to play them." Pivoting, he found Kate coming through the door with an armload of towels. Her hair framed her face wildly, and the red strands shooting through it were highlighted by the pale pink sweatsuit she wore.

"It's all right. I don't mind."

"You will," she'd called out, a light chuckle following her to the bathroom.

Since then he'd played four games of Sorry, two of Chutes and Ladders, and three of Uncle Wiggly; he suspected he'd be in for more before the night was over. For a man used to having dinner at Club 21 on Friday nights, he wondered why he was so cheered by the prospect of a game of Uncle Wiggly or checkers with the girls.

All just part of the investigation, he told himself.

Liar, said the voice from inside.

BALANCING BAGS in each hand, Kate followed the twins through the farmhouse's back door. "I hate grocery shopping,'' she muttered under her breath as she kicked the door shut and plopped the bags on the table in the kitchen.

The girls stood before her somberly. Hope stuck her fingers in her mouth.

''Sorry, Mommy.'' Hannah's eyes were downcast in the perfect imitation of a penitent sinner.

''Sorry won't cut it, young lady. Go straight to your room.''

''For the whole night?''

Kate glanced at the clock. ''Until eight. You can watch a half hour of TV and then bed. And no arguing. I'm not happy, Hannah.''

''...didn't mean to...'' Hannah grumbled as she trudged down the hall.

Hope said, ''Can I go, too?''

''No, Hope. Hannah's being punished. Stay out of your room. You can lie on Mommy's bed and look at books or watch TV if you want.''

''Is everything all right?''

Kate was startled by the male voice coming from the semidarkness of the family room. ''Oh!''

''Sorry, I guess you didn't see me sitting here.''

Her heart settled a bit in her chest. Until he crossed into the light and she got a good look at him. He'd obviously just showered. His hair was wet and combed back off his face, appearing brown, not dark blond. And he smelled heavenly, like the expensive cologne in those scratch-and-sniff ads in magazines.

''No, but it's okay.'' She glowered after her daughter. ''I'm just on edge.''

''So I see.''

''Mommy's mad at Hannah again.''

"Surely she didn't misbehave in the grocery store."

Even Hope caught Jay's teasing tone and rewarded him with a conspiratorial smile. "Aunt Ruth says she's a devil sometimes."

"What did she do?" Jay asked after Hope headed toward Kate's bedroom.

"I'll tell you as soon as I bring in the rest of the groceries."

"I'll help."

"You will not. Sit and have some coffee. We can talk while I put them away."

"Yes, ma'am." His voice was playful again. It drew Kate in, as if a spell was being cast with each syllable. She shook off the whimsical thought, telling herself this wasn't a Stephen King novel.

After she retrieved the other eight bags, she found him seated at the table, sipping coffee and watching her; she propped the groceries on the counter and opened the cupboard to stow things.

"So what did the little Wild Thing do tonight?"

"Have you read Sendak's book?" Naturally, *Where the Wild Things Are* was Hannah's favorite story.

"Yes." He seemed uncomfortable answering. "Hannah?"

"She hid from me."

"Hid?"

"Yep." Kate had to keep herself from slamming the coffee cans onto the shelf. "One minute she was by my side, the next she was gone."

"Did you panic?"

"If it had been Hope I would have. She'd never trick me like that. But Hannah plays pranks." Kate pushed the hair off her face. "At least this was less visible than the others she's pulled in the grocery store."

"I'm not sure I want to hear this."

She bit back a grin. "They're funny now, but they weren't then."

"I have to know."

Stopping with a can of tuna in her hand, Kate stared off into space. "Well, there was the time when they were two years old and I had them both in those carry seats in the cart. They cracked a half carton of eggs on their heads in the time I reached for a gallon of milk and turned back to them."

Jay chuckled.

"Then there was the time Hannah had just learned about 'stranger safety' in prekindergarten. We were in the supermarket and she wanted a cookie. I said no because it was too close to dinner. When I reached for Hannah's hand to go check out, she threw herself on the floor, screaming exactly what she'd been taught. 'You're not my mother. You're not my mother. I won't go with you. Leave me alone.'"

Jay threw back his head and laughed heartily.

Kate stilled, tightly gripping a package of paper napkins. Though rusty, the sound of his laughter was deep and masculine.

And sexy. It touched something inside her, some feminine part that hadn't been…stirred in a long time. She swallowed hard, unable to remember when she'd been so entranced by a man's laughter.

"…is the most incredible story I've ever heard."

Shaking off the sensual haze, Kate chuckled. "I know. I can't believe what that child does sometimes."

After she finished unpacking the groceries, she reached for the coffeepot. "Oh, messages," she said when she got a glimpse of the machine.

"Would you like me to leave while you listen to them?" Jay asked. Rather stiffly, she thought.

"No, of course not. I don't have any secrets."

She noticed his eyes shift from her as she pressed the button.

"Hmm." She scribbled a reminder on a notepad while a message from Rachel about a problem at work played. "I can't imagine what that's about." Billy was next. Just the sound of his voice, spouting his trademark excuses, set her teeth on edge. And allowed her female insecurity to kick in. Normal response after catching him in bed with another woman, she figured. "Damn him," she muttered, then looked up at Jay. "The girls will be disappointed." Another message— this one from Paul. "Well, that can't be helped." Kate had been looking forward to an afternoon with only adult company, but it wasn't the end of the world.

"Who's Paul?"

"Paul Flannigan. A pharmacist in town."

"Is he a boyfriend?" Jay asked, again with the playful note tingeing his deep baritone.

"I guess. At least he wants to be."

"What about you?"

"I like Paul. But it's not serious."

"He sounded anxious to see you."

"He's…interested." She cocked her head, taking in Jay's Ben Affleck jaw, his Schwarzenegger shoulders and the Tom Cruise glint in his eye. "How about you? Are there women who are missing you?"

"Scores, I'm sure."

She smiled, then glanced back at the phone. "I'm more upset about Billy."

"Your ex?"

"Uh-huh. He isn't very reliable."

"I'm sorry."

Weary, she sighed and rubbed her neck. "Let's not talk about him. What did you do while we were gone?"

Again the slight grin, the faint glimmer in those dark eyes. "I fulfilled the 'one hour of work per day' on your Spare Room to-do list."

Kate's jaw fell open. "You what?"

"Don't worry, I know how to spackle."

"You actually did the work for me?"

"Yes."

She glanced down. "What about your leg?"

"I wore my brace. It was fine."

"Why did you do it?"

He shrugged. "I was bored. I thought I could pay you back for all this," he gestured widely, "by tackling some odd jobs." Another sexy male smile. "And I guessed you might like an hour to yourself tonight."

"I don't know what to say."

His dark eyes narrowed on her. "If you could do anything with a free hour tonight, what would you do?"

She swallowed hard, watching his face for hidden meaning. Just because the husky timbre of his voice kindled something inside her didn't mean that was his intention. She looked away, and her gaze landed on the counter where *her* weekly treat rested. "I'd take an hour-long bubble bath with no interruptions."

Jay glanced at his watch. "Tell you what. Spring Hannah out of solitary confinement, get them ready for bed and I'll read to them, or we'll play games while you have your bath."

This was better than finding a rare book buried in a box at a garage sale. "Really? Do you mean it?"

She didn't understand why his face darkened. "Kate, it's a simple thing."

"Not to me it isn't."

"No, I can see that." His voice was hoarse. "All the more reason that you should have it."

"But—"

Reaching out, he grasped her hand. His was big and warm and cradled hers like a lover's. "You've opened your home to me. Taken care of me for almost a week. Let me do something for you."

"You've already spackled," she joked. But she could feel her breathing speed up and a warm flush sweep through her.

"Go get the girls ready. Then take your bath." He squeezed her hand and her heart somersaulted in her chest. It did cartwheels when he arched a brow and smiled. "I insist. And I'm a man used to getting my way." He left off the *with women,* but she got the meaning. Too loud. And too clear.

"UNCLE WIGGLY says go back three spaces."

"How do you know what that says, Hope?" Jay stared down at the child whose blond ponytail bobbed up and down as she spoke. The girls were dressed alike tonight in yellow footed sleepers, but had different colored ribbons in their hair. "You can't read yet, can you?"

"We know all the markers by heart," Hannah answered for her. "So does our friend Allison."

Hope lowered her eyes, but he caught the sweet smile she threw his way. It made him think of things he'd never have—children and a wife who belonged to him. He sat back and stifled a groan. He had to get a grip, because he was beginning to like these kids. And their mother, who right now was...

With firm resignation, he banished whatever thought was about to take shape in his mind. Especially if it dealt with where Kate McMann was at this very moment, and what she was doing.

He had no business liking or thinking about the McMann family this way. Not when he was going to pull the rug out from under them all in a few short weeks.

Hannah's squeal of delight dragged his attention away from his misgivings. "I only got one... two...three—" she punctuated each word with a jab of her stubby finger on the board "—four spaces to go then I win."

Without thinking, he reached over and brushed the bangs from her eyes. Her fine hair felt like cornsilk. And it was almost the same color. He whispered, "You don't want to brag in front of your sister, do you, Goldilocks?"

Big blue eyes widened. She shook her head.

Hope's fingers crept to her mouth. Thoughtful. Watchful. Not expecting anything from anybody. Just like her mother.

He wondered if Hannah took after her father.

The bastard who'd called and canceled his afternoon with these two precious little girls. The guy had to be nuts. Of course, he'd dumped Kate, too, which made no sense. Unless there was more to her than met the eye, as Jay had first suspected.

But was beginning to doubt.

The game ended with Hannah indeed as the winner. Glancing at Jay, she matched his sober look and faced

Hope. "You only had a couple squares left, Hope. You'll win next time."

Hope smiled at her sister. Jay patted Hannah's head in approval.

Kate appeared in his line of vision. "Now that the game's over, I think it's your bedtime."

Jay turned his head to see her standing behind the couch. Like a lawyer before a judge, he schooled himself not to react. But it was almost impossible to suppress his response to the way she looked. Her hair was up in some kind of knot, from which several tendrils had escaped. They were moist, framing a dew-kissed face. Her cheeks were the color of ripe peaches, and her eyes were slumberous. She'd thrown on a plaid bathrobe, but he could see some purple lace peeking out from underneath. He shifted in his seat.

"Did..." He cleared his throat. "Did you enjoy your bath?"

"It was positively sinful."

Jay's thoughts turned to sin, all right.

"Come on, ladies. Say good-night to Mr. Lawrence and it's off to bed."

With no warning, both girls launched themselves at him for hugs. He caught one in each arm. They felt so good, their sleepers fuzzy against his hands, smelling fresh and clean like baby powder. Billy McMann was an idiot. He hugged them back, then stole a glance at Kate. She was watching him, her eyes glowing. For a brief instant, he wished she knew the real him, wished she was looking with such approval at the man he *really* was.

The girls drew away, planted sloppy kisses on his cheeks and skipped down the hall. "Brush your teeth," Kate reminded them before facing Jay. "Thank you so much." When he didn't respond, she bit her lip in a totally feminine gesture. "For the bath."

He only nodded, unable to speak for the emotion swirling inside him.

Her eyes sought out the clock. "Should I...would you like some company? I can put the kids to bed and come back."

It took the strength of Hercules to shake his head. Standing awkwardly, he reached down and rubbed his knee. "No, I'm tired. And my leg hurts. I'll just go to bed."

He tried to ignore the disappointment in her eyes. He tried to stop his gaze from dropping to the purple lace. He tried to keep his body from hardening at the thought of her in the bathtub. With willpower he didn't know he had, he forced himself to step past her, toward his room.

She halted him with a firm grip on his arm. His hands fisted at his sides. He wouldn't look at her. Couldn't. "Good night," she said simply, then let go and crossed to the kitchen. Switching off all but the light over the stove, which she kept burning like a beacon all night, she left the room.

Grimly, he stood for a long time in the dimness of the farmhouse that had once been his haven. Then he, too, went to his room.

CHAPTER FIVE

KATE TURNED from the sink where she'd been washing dishes. "Good morning."

"Good morning." The crutches scraped on the floor as Jay crossed the kitchen.

"Did you sleep well?" Gulping back her reaction to her initial glimpse of him, she prayed the words came out sounding neutral. He was dressed today in jeans that fit him like a cover model's. Other than last Sunday, she hadn't seen him in anything but sweats. He looked good. Too good, with the rangy, loose build of a natural athlete. The burgundy, thermal, long-sleeved shirt he wore was pushed up to the elbows, revealing the ropy muscles of his forearms.

"Sleep well? Um, not really. I was restless."

So was I. "Oh, dear. Did you overdo it with your leg yesterday?"

"Maybe." He scanned the kitchen, then sniffed. "What smells so good?"

"Chocolate-chip pancakes."

He smiled, but it was colored with melancholy, like most of his responses. He reminded her of Jay Gatsby, whose every expression and gesture was tainted by the sadness he carried within him. She also sensed he was a loner, just like Fitzgerald's hero.

"Do you like chocolate chips in your breakfast?" she asked.

"I used to. When I was young."

Pivoting around, she flicked on the electric frying pan and went to the refrigerator. He set aside the crutches and limped to the coffeepot. She stifled the urge to serve him, given his week-long resistance to her caretaking, and let him pour it himself.

But she'd cook him breakfast.

From the table, after he sat, he asked, "Did *you* sleep well?"

She tugged at the collar of her red plaid flannel shirt and rolled up the sleeves. She was nervous today. "The bath relaxed me." It wasn't a lie. She'd been relaxed. Unfortunately, a little too much. Defenses down, she'd lain in her big bed, acutely aware of its emptiness. She'd begun thinking about sex. And how much she missed it. When she'd finally fallen asleep, she'd dreamed of a tall stranger making love to her.

"This isn't necessary." He nodded to the pancakes, which sizzled in the pan and smelled like mornings at the Sunnyside Café, a popular eatery in town, not far from the bookstore.

"Hey, you're saving me from leaf raking."

"I thought you didn't work on Saturdays."

"The girls view raking leaves as fun. More accurately, jumping in them after *I* rake them is fun." She stared out the window at the lawn, covered with layers of maple leaves. When she turned around, she saw that he'd followed her gaze. His face was transfixed as he watched the red and yellow leaves swirl in the yard. "Did you ever play in the leaves?" she asked, dishing up his breakfast.

"In another lifetime."

She set the pancakes in front of him. "You can come

outside with us and watch. The fresh air will do you good.''

He shook himself, a man returning from the past. ''No, thanks. I have some work to do.''

''I don't even know what you do for a living.'' Refilling her mug, she dropped into a chair and sipped her coffee. Last night, she'd made a mental *What I Don't Know about Jay Lawrence* list. It was very long.

Taking a bite of food, he sighed. ''These are great.'' Evasion again. He rarely answered personal questions.

''What do you do for a living, Jay?'' she asked directly.

There was a long pause. Finally, he spoke. ''I work in computers.''

''So you said. What do you do?''

''I own a company that makes software.''

''In Chicago?''

He cocked his head.

''I noticed the plates on your car,'' she said.

''I came from Chicago,'' he told her. It was an odd answer.

''Is it a big company?''

''No, that's why I'm merging with a larger firm.''

''You're selling out?''

''I'm becoming a partner in ComputerConcepts.'' He studied the room, looking for a distraction. ''Where are the girls?''

''Watching cartoons in my bedroom. They don't watch much TV, but I try to make Saturdays special.''

''So you said.''

Disturbed by his curt manner—emotional armor obviously had been erected when she questioned him about his work—she stood and crossed to the sink to finish the dishes.

"What about you?" he asked, surprising her. "Do you like working at the bookstore?"

"I love it. Next to the girls, and Ruth and Rachel, it's the most important thing in my life."

Silverware clattered to the floor. She pivoted.

Before he concealed it, she saw a hard, suspicious look on his face. "Jay? Is something wrong?"

"I'm just clumsy in the morning." He bent down and retrieved the fork. "Tell me about the bookstore."

Immersing her hands in the soapy water, she stared out the window again. It was a cool November morning, but sunny; though it was unusual for 10 a.m., the wind was starting to blow a bit, which was good because the girls could fly their kites today. She shivered at the thought of what had happened last weekend with the kites. On her Twins to-do list, she put, "Talk about safety again." She replied to his question. "Not much to tell. Ruth and Rachel Steele own it. They started it years ago, and they've built it into a thriving business."

"Unusual for a small town, isn't it?"

"Maybe. Even without the rare books, the main store does all right on its own. We're the only game in town, and people like to read here." She shrugged. "There's not a lot to do in Riverbend."

"Basketball and books," he said sarcastically.

She circled around, stung by his tone. "I guess for a big-city guy, we do seem provincial."

After a moment of silence, he said, "No, I'm sorry. I didn't mean that the way it sounded."

He was a good liar. She almost believed him. "Anyway," she said wiping the counter, "Ruth and Rachel have collected rare books since they were in college in Chicago. Lately, the beat-generation writers." Kate smiled. "Jack Kerouac, if you can believe it."

"On the Road."

"Yes, though he wrote several others." Kate couldn't control the amusement that tugged at her lips.

"What?"

"Oh, I guess it's common knowledge. There are rumors that Ruth had a fling with Jack Kerouac."

"Aunt Ruth?"

She scowled. "Aunt?"

Jay's face reddened. "I guess I hear the girls refer to the Steele sisters like that, so it's how I think of them."

"Oh." The explanation didn't ring true.

"She's gotta be, what? Sixty-five?"

"Uh-huh. You should read some of the inscriptions."

"The books are signed?"

"Some. There's a difference between inscriptions and signings, though. The latter is just the name of the author with maybe a generic Best Wishes kind of thing. An inscription is more personal, like, 'To Kate. Thanks for last night.'"

"Kerouac wrote *that* to Ruth?"

"No, though there *are* a couple inscriptions that read, 'Thanks for your inspiration' and 'You've been a good friend to a lonely writer.' But they're first editions, with dust jackets in A-plus condition. Ruth has been the only owner so..." She shrugged. "You do the math."

A broad grin spread across his face. "Unbelievable."

"Since then, they've collected Kerouac books. We have a huge selection."

"Do you sell them?"

"Some. When Simon thinks it's a good idea."

"Simon? Don't they belong to Ruth?"

"Only a few are her personal possessions. And Rachel owns two. The rest they bought for the store. Along with Ginsberg, Burroughs and Ferlinghetti."

"I see."

A crash sounded from the bedroom. "Oops, I'd better go see what that's about." She bounded from the chair and called over her shoulder, "You really should come outside with us."

SAFE BEHIND his locked bedroom door, Jay could hear Kate and the girls' laughter bubble through his open window. He booted up his computer, clicked into a search engine and typed in "rare books." In no time, he was in the Advanced Book Exchange, which listed books for sale in the collectible market. Steele Books had to be represented on the Internet; even Riverbend was out of the cyberspace Dark Ages.

Sure enough, there it was. A dozen of Jack Kerouac's books were listed. He whistled. A couple were going for thirty thousand dollars. Some twenty. Many in four figures. He leaned back and sighed. No wonder the store was doing well. The rare books alone would give him the cash he needed. And for all but a few, he owned this gold mine.

Ruth is rumored to have had a fling with Kerouac...

Suppressing the thought, Jay searched the desk for paper. He'd make some notes, do some calculating. He came up with nothing. Leaning over, he pulled out a drawer of the filing cabinet next to the desk. It was empty except for some pretty pink paper. He picked up a piece and uncovered some manila folders. The one on top was decorated with daisies and other flowers.

In neat calligraphy were the words "Kate's Wish Folder."

He lifted it out of the drawer. Two more folders lay underneath it, "Hannah's Wish Folder" and "Hope's Wish Folder." What the hell were these?

Torn, he blew out a heavy breath and stared at Kate's. Did he want to read this? Somehow it seemed different from rifling through her computer records— legally most of those records belonged to him. This, however, was clearly personal property.

Didn't stop you from searching her room.

For a minute he was bombarded by the images of the very feminine bedroom he'd explored Friday morning. White wicker furniture, which she'd most likely painted herself, included a bed, dresser and an old-fashioned chaise longue. The floor was hardwood, partly covered by a woven green-and-white carpet. Subtly striped wallpaper in several shades of green. A bed big enough even for him. A mint-green comforter that she'd probably sewed on that machine in the corner, and curtains to match, with soft shades underneath.

Her closet had revealed a paltry booty—a few skirts, some dressy pants, lots of jeans. In the bureau he found sweaters, shirts and plain cotton underwear. Of course, she couldn't afford Victoria's Secret, though she'd be dynamite in those little push-up bras and skimpy thongs that made a man's mouth water.

Damn, why was he thinking about her in underwear?

Because he couldn't sleep last night picturing that purple lace he'd gotten a glimpse of. And the body that it covered. Though *why* he was thinking of her this way, he couldn't say. He fingered the folder. She certainly wasn't his type. Freckles, untamed hair and colt-ish legs had never appealed to him before. He preferred cool, slick women like Mallory who knew how to please a man in bed. Briefly he wondered about Kate's sexual experience. She had such a naive quality he had trouble imagining her coming on to a guy. He'd bet the right man could bring out passion in her, though…

He swore again, this time vilely, and glared at the folder. He was getting soft and couldn't afford it.

"Know thy enemy," he said aloud as he opened the folder.

There were pictures in here, cut from magazines—one of a huge bouquet of wild daisies that looked so real he could almost smell them. Another of a bottle of Paloma Picasso bubble bath—with a big price tag. Others of an electric drill? A sander? He shook his head. Less surprising were pictures of clothes—a cashmere sweater dress the color of ripe cherries that would look terrific clinging to her slender hips. A heavy suede coat from Neiman Marcus. A leather-bound edition of *Romeo and Juliet*. Another normal wish—a brochure from Florida's Disney World. He couldn't keep himself from smiling as he walked through her fantasy world. Until he got to the last picture.

This one Kate had drawn—sketched really. It was a sign like the one over the bookstore. But instead of reading Steele Books, it read *McMann* Books.

So, it looked like he wasn't the only one after Ruth and Rachel's collection.

With the knowledge that she was indeed after the bookstore, his heart, for some reason, plummeted.

"I'M SORRY. They can be really insistent." Kate watched the thunderclouds pass over Jay's face. "You don't have to eat out here with us."

"It's fine, Kate."

It wasn't fine. His tone was clipped. "No, really, it's okay."

Hannah crawled up on the picnic-table bench and snuggled up next to him. "You like white or red hot dogs?"

"White."

"So does Mommy." Hope stood guard next to the table, holding down the paper products so they wouldn't blow away.

"They're almost done," Kate called out.

Jay stared at her as if he was X-raying her. Had she done something to offend him? She hoped not. *Oh, God, please don't let him have seen my reaction to him this morning. I can't help it if I'm attracted to him. But I won't act on it. He's way out of my league. Besides, he scares me a little.*

"Mommy, you look sad."

"No, sweetie. I'm starved." She flipped the hot dogs once more. "I'm going into the house to get the rest of the food." She glanced toward the road. "Come on, girls."

"I wanna stay here."

"Me, too."

Kate sighed. "Not on your life."

"I'll watch them." Jay's voice was deep, husky. Warmer. "They'll sit right on this bench with me. Won't you, ladies?"

"Will you tell us a story?" Hannah asked.

"Yes, about little girls who disobey their mothers and what happens to them."

Hannah got the message. "We'll be good for Mr. Lawrence, Mommy. I promise."

Kate left them settled on the bench, thinking about the mercurial man staying with her. He'd been warm and friendly this morning, and now he was distant. Maybe he was in pain. Maybe the twins were bothering him. Maybe he was bored. Gathering the potato salad and raw vegetables, she entered onto her Self-Improvement list, *Don't take on other people's issues.* Jay's moods weren't her problem. She just owed him, big time.

When Kate had the food ready, she trundled back outside.

But the picnic table was empty. She surveyed the yard and found them by the shed. Jay was sitting down on the old wooden stump, his leg outstretched, patiently instructing both girls. "Hold the string like this...then let it out a little at a time...take a few steps—you'll have to run to get it started..."

He was teaching them to fly a kite. Like a father would. The scene made something inside Kate shift. She glanced at her own kite lying on the ground. The one decorated with a whole, normal, healthy family. For a minute her eyes stung. No matter what she did, no matter how long or hard she worked, she couldn't give her daughters—or herself—what they wanted most in the world. A whole, complete family.

As she watched both Hope and Hannah get their kites up and shout with glee, a list buried in the deepest recesses of her soul surfaced. She hated this list, fought it back, refused to put entries on it. But it was there. Detailing all her inadequacies.

The Failure list.

SOMETHING WAS WRONG with Kate. As Jay sat down to eat with a little blonde on each side of him, their mother took the bench opposite them. *He* felt better—breathing in the fresh air, watching the kites soar, hearing Hope and Hannah's squeals of delight, which almost made him forget why he was here and what he was doing.

The silent woman across from him was a sobering reminder. Still, he couldn't let it go. "Are you all right?"

"Of course." Her smile was as phony as Mallory's when she was trying to coax him into or out of something.

He fixed his hot dog by rote, stealing glimpses at Kate. *Sad.* She seemed sad. He'd never seen her like this in the six days he'd been staying here. Not that she didn't have reason to be a lot more than sad. Her life was tough. Hell, she was probably tired.

"Just like Aunt Rachel." Hope's voice startled him.

"What did you say, Hope?" he asked.

"You eat your hot dog just like Aunt Rachel." Her face scrunched up in displeasure.

"How's that?"

"One line of mustard. One of ketchup. That pickle stuff. Some smelly onions."

"Honey, a lot of people like hot dogs with everything on it." Kate smiled indulgently at her daughter.

"He puts it together like her."

This time Kate's smile was nonplussed. "You know, she's right."

Jay shrugged. "Small world, I guess." Damn, he'd forgotten. Thinking about Kate's mood and enjoying the kite flying, he'd forgotten to watch himself.

Riverbend is turning you back into Jacob Steele.

Like hell.

Promising himself he'd go inside right after lunch, he ate his food.

But he didn't return to the house. The girls enticed

him into staying out and watching them fly their kites, while Kate raked leaves. Her melancholy mood seemed to dissipate with the exercise and the brisk air. As she worked, she glanced over at her daughters and smiled or joked with them. They even nagged her into flying her own kite. Jay was mesmerized by her girlish laughter and youthful surprise when it soared above them. He didn't miss the decoration on hers, either—the myth of the big happy family.

The wind took an unexpected turn and her kite nose-dived. Right into him. It bounced off his arm and landed on the ground. He grabbed it before it blew away. She jogged toward him, giggling. Her cheeks were ruddy, her freckles more prominent today. Bits of leaves nestled in her hair, which had long ago escaped her ponytail.

"Sorry," she said, the genuine smile back.

He couldn't keep himself from staring at her. "You have leaves in your hair."

"I do?"

Standing, he held the kite with his right hand. He was almost a head taller than she, and she was forced to look up at him. Her eyes were grass-green, deepened by the color of the soft fleece jacket she wore. Her lips parted as he scrutinized her face.

Slowly he reached out and brushed the leaves from her hair. When they were gone, he ordered himself to take his hand away. Instead, he gently grasped several strands and tucked them behind her ear. He turned his knuckles to brush a cheek that felt like cool, expensive silk.

Her eyes widened. But she didn't step away.

She'd let him touch her.

The meaning of that hit him like a sucker punch to the gut.

Without a word, he backed off, grabbed his crutches and unsteadily made his way to the house.

THEY STAYED OUTSIDE like the Wilderness Family all afternoon. It wasn't until late-day shadows crept across the wall, etching out the soon-to-be bare trees, that Jay heard them scuffle in the back door. He'd fallen asleep, but dreamed of her. She was wearing the cashmere dress, a yellow daisy kissing the soft strands of her hair. When he eased the dress off her shoulders, he could smell the expensive bubble bath on her creamy skin. He'd awakened hard and hurting, and had stumbled to the shower to scour away the vision of her that stayed with him.

He'd taken his time dressing, but continued listening to the three females outside his door. There had been kitchen sounds—the clanking of cups, the rush of water. He could smell hot chocolate. They'd be drinking it with gooey marshmallows and maybe a warmed-up cookie. Then he'd heard the TV. Some children's show, given the tinkling sound of laughter and the mellow, family-oriented music.

At six, he'd given up the struggle and thrown open his door. He couldn't stay away any longer, no matter how much he warned himself he was getting sucked in to this family. The sight that greeted him should have sent him running.

The three were lying on the floor in front of the TV, a patchwork quilt over them, heads nestled on bed pillows. Kate was in the middle, her hair fanned out in silky waves on the light-green case, making him wish it was his pillow. In his bed. A twin snuggled, one into each of her arms; two of the three were sound asleep. Hope's eyes were open, but she was sucking her fingers, drowsily watching the end of the show. As Mr. Rogers bade everybody goodbye, inviting them to return to his neighborhood tomorrow, the music began. Hope turned and nuzzled her mother's breast. Then Hannah bolted awake. "Mom-om," she began. Dropping to his good knee, Jay gently laid a hand over her mouth. "Shh, Hannah, let Mommy sleep."

Hannah gave him a sideways, what's-in-it-for-me look.

Winking at Hope, who watched them wide-eyed and silent, Jay answered, "How about if you, Hope and I make dinner?"

Hope sidled out from under her mother's arm, causing Kate to turn on her side and burrow into the pillow. He stood and helped both girls up.

"We can't cook, silly," Hannah told him.

You're only eight, Jacob, but you should help around the house. Let me show you how to make scrambled eggs. Ruth always pushed him to test his limits. He'd forgotten that, along with the billion other things they'd taught him, believing their lessons would help him become a good man.

They'd be disappointed by how he'd turned out.

"Of course you can cook," he whispered. "I'll show you how."

Reaching down, Jay pulled up the quilt and tucked it around Kate. His knuckles grazed her shoulder. She sighed and dug her face into the pillow. Drawing back, he took each child by the hand and led them to the kitchen.

"Now what should we make?"

"Mommy was going to cook pork chops," Hope informed him dutifully.

"Yuck." Hannah crinkled her nose.

Jay thought back to when he was young. His aunts had served things like soup, tuna casserole and, ahh, fritatta—one of his favorites. He wondered if Kate had the ingredients. Checking the fridge, he found eggs, onion, peppers. In the freezer was hot sausage. Of course Kate had bought the fixings—she made a lot of his aunts' recipes.

Just like a daughter.

The thought niggled at him as he set the twins up at the table, showed them the right way to crack an egg and, remembering the incident in the grocery store, warned them that they needed to get all eight *inside* the bowl. They giggled at the reminder of a story they no doubt had heard told over and over.

When the sausage was thawed and cooking, he joined the girls at the table to slice the onions and peppers.

"Look, Mr. Lawrence, we didn't spill any."

Leaning over, Jay checked the eggs. "Great job." He kissed Hope's nose. "Now you have to scramble them." He rummaged in the drawer for a whisk and showed them what to do with it. Hannah was eyeing the eggshells—no telling what she had in mind for those—so he set *her* up with the tool while Hope held the bowl and he disposed of the shells. He ruffled Hannah's hair. For a minute, she leaned into his hand, looked up at him and smiled.

His heart turned over in his chest.

By seven, the food was simmering in the electric frying pan, and the girls were sipping warm cider as they colored at the table. Jay found a beer in the refrigerator and had just taken a seat, wondering if it was Paul Flannigan's beer. He wanted to know about this pharmacist who'd had a date with Kate tomorrow. What was he like? What kind of man did she prefer?

"What's going on?"

The three turned to see Kate in the open space between the family room and the kitchen. Jay gripped the bottle hard. Flushed from sleep, her skin glowed like the prettiest of sunsets. Her hair tumbled in wild disarray around her face, and the top button of her flannel shirt was undone. Her sleepy eyes seemed to beckon a man to bed.

"Mr. Lawrence and us made supper."

"Supper?" She glanced at the clock over the stove. "Oh, my God, I slept all this time?" Her eyes darted to the girls. "They could have... Sometimes I take a nap with them, but I can feel them move. At the very least, they always wake me up." The woman couldn't even steal a nap Saturday afternoon. Her responsibilities overwhelmed him.

"It's all right, Kate. They would have wakened you. I came out and spirited them away to cook dinner."

After shooting him a grateful look, she sniffed. "Rachel's fritatta?"

Clearing his throat, he said, "I don't know about that. Some of the best restaurants in Chicago serve it for lunch."

"Oh." Her eyes focused on him. "This was so sweet of you—letting me sleep, cooking." He knew she didn't mean to give him a Jezebel smile. Nonetheless, it claimed her lips. "How can I thank you?"

A dim bedroom with tangled sheets would be a good beginning, he thought. Lord, what was happening to him?

DESPITE THE ARTHRITIS acting up in her knee again, Ruth bent down and hugged little Hannah. She'd watched the girl during the services and concluded, by the child's lack of fidgeting, that something was wrong. Since Hope flew to the altar to find Rachel as soon as the organ played its final note, Ruth decided the McMann girls were unhappy on this sunny Sunday morning. While Kate was talking with Lynn, Ruth resolved to get to the bottom of it.

"What's wrong with my girl, Hannah Ruth?"

Hannah's big blue eyes were wounded, like a baby bird's with a broken wing. It wasn't often that she saw Hannah so subdued; like Ruth herself, Hannah was tough. "Daddy doesn't want to see us today."

"I thought you were spending the day with him."

"He said he couldn't come." The little girl scowled. "I hate him."

"It's not nice to hate in church, love." But understandable. Ruth's own feelings were none too Christian where Billy McMann was concerned.

"Can we come and see you today?" Hannah asked.

"Oh, dear, Rachel and I are volunteering at the seniors' residence all afternoon. Or we'd love to have you." Ruth glanced over at Kate. She had a date later with that handsome Paul Flannigan. Another reason Ruth wished she and her sister could take the girls.

Seeking out Rachel's help, she turned toward the organ. Hope was cuddled against Rachel's ample bosom. Tearful. Hurt. Ruth caught Rachel's eye. God wouldn't like all these negative emotions bouncing around in His church; even angelic Rachel looked angry. She coaxed Hope up and, grasping her hand, led her toward Ruth and Hannah.

The two sets of twins met in front of the sanctuary.

Rachel drew in a deep breath. With no prelude necessary, she said, "What shall we do?"

"We could cancel our afternoon at Golden Fields."

"You'll do no such thing." Kate had come up behind them.

Again, Ruth sought out her sister's silent opinion on how to proceed. Rachel nodded to her. Ruth said, "Maybe they could spend the day with Allison."

"No, Grace and Ed were taking their three to visit their grandparents. I'll do something special with Hope and Hannah."

"You have a date," Ruth said. At this rate, Kate was going to end up a spinster, but unlike Ruth and Rachel, she didn't have a sister to keep her company in her old age, so it wasn't acceptable. "Maybe you and Paul could take the twins somewhere."

Kate shook her head. "No, I've canceled our date." She bit her lip, obviously exasperated and embarrassed, much as she'd been when that rat had cheated on her and the whole town found out. "What would you like to do today, girls?" she asked with false cheerfulness.

Both were silent. Hope hid her face in the folds of Rachel's long flowered skirt.

"I'll think of something fun," Kate promised.

Rachel knelt again and faced both little ones. "When Jacob was small, sometimes his father backed out of his promises to spend time with him, too." Bless her heart, Rachel really knew how to make people feel better.

"What did Jacob like to do, Aunt Rachel?" Hope asked.

Rachel smiled. So did Ruth. "He liked to fly kites."

"And jump in the leaves."

"And this time of the year," Rachel said, her throat tight, "we used to take him on hayrides."

"Tell you what," Ruth suggested. "Why don't you plan to stay with us next Saturday, overnight. Maybe Allison can come, too." The girls' eyes brightened. They loved sleepovers. "We'll do something special Saturday, then bring you to church Sunday and your mom can meet you here."

As consolation prizes went, it was a good one. Kate smiled at the sisters. "Great idea. Let's get on home and see what we can find to do in today's paper." She leaned over and kissed Ruth's cheek, then Rachel's. "Thanks. Again. What would I do without you two?"

As Kate trekked out of church with her solemn, but less-sad girls clinging to her, Rachel said, "Some things just aren't fair, are they, Ruthie?"

Ruth sighed. "I wish she'd find a man." She faced Rachel. "Why don't you talk to God about that, sister?"

"Why don't you?"

Ruth rolled her eyes. "We all know who's got an in with You-Know-Who."

Rachel tried to smile, but Ruth knew that she was thinking about Jacob. She probably felt that if she'd *really* had an in with You-Know-Who, Jacob would be back in town this very minute.

CHAPTER SIX

DEPRESSION DIDN'T often rear its ugly head in the McMann household, but Kate was having trouble keeping the black monster in its murky depths. As she drove home from church, she cursed the catch-22 situation she found herself in with Billy and the girls. If she allowed them to see him, they were destined for these kinds of disappointments. If she didn't, they'd resent growing up without a father in their lives. Uncharitably, she admitted that Billy would never be a father to the girls in the real sense of the word. She added *Check out self-help section of the store* to her Good-Parenting list.

"Mommy, Hope's *looking* at me."

Kate peered into the rearview mirror as she signaled her turn into the farmhouse driveway. "Hope can look at you, Hannah."

"Uh-uh. Not like that. Tell her to stop *looking* at me." When Billy pulled one of his no-shows, Hannah got difficult.

Hope's eyes teared. She, on the other hand, cried over her daddy's neglect. Kate empathized with both her daughters. Her own father had left town when Kate was the twins' age and they'd never heard from him again, so she knew what abandonment felt like. And then, of course, there was the fact that she wasn't able to hold on to her own husband.

With the sluggishness of old women, the three of them exited the car and dragged their feet all the way to the back porch and into the farmhouse.

"What do we have here? I thought Halloween was over. You two look like zombies." Jay Lawrence sat on the family-room couch; he put down the paper he'd been reading as they entered. Kate groaned inwardly. He was dressed again in jeans, which seemed to caress his long, muscular legs. With them he wore a denim shirt and a bulky navy-blue sweater. She didn't need the epitome of maleness facing her when she felt like a world-class loser.

"What're zombies?" Hannah asked, climbing onto the sofa next to him. Hope followed suit.

"Living people with no life in them."

"They were in that Halloween book Aunt Ruth got us," Hope put in. She smiled so ingenuously at Jay that Kate's heartbeat stuttered. Her children craved male attention.

To cover her reaction, Kate headed for the kitchen and the coffeepot. From the corner of her eye, she saw Jay ruffle Hope's hair. Then Hannah's. "So why the glum faces?" he asked.

"Daddy's not coming today. And Aunt Ruth and Aunt Rachel are too busy to take us." The fact that Hope's tone was so resigned hurt.

"Even the Penningtons are away. Nobody wants us today," Hannah told him bluntly.

Her back to them, Kate swallowed hard and gripped the mug. How did she deal with this kind of rejection? Keep them busy, she guessed. Turning she made her way to the family room. "I want you! Why don't we—"

Jay spoke just as she did. "*I'd* like to spend today

with you." From the coffee table, he retrieved a torn page from the newspaper. "As a matter of fact, I found this advertisement for a special event in Graysberg."

Graysberg. The next town over from Riverbend. Where Kate had walked in on Billy with another woman.

Hannah grabbed the paper and the two little girls pored over it as anxiously as kids making a Christmas list. Both looked up at him. "A hayride," they said together.

"Uh-huh." His smile made Kate's toes curl. Not only was it rare, but it was so big and broad and earnest it altered his whole appearance.

"Aunt Ruth just told us she used to take Jacob on hayrides, didn't she, Mommy."

"Yes. This is quite a coincidence." *And a blessing.* What had she done to deserve the appearance of Jay Lawrence in her life?

Jay did not meet her gaze. "I called while you were gone and reserved four spaces." He glanced at his watch. "But we have to be there in thirty minutes." At last he looked at Kate. "What do you say, Mommy?"

She knew her eyes were bright with emotion. She couldn't control it, though she did gulp it back. "I say yes." She addressed the girls. "Run in and change."

As the twins scooted to their room, Kate followed them. But in the hall, she turned back. Jay was watching her with something different in his eyes. Pleasure, but once again tinged with sadness, almost worry. "Thanks. For this."

"It's not much. After all you've done for me."

"You really are a lifesaver."

His look was pained. But he said, "Go change." She

was halfway to her bedroom when he called out, "Dress warmly."

THE PUNGENT SMELL of hay and the rich loam of the overturned earth catapulted Jay back to his childhood more than anything in Riverbend had done so far. As he assisted Hope up onto the wagon, while Kate got Hannah settled, he was swamped by the memories.

Jacob, look at the horses. Aren't they beautiful? No, sweetheart, don't throw hay in Aunt Ruth's hair. She's trying to impress that handsome gentleman driver...

"Can you get on without help?" Kate asked him.

Retreating from the images, he focused on Kate. Her well-worn jeans were not designer. But his very male libido appreciated how they molded to her bottom. Under her green fleece jacket, she wore what looked like a handmade, off-white, fisherman's sweater. She was pointing to his brace, which he'd put on over his jeans. He was thankful he'd thrown on his leather jacket, because it was cold out here. He worried her coat wasn't warm enough.

"I can get on just fine." Expertly, he faced away from the wagon, braced his arms on the flatbed and hiked himself up; he slid over next to one of the bales and stretched out his leg. Immediately, both girls clambered over their mother to sit on each side of him. A strong rush of emotion for these little ones swamped him. He averted his gaze to control it, but caught sight of their mother staring at him as if he were a superhero.

He should have known this excursion would cost him emotionally, bringing back all kinds of memories and longings he thought were dead and buried. But he couldn't resist alleviating the gloom that had settled on the McMann household this morning when Kate finally told the twins their father wasn't coming for them to-day.

He'd like to beat the shit out of the jerk.

Oh, and you're such a saint. What he was going to do to Kate surpassed anything Billy McMann had ever thought of doing. Jay's actions, after all, were conceived with malicious intent.

A bump, a jostle and the voice of the driver distracted him as they got under way. All the kids aboard squealed with delight when the horse picked up speed and the driver pointed out the sights. Ignoring the scenery, Jay surreptitiously watched Kate, who was as excited as the twins. A world away from this morning when she'd been truly upset by the bad news she'd brought them. But he sensed an underlying anger in her then, too. Good. She needed to develop some armor.

Especially when you show your true colors, Lawrence.

The only way he could live with himself was by promising that inner voice he'd end this charade soon. Somewhere this week, he'd decided that Kate had never been sexually involved with his father. He'd also realized she wasn't milking his aunts for money; true, he'd discovered she was interested in owning the store, but during a restless night, he'd decided she meant to come by it honestly. Deep in his heart, he'd admitted she was everything Nick Harrison had said she was. So he had to tell her who *he* was, what he'd come to do, and leave the farmhouse.

Because something had happened that he hadn't counted on. Last night, after he'd tossed and turned for hours, he'd finally admitted he was attracted to Kate.

He didn't know how it had happened. He hadn't intended it to, certainly. But somehow, over the past several days, living in their home, he'd developed very male feelings for Kate—and worse yet, he'd come to care deeply for all three McMann females.

He struggled to banish the dread over what he had to do, despite his feelings. "Great weather, don't you think?" he said companionably.

"Mommy loves the sun." Hope's gaze was misty-eyed with dreams of the future. "Someday, we're going to Florida."

"To Disney World." Hannah was certain of it.

Yes, I know. It's in her Wish Folder.

"It's a great place."

"You been there?" Hannah wanted to know.

"Yes. As a child and as an adult."

"Tell us 'bout it."

So Jay talked. Remembering Main Street USA, Cinderella's Castle, Space Mountain, he drew verbal pictures for two little girls who'd never had all the opportunities he'd had. Would probably never have them now.

Because of him.

For the first time, he let himself consider what would happen to Kate and the kids financially when he sold off the bookstore and their home. It disturbed him.

Kate smiled at him as he talked, not knowing he was a snake in the garden of the small Eden she'd created for her girls. "You've probably traveled a lot."

"Yes, I have."

Hannah squealed, "Look, Mr. Lawrence, cows."

Over the girls' heads, Kate and Jay shared an amused look, just like a mother and father would when their kids said something cute. Though it made Jay nervous, it felt so good he allowed himself to bask in the exchange.

As he basked in the rest of the delightful day. The bumpy trip lasted a couple of hours; afterward, they gobbled up hamburgers grilled by the farmer who sponsored the hayride. Then they played hide-and-seek in the corn maze.

Though his brace slowed him down, Jay dashed in and out of the cornstalks and bales of hay holding Hannah by the hand. Kate kept Hope with her. At one point, the duos backed into each other, and the girls yelped with joy as the two of them fell onto their bottoms.

Jay grasped Kate by the shoulders to keep her upright. Her hands clutched at his arms. "Steady now," he murmured hoarsely, staring down at her. Her freckles had been lured out by the sun and covered her cheeks and nose. But it was her eyes that glowed. As the kids lay back on the straw and kicked their legs in the air, Jay allowed himself to drink in the sight and smell of Kate McMann. He was sure he'd never seen anything lovelier, smelled anything sweeter, touched anything softer.

The air was cooler now. "This coat's not warm enough," he said huskily. "You need something heavier." Without thinking, he reached down and tugged up its zipper. Her breath caught at the intimate gesture, but she didn't draw back. Instead, and unconsciously he was sure, she leaned into him. Her breasts brushed his chest and his whole body reacted with a violent surge. Of need, of desire, yes. But also with an overwhelming tenderness that he hadn't felt for years. Ever since he'd left Riverbend, Indiana.

Still, even that reminder couldn't break the spell. It

intensified when Kate reached up and brushed her palm down his cheek. "Thank you so much for all this, Jay. It means a lot to me."

He didn't answer. He just stared at her, wanting to kiss her so badly he ached with it. He even started to lower his head, until he remembered where they were and that their little audience watched from below with owl eyes. Ordering himself to back off, he gathered her close for one generous hug, then stepped away.

She averted her face and the kids jumped up.

"What do you wanna do next?" Hannah asked.

Jay didn't answer. His X-rated thoughts were not for their chaste ears.

"ARE YOU SURE you can carry her?" Kate asked as she lifted Hope out of the car and into her arms. Jay was so big she felt foolish questioning him. But he *was* injured.

"Yes, of course. Now go, they're heavy."

Heavy? Kate could have scaled Mount Everest with fifty pounds of gear on her back. Her tread was light as she followed the walkway to the porch, unlocked the door and entered the semidark house. She made a beeline for the girls' room and Jay followed. Kate placed Hannah on her bed; Jay set Hope down and chuckled. "They're worn-out."

"It was that last game of Ring around the Rosy with the other kids that did it."

He checked his watch. "Must be. It's only seven o'clock. Should we wake them up to get ready for bed?"

"No, I'll get them out of their coats and shoes. They'll be up early and they can bathe then."

His exit cue. "Oh, fine." He meant to leave right

away. But knowing what he was about to do in the near future and realizing he might not get the chance again, he leaned over and kissed each child on the forehead. Their noses were cold and they smelled like the outdoors.

He was in the kitchen, sipping decaf coffee when Kate joined him. After pouring herself a cup, she sat down at the table, smiled and opened her mouth to speak. He held up his hand. "Don't thank me again. I can't remember the last time I enjoyed myself as much."

"Really?"

"Really."

"Aren't you bored with all this?"

He shook his head.

"Leg hurt?"

"No." He focused on her with an intense stare. Best to put the machinery in the works now. "My leg's better, Kate."

It was a long time before she spoke. "I know."

"I should—"

She reached up and stopped him by covering his mouth with her fingers. They were rough, but had warmed up with the coffee. He parted his lips slightly to taste them. She whispered, "I know you're better. But stay. Just for a while."

He grasped her hand and kept it near his mouth. "That isn't such a good idea." He kissed her fingers.

"I want you to stay."

Something inside him pushed to try. "I'm not the man you think I am, Kate."

"You're the man who saved my girls and have brought joy to this household every day since."

Oh, God.

"Please, stay a little longer. We all like having you here. You still have business to take care of, don't you? And you can do it from here."

"Yes, but—"

"Only a few more days."

He sighed and held her hand tighter.

And made a monumental decision, one he would be damned to hell for, but he simply couldn't resist. "All right, I'll stay. A little while longer." He buried his mouth in her palm and lowered his eyes from hers. He was afraid she'd see guilt there. And deception.

But, typical of corporate-shark Jay Lawrence, he was going to take from this woman, as he'd said, a little while longer.

"YOU CUT IN pretty well, for a girl." Jay's voice was teasing, husky. Though he wasn't completely relaxed around her, something had changed in their relationship two days ago, when she'd asked him to stay. He seemed to let go of whatever yoke he was carrying on his back and enjoy himself.

They'd had fun Monday night cooking a dinner of breakfast food when Kate realized she'd forgotten to buy the ground beef she was going to use for meat loaf. She'd done the pancakes, Jay had fried the bacon and the girls had been put in charge of the toast. At bedtime, he'd read Tommy DiPaolo's book, *Nana Upstairs, Nana Downstairs* to them, which Kate refused to read because it always made her think of losing Ruth and Rachel and she'd cry. Hannah had taken great delight in seeing the tears sparkle in Jay's eyes at the book's ending.

Tonight, she'd brought home pizza with his choice of toppings on half, and he'd actually persuaded the twins to try anchovies. Then he'd sat with them while they'd baked cookies for a shower they were giving tomorrow for Tessa, Mitch's friend—and a lot more if Kate knew anything. When she went to work on the spare room after Hope and Hannah were in bed, he'd joined her here. All in all, the three of them had been walking on air this week—and it was because of him.

She felt comfortable enough to tease him back and flirt. Dipping the paintbrush in the can, she covered it with eggshell white and bent down to draw the small strip above the wooden baseboard. "For a girl? I'll have you know, in my Home-Repair class, I ran circles around the guys."

No answer. After she finished with the strip, she looked up at him. He was staring at her. She'd thrown on gym shorts, a ragged T-shirt and sneakers, as had he, along with his brace, to paint the newly spackled spare room. She hadn't given a thought to modesty, only comfort, because she worked up a sweat painting; now she was embarrassed by the pose she'd just struck and what it revealed. She smiled weakly at him when she recognized his look.

It was the look of a man aroused. She knew the expression, had seen it on Billy's face, on Paul's and on a few men she'd dated since her divorce. On Jay Lawrence, however, it elicited a swell of response in her. Just as it had Sunday night when she'd begged him to stay.

The thought made her wince.

"What is it?" he asked. "Did you hurt yourself?"

"No. I was just thinking that I asked you to stay and then I put you to work." She gestured to the room, complete now except for the coat of paint over the primer. "It wasn't to paint or spackle."

"You said you wanted to finish this room by Thanksgiving. I wanted to help." His eyes were filled with that guilty look again; he turned away from her and began to roll paint on the drywall.

"I do want to finish it. I always have a houseful for the holidays. I'm going to surprise Ruth and Rachel by having this room done by then." She glanced over at him. "Will you be here for Thanksgiving? We'd love to have you."

"No." His voice was I-won't-discuss-it cold. "What do you mean you're going to surprise Ruth and Rachel by having it done?"

"This isn't my house."

His hand slipped, getting a glob of paint on the wall, which he promptly smoothed out. He glanced over his shoulder. "It isn't?"

"No, it belongs to Ruth and Rachel. It's the Steele-family homestead. Ruth, Rachel and Celia, Tom Bainses's mother, grew up here with their brother, Abraham. He moved out when he married, and Celia moved away, but the sisters stayed on until four years ago when they wanted to be in town."

Nervously, she thought, Jay cleared his throat. "You rent it from them?"

"Nope." Slathering more paint on the brush, this time she knelt down more modestly. She talked as she covered the wall above the baseboard. "They won't take any rent money, since the place is paid for."

"Oh, well, that's good for you, isn't it?"

"I suppose it could be. But I can't accept charity."

"I don't understand."

"We have an agreement. I've been repairing and redecorating the house at my expense in return for living here. I decided on a fair monthly payment and I put the equivalent away in a separate account every month. I use it to fix things up. All except for the room you're sleeping in.''

He took in the information greedily, as if he'd wondered about it. Finally he asked, ''Why aren't you redecorating that one?''

''Because Rachel asked me specifically not to touch it.'' She remembered the old woman's face and the pain she saw there. ''Apparently, Jacob Steele stayed out here a lot. He had his own room. Rachel wanted to keep it just as it was. Why, I don't know. It's almost a shrine. Not that I think the man deserves it.'' Kate reached a corner and angled the brush. ''Anyway, Ruth doesn't agree with Rachel. She wanted it redone, too. But Rachel can be stubborn. It's why my computer is in there. I never work on that room.'' She shook her head. ''I feel like I know this guy from his things.''

''Really?''

''Yeah, he was a big basketball star for Riverbend High and went on to play at the University of Indiana under Bobby Knight. His trophies stare me in the face almost every day. But apparently his books were his most precious possessions.''

''I didn't see any books in there.''

''No, I asked Rachel if the girls could keep them in their room. They were always stealing into Jacob's room to look at them. In case you haven't noticed, they treat those books like sacred scripture.''

''I noticed.''

''We got off the track, I guess. It was a long route to telling you why I'm fixing the house up.''

They painted in silence for several minutes. Finally Jay said, ''You could hire someone to do the work if you've got the money saved for it, couldn't you?'' He hesitated. "Maybe Charlie Callahan or Mitch Sterling could do it."

She shot him a quick glance. "Why should I hire someone?"

He chuckled. "So you could take advantage of your Relaxation to-do list?"

Always able to laugh at herself, Kate giggled. "Am I that obvious?"

"You're an open book, sweetheart."

The endearment was made in a teasing, brotherly tone, but nonetheless it stopped her. Her whole body flushed. Since Sunday night her hormones had been working overtime, and she'd become so aware of Jay's scent and size and overriding masculinity that it almost hurt to be near him. Her skin prickled now with that awareness.

For a man she knew nothing about.

"You're not." At his quizzical look, she added, "An open book."

"I'm a boring volume."

"Are you kidding? Riverbend is boring." She grinned, imagining his life in Chicago. "I'll bet there are big fancy bookstores near where you live and you drink cappuccino and see famous people there."

When he didn't respond, she said, "It's how the aunts described Chicago."

"And the mysterious Jack Kerouac."

"It's so romantic, isn't it? Like a romance novel." She stopped and turned to look at him. "That's who you remind me of."

"Who?"

"The cover model on one of the romance novels in my bedroom." When he made no reply, she asked, "Is something wrong?"

He shook his head. "I'm no hero, Kate."

Embarrassed, she turned away and resumed painting. "I, um, didn't mean it that way. I just meant that ever since you came here you've reminded me of someone. It's the guy on *Passion's Fury*." She grinned. "Well, him and Heathcliff from *Wuthering Heights*."

"Yeah, he's more my prototype."

"No, he's not. Heathcliff turned into a manipulating, vengeful jerk who hurt those he loved most. Even if it was because somebody hurt him irrevocably. You're nothing like him."

Absolute silence made her turn to look at him. His face was a cold, brittle mask. "I'm every bit as jaded and selfish as Heathcliff, Kate."

A foreboding worthy of Greek literature flashed through her. She shook it off. "Why, Jay? What happened to you in the past?"

"Nothing. At least nothing I want to get into now." When he turned back to the wall, he mumbled, "You really don't want to know."

Unnerved, Kate didn't ask why.

ON FRIDAY NIGHT, Jay was still telling himself he had to leave. And he still wasn't listening. He just couldn't bring himself to go, plain and simple. So tonight, at six o'clock, prowling around his old bedroom, he vowed he'd tell Kate everything tomorrow, when the girls were with Ruth and Rachel. Then he'd take off. After she knew what a truly despicable human being he was.

Her view of Jay was so skewed it was almost funny. Except he hadn't laughed when she'd told him about Heathcliff or the romance cover or any of the other times she called him a hero.

Studying the trophies and posters and other personal

items in his room, he admitted why he'd read his own books to the girls, cooked with them, taught them to fly the kites, played his old board games; it was to make up in some small way for ultimately destroying the life Kate had so carefully built.

"Who the hell are you trying to kid, Lawrence?" he asked himself, pounding a fist into his other hand. Like everything else, all he'd done this week was for purely selfish reasons.

He cherished every single minute with Kate and admitted it would be a long time before he'd forget her. He viewed it as his personal purgatory—that he'd remember vividly what she looked like fresh from her bath, with hay in her hair, bending over to paint the room and revealing long bare legs, which sent his blood pressure skyrocketing. And last night, she'd made them Spanish coffee and he'd built a fire; for hours they'd sat discussing their favorite books and authors. He'd been so distracted by the burnished highlights of her hair and how the fire brought out the green in her eyes that he'd become a tongue-tied teenager trying to argue her out of defending James Joyce's *Ulysses* as good literature.

He should have left this house. That she'd pleaded with him not to go was no excuse. He'd wanted to stay. He'd needed to stay. But he knew, in his own perverse heart, that everything he did, including his little surprise for her tonight, would make the whole revelation that much worse.

He deserved more than purgatory; he deserved to burn in hell.

The main door to the house opened and closed with a bang. Then Kate's voice, filled with exasperation, filtered back to him; she spoke more loudly than normal. More firmly. "Wait here. Let me get those wet things off you."

No response from the girls.

After a few minutes, "Now wrap up in these towels and get in your room. Put warm clothes on there."

Not a peep out of Hope or Hannah.

Kate called out even louder, "And think about the fact that I may not let you go to Ruth and Rachel's tomorrow."

"No, Mommy, you can't. I'll die!" Hannah's voice was a strident whine.

"It's what you deserve. Now go. Mommy's livid, and she's going to regret what she says if you don't leave her sight." A pause. "Immediately."

Jay waited through a few minutes of silence, then approached the doorway to his room. From here, he heard rustling, a beleaguered sigh, then Kate grumbling something he couldn't make out. He stepped into the dimly lit hall and found her coming toward him— dressed only in a big, thirsty towel.

Jay envied that strip of terry cloth more than he envied Donald Trump. It was emerald-colored and tied at her breasts. Generous cleavage strained against that knot. Beautifully bare shoulders with just a sprinkling of freckles could be seen above the tight terry cloth. The towel hem ended in a tantalizing display of exquisite bare legs. Her hair was slicked off her face and wet, as if she'd just stepped out of the shower. On the floor of the porch behind her, soggy clothing and shoes lay heaped in a pile. His eyes traveled back to her body.

She'd frozen, like a mannequin in a store. Finally she gasped. "Oh, my God, I didn't think—"

"Lucky me."

Gathering her wits, she glowered at him. "I…" She

threw up her hands, the action tugging mercilessly at the knot. He prayed that it held. He prayed it didn't.

She grasped it. "I'm...so furious. I wasn't think-ing..."

A little of young Jacob Steele's devilment sur-faced—the influence of this house, no doubt. "This must be my day."

The gleam of sexual interest in her eyes was unmis-takable. She smiled a woman's smile. Then averted her gaze. "Excuse me. I need to dress."

"Not on my account," he called after her. Though he meant it—oh, God, did he mean it—he was also trying to dilute her embarrassment.

Wandering into the kitchen, he poured the coffee he'd made earlier and leaned against the counter, for-getting all about his self-recrimination; instead, he lan-guished in the vision of Kate standing before him in only a green towel and a delicate pink blush.

She returned a few minutes later wearing a navy sweat suit. "Sorry," she said sheepishly, as she dried her hair with a towel.

"I'm not."

"Jay, please. I'm embarrassed."

He turned away from her, grabbed a mug and poured her coffee. Handing it to her, he said, "Sit, and tell me what happened to bring you to a state where you'd forget I was here."

She sat. "All right. But I still have to go grocery shopping." She raised her eyes to the ceiling. "I swear if that imp pulls one thing in the store tonight, she'll be in solitary confinement till she's a teenager."

Joining her at the table, he bit back a smile. "What did she do?"

Kate took a deep breath. "We stopped at the car

wash on the way home. Usually, I wash my own car, but I had a coupon for Rite-Wash that I bought from the Booster Club, and it expired today.''

"She didn't!"

Her eyes were rounded with disbelief. "Hannah pressed the button on her side of the car and opened the window in the middle of the cycle. She goaded Hope to follow suit." Kate rolled her eyes. "Do you have any idea how much water can come through the back windows in a car wash? Not only were we drenched, the whole inside of my Jeep looks like Noah's Ark on a bad day at sea." She shook her head fiercely. "I forgot to put the window locks on.''

"Kate, it wasn't your fault. Hannah's a devil. Hope imitates her."

"I know. That's the worst of it. I'm worried about Hannah in her own right *and* her influence on Hope. She does these things without even thinking about others. What did I miss bringing her up?"

"Nothing. It's not so much selfishness as a little gene that makes her curious. Daring." He shrugged. "Mischievous."

"Maybe. Everybody says Ruth was that way and she turned out all right." Kate grinned. "And her influence on Rachel didn't do that sainted woman any harm."

Jay had to smile. He remembered stories about his black-sheep aunt dragging poor Rachel into dicey situations. "See, it'll work out."

Kate sipped her coffee. "I guess." She checked the clock. "I need to get going. The girls had sandwiches at five, so I'll fix you something to eat and then leave for the store."

"Did you eat?"

"No. I've had a vicious day. I'm not hungry."

"What else happened?"

She scrubbed her fingertips over her eyes. "Where would you like me to begin?"

"The store?"

Her forehead furrowed. "I got this odd, official-looking letter from some accounting firm asking to meet with me."

The auditor. Jay had forgotten about that.

"Accounting firm?"

"Yes, and I don't understand why. I couldn't get through to the right person on the phone to ask him."

"Is that all?"

She shook her head. "As you know Izzy's sick, which is why I stayed till six. And Rachel seemed depressed this afternoon, because it's getting near the holidays, and there wasn't a minute to talk to her. And—" She stopped. "That's enough. The icing on the cake'll be taking Satan's spawn grocery shopping."

"Kate, I—"

"No, don't say anything. These aren't your problems. And I hate to whine." Abruptly she stood, crossed to the refrigerator, and before he could stop her, she pulled the handle. "I don't know exactly what's here..." Her voice trailed off. After a long pause, she said, "The fridge is full." She stared at the food as if it might disappear. Then she pivoted. "Jay? Did you stock the refrigerator?"

He nodded, and her eyes narrowed. Then she went to the cupboards and opened each one. They were, he knew, filled, too.

Facing away from him, she said softly, "You went grocery shopping for me."

"Uh-huh."

She gripped the edge of the counter. "How—" she cleared her throat "—did you know what to get?"

"Your list was on the counter."

"You paid for them?"

"Yes."

"I'll reimburse you."

"No, you won't." He added tightly, "I can afford a few groceries."

Another longer pause. "Why did you do this?" It was then that he became aware of the quiver in her voice. Goddamn it, she was going to cry. Over somebody doing an errand for her. He stood and went to her. Sidling up behind her, he grasped her shoulders. "Honey, I did a chore for you."

"Why?"

"Because you hate doing it. Because you had to work late." He kissed the top of her head, her hair still damp. "Because you deserve to have somebody do things like this for you all the time."

Her shoulders began to shake.

His throat clogged. "Shh, don't cry. This was supposed to make you happy."

"It does."

"So I see." His tone was dry.

She didn't laugh.

He tugged on her arms to turn her to face him. She resisted. Exerting pressure, he forced her around as gently as he could. Her chin rested on her chest. He tipped it up.

The sight of her eyes awash with tears for such a little thing floored him. "Kate, please, I didn't mean to make you cry."

"I...I can't remember when someone's done anything this nice for me."

"Your life should be filled with these things." He couldn't keep the harshness from his voice.

For a minute she just stared at him, then buried her face in his chest. Overcome with feeling for this more-fragile-than-she-looked woman, he slid his arms around her. Widening his stance, he fit her body to his. Every curve, every slope and indentation felt like pure heaven against him. He stroked her hair as she cried quietly. He held her, unable to remember any woman in his whole life feeling this good in his arms, so close to his heart. Every single cell reached for her, yearned for her.

She only cried a minute or so, then finally she raised her face to his.

He recognized the craving in those hazel eyes. Lifting his hand, he brushed back her hair. With his fingertips, he traced the beautiful arch of her eyebrow, her upturned nose, a couple of freckles on her cheek. Her eyes said, *Kiss me, please.*

Tonight, he didn't have the strength to resist.

Her lips were softer than a duck's down. They parted slightly then pressed into his. He gathered her closer, felt her breasts crush against him. His mouth became more insistent, refusing to listen to the inner voice that told him to go slow. He parted her lips, and his tongue delved inside. Her response was unexpected—she clutched at his shirt, met his tongue with hers, arched into him. She was sweet and untainted, and the beast inside him struggled to get out and devour her.

He contained it. Instead, he responded to her with a tenderness he didn't know he possessed, hadn't ever demonstrated in his adult life; it was as though some remnant of the gentle boy he used to be had swum to the surface of his consciousness.

Thoughts of that boy, of Jay's true identity, brought

him back to reality. *You don't deserve to kiss her feet, let alone her lips.*

Abruptly, he broke the contact.

Still in a sensual haze, she swayed toward him. He held her away, gently but firmly. She steadied herself and looked up at him with passion turning her eyes the green of new grass.

He stepped back. Searched inside himself for Jay Lawrence, the man he could count on. After a moment, he found him. "I'm sorry. This shouldn't have happened."

"I...I don't understand."

"I know. I'm leaving tomorrow."

"Leaving? Because of this?"

"Partly. But there's more to it than that." He turned his back on the hurt etching her face, knowing he was about to cause her deeper pain. He almost groaned at the thought of it. "Kate, I have something to tell you."

CHAPTER SEVEN

HE *WOULD* HAVE told her, Jay convinced himself as he threw the last of his clothing in the big leather suitcase that lay on his bed. He *would* have if things hadn't become crazy just after the words left his mouth.

Hope had gotten ill. A desperate yell from the twins' bedroom had sent both Jay and Kate running, only to find Hannah jumping on her bed, crying, and Hope bending over a pool of vomit on the floor. He'd been petrified, and all thought of confession had fled. Kate had stayed cool. She'd cuddled Hope on her lap and crooned softly; Jay had picked up Hannah and walked the floor with her head tucked into his shoulder and her chubby little legs clamped around him. When both girls were calm, Kate had whisked Hope to the bathroom and cleaned her up, then taken the children to her bedroom alone. She'd stayed there, while Jay prowled the house, for a good hour.

When she'd come out, she'd looked so pale and distraught, all he'd wanted was to hold her and make everything okay.

"It's happened before," Kate had told him. "The pediatrician said this is how Hope deals with stress—she turns it on herself. I need to be better with them. I think I'll let them sleep in my room tonight. They'll probably be all right to go to the Steeles' tomorrow. Can we wait and talk then?"

He would have agreed to walk barefoot over hot coals at that point, anything to make this easier for her. He'd stepped closer and brushed his knuckles down her cheek. "Go take care of the girls," he'd said simply. Then he'd spent a sleepless night alternately berating himself for his behavior and reliving in Technicolor the glorious moments Kate had been in his arms.

As he dumped all his toiletries into his shaving kit, Jay thought about how she'd left the house this morning without waking him. He wasn't surprised he'd missed her exit. He'd fallen into a deep and haunted sleep at dawn and awakened at eleven to find them gone.

Quickly, he scanned the bathroom, then the bedroom, for anything he'd left. Apparently, he'd packed everything. His gaze lingered on his poster of Larry Bird, his basketball lamp, his trophies. So many good memories of his days in this house. He glanced out the doorway to the kitchen. Now he had one more. The image of a sweet kiss that had turned him inside out in a way that even the kinkiest sex had never done for him.

The fact that he'd had kinky sex underscored how much he didn't deserve her.

Every nerve ending in his body tingled when he heard the back door open and close, then her light footsteps across the kitchen floor. In seconds she was standing in his open doorway. Though he was afraid to look at her, he forced himself to meet her gaze.

"So you *are* leaving." Her voice was gentle—and filled with a resignation that tore at him.

"Yes." He watched her closely. "Are the girls all right?"

"Uh-huh. As I said, this has happened before. I need

to deal with their antics better.'' She stuck her hands in the pockets of her jeans. She shrugged slightly and glanced at his suitcase on the bed. ''I didn't mean to drive you out of here by falling all over you last night.''

Briefly he closed his eyes at the pure error in her statement. ''You didn't. Fall all over me or drive me out of here.''

''Of course I did. And now you're embarrassed enough to lie to spare my feelings.'' Again, delicate shoulders that already bore too much responsibility moved up and down. ''It's all right. You had to go sometime.'' She shook her head. ''Can I help?''

''No.'' He crossed to her. ''Kate, what are you thinking? You look…I don't know. Sad. Uncertain.''

''I'm just not very good with men, Jay.''

He would have laughed out loud if her expression hadn't pierced his heart so badly. ''That's bunk.'' He squeezed her arms.

She tried to back away from his touch. ''No, really I'm not. I went with Billy in high school and we got married right after graduation. I divorced him when I was pregnant with the twins. Needless to say, I haven't had much time to hone my feminine wiles.''

''Your feminine wiles are just fine.''

''Don't patronize me, okay? I'm sure a big-city guy like you is used to more sophisticated…game playing. It's not my style. I just let my feelings show.''

What she said was true. What she didn't know, what *he* hadn't known until right now, was that he hated the game playing.

''What happened with Billy, Kate?''

At that she turned away. ''Please, don't humiliate me any further. It's best that you leave now.''

Before he could stop her, she escaped out the door. He followed quickly and grabbed her arm as she headed toward her room. "Wait a second. I want to talk about this."

Still with her back to him, she crossed her arms over her chest and gripped her elbows with her hands. "Please don't make me do this."

"I want to know."

She pivoted and, biting her lip, stared at him, a grim expression on her face. "All right. First, I want you to know I've gotten over it pretty well, and I realize none of it was my fault. There's no reason to feel sorry for me."

"What wasn't your fault?"

"Billy had an affair."

"I'm sure it hurt, Kate, but it's not uncommon."

"I walked in on him and his mistress in a dingy little room in Graysberg where he was working. He was in construction and followed the jobs. He often stayed overnight in different towns."

Jay nodded for her to go on.

"I'd gone there to tell him I was pregnant with the twins."

"Oh, God."

"We'd been trying for seven years to have children. It had strained our marriage." She raised her eyes to the ceiling. "Do you know what it's like to go from pure bliss to absolute despair?"

Jay saw Sarah's face, then Abraham's, as they'd been the winter break of his senior year. "Yes, Kate, I do."

She cocked her head. "I believe that. In any case, the marriage was over. Billy made a halfhearted attempt to reconcile. But I couldn't bear the thought of

his touching me after seeing him naked in the arms of
another woman.''

"I understand.''

"Obviously, I steered clear of men during my pregnancy and for a few years afterward.'' She raised her
chin. "But I've had some experience since then.''

Mitch Sterling? Probably the pharmacist. Maybe
Nick Harrison. The thought made Jay's fists curl. "So
what did you mean in there that you weren't good with
men?''

"It was never as right with anybody, after Billy. I
responded but not so...passionately.''

He glanced toward the counter where he'd held her
last night. "You responded just fine with me.''

"Don't remind me.'' She shook her head. "Look,
Jay, we both know I'm not in your league. You're used
to sophisticated women. I can't compete. I don't want
to compete. I just wish I hadn't discovered I still
could...that it could be so good...that I could feel...''
Again, she turned her back on him. "I wanted you,
Jay, more than I've wanted anyone in a long time.''

"I wanted you, too.'' He cleared his throat. "I still
do.''

She spun around, her eyes blazing. "Don't *patronize*
me,'' she repeated. "You said you were leaving because of the kiss.''

"I'm leaving because of what I have to tell you.''

For a moment, she watched him carefully, apparently
thinking about something. Deciding something. Her
chin lifted and she stood tall. "Be straight with me.
How do you really feel about me?''

The control he kept on what he allowed himself to
feel, on how he let himself react, snapped. He stepped

closer. "I want you more than I've ever wanted a woman."

Her pupils dilated and her breathing sped up. "Then take me."

"What?" Nothing could have surprised him more.

"I said, 'take me.'"

"I can't. You just don't know…"

As naturally as a long-standing lover, she leaned into him. Running her hands up his chest, she aligned her body with his. "I know you're a good man. You risked your life for my girls. You're kind and giving and you carry an unbreachable sadness within you." She paused. "That's all I need to know."

Without his permission, his arms went around her waist. "No, honey, it's not enough."

She bumped his hips with hers. He was violently aroused. "Yes, Jay, it is."

His hands clamped on her bottom. His heart thrummed. For the first time since he left Riverbend, he felt truly alive, felt as if the world held some hope, some reparation for what he'd discovered here fifteen years ago.

He pulled her to him and buried his face in her hair. Standing in Ruth and Rachel's kitchen, surrounded by the reminders his childhood, he could almost convince himself he deserved this sweet guileless woman in his arms.

Almost.

With one last burst of sanity—possibly thanks to the integrity of the boy he'd once been—he let go of Kate and stepped back.

There was a trace of insecurity in her eyes and a tension in her shoulders that stopped his words of rejection. Suddenly he was infused with myriad emotions—indecision, arousal, decency, and the over-whelming need to prove to this woman that they were both good people, deserving of the joy they could find with each other.

Torn, he grasped her hand and brought it to his mouth. "Are you sure, love?" he whispered against it.

"Very sure."

"All right, then."

Without another word, she turned and led him to her bedroom.

WHO WAS THIS WOMAN in the mirror? Not the Kate McMann she'd known for almost thirty years. The man standing behind her had changed her into someone else. The metamorphosis was thrilling.

First he'd removed her clothing and his, with the fumbling hands and fast breathing of a lover on the edge. Then he'd brought her here, to the beveled mirror she'd found at a flea market and lovingly restored.

He held her eyes in the glass. His were dark with desire. His naked body blocked out the rest of the world, narrowing their whole universe to that spot, that moment. "You take my breath away." Sliding his hands around her, he caressed her breasts.

Her eyes drifted shut.

"No, watch," he said.

She lifted her lids.

He kneaded her gently. The sight of his dark fingers on her pale skin made her moan; her head fell back to a chest sprinkled with dark blond hair, but she kept her eyes open. She watched one of those big masculine hands as it drifted lower. The very air around her crackled with need—emanating from her, radiating from him. "You are so lovely. So desirable." He repeated the words like a prayer.

Somewhere in the dim drugged corners of her mind, she knew what this was all about, what he was trying to do. And it worked. She felt like the most alluring of courtesans.

He kissed her neck. "I want you to remember me. Remember us. Always."

"I will," she uttered hoarsely.

"Promise."

"I promise."

HE POSITIONED HER in the center of the large bed. The window blinds were drawn, allowing only a soft glow of afternoon light into the room. The air was cool, but their bodies burned with sexual heat. Gently he raised her arms until her hands grazed the headboard. The action plumped her breasts; his mouth found one. Her body arched when he took the beaded nipple between his teeth and scraped lightly.

She gasped for breath. "I can't…oh…Jay… please… where are you go…what are you doing?"

His dark head moved down her body. "Loving all of you," he whispered against her slightly rounded stomach. She felt him grin. "This is on my Making Love to Kate list."

Kate laughed, then moaned loudly as his mouth closed over her. She felt as if she was some newly born creature—Eve from Adam's rib, Athena from Zeus's head, Pygmalion come to life—and she reveled in it.

She called out his name, over and over, a name she knew she'd never forget.

THANKFULLY HE HAD condoms in his wallet. His hands were trembling so badly he'd barely been able to rip open the package. He couldn't imagine trying to search his bags for protection. Her cries had stripped him of the veneer of civilization. He felt the beast inside him rumble to get out. He battled it back and covered her body with his.

"You feel so good," she said, arching against him.

"I need you," he told her. "I...I need to be inside you."

"I want that." She kissed his jaw, nibbled on it. "Don't wait."

He didn't.

Never, *never* in his life had anything been so right. "Kate..."

Those were the last words they spoke. Instead, together, they created a unique sexual language that Jay knew he'd remember the rest of his life.

WITH THE GIRLS gone for the night, they'd made love in the family room in front of the fire after eating an early dinner of wine, cold meats, cheese and fruit. Later, they'd come together frantically in the kitchen, against the refrigerator, when they'd been cleaning up. But there had also been the intimacy of shared confidences.

It was morning now, and Kate could hear him moving around the kitchen. Maybe he was cooking breakfast. Instead of wondering what would happen, where this would all lead, she rolled over, grabbed her pillow and lost herself in the images of the night, reassuring herself that he wouldn't just go away...

After they'd made love the first time, he'd nuzzled his face close to her ear. The masculine smell of him had spread delicious warmth through her.

"What's the thing you regret most in life?" she'd asked.

He'd hesitated a long time. "I hurt two people I loved more than anything in the world."

Kate wondered if it was a woman and a child. Had he been married?

"What about you?" he'd asked.

"I wish I'd gone to college."

He nipped her shoulder. "What would you have studied?"

"English Literature, of course."

By the fire, he'd lounged back against the sofa in a pair of navy sweats and nothing else. A scratchy stubble had appeared on his cheeks and jaw.

"What's your greatest ambition?" she'd wanted to know.

He'd stared at her intensely. "Right now it's *not* to hurt the people I care the most about."

Had he meant her? She hoped so.

"You?"

She'd curled herself on his lap. "To be independent, but to have somebody to share that independence with."

And just before they fell asleep, once again spoon-like and safe, she's asked, "What's your best quality?"

Again, he'd thought a long time. "I'm shrewd."

"Mine's hardworking."

He'd chuckled. "No kidding."

But he'd scared her when he'd tugged her closer and said, "My worst quality is that I'm selfish, Kate. And I can't be trusted to do what's right for others."

Picturing him racing across the road to rescue the twins, she didn't believe that for a minute. With utter confidence in his integrity, she'd fallen into a deep and peaceful slumber.

Now it was morning; she slid out of bed and into a long white terry-cloth robe. Padding barefoot to the kitchen, she found him at the sink, facing the window.

He vibrated with an almost tangible tension, as if he struggled to keep something within him restrained. And he wore clothes she'd never seen before. From behind him, she observed how the wool of his blazer hugged his shoulders. Sharply pressed black slacks contrasted with the gray tweed. When he turned around, she took note of an expensive, open-at-the-collar white shirt underneath. He was dressed like a man she didn't know.

"Good morning."

"Good morning, Kate." His voice sounded like a rusty hinge. And for someone who'd indulged in a night of lovemaking, he didn't look sated or peaceful. His face was lined with strain, his jaw was stiff. He hadn't had much sleep, she guessed.

"Something's wrong."

He nodded. "We have to talk."

She suddenly felt vulnerable wearing just her robe. Her legs went wobbly and she sank onto a chair at the table. He set a steaming mug of coffee in front of her. That his hand went to her hair and trailed down it to squeeze her shoulder comforted her some. He returned to the counter; she smiled up at him. "All right, tell me what you've been trying to get out since Friday night."

His face blanked, as if the only way he could utter the words was by bracing himself against them. But he couldn't stifle the regret in his eyes. For the life of her, she couldn't fathom what he had to tell her.

"My name, the name I was born with, isn't Jay

Lawrence. I've legally shortened my first name and taken my mother's maiden name as my last.''

She hadn't expected this. ''Why?''

''Because something happened to me when I was twenty that caused me to reject every aspect of my upbringing.''

''Oh, Jay, I'm so sorry.''

Impatiently, he looked to the ceiling and blinked fast. ''Kate, don't be nice about this.''

''Why not? Changing your name isn't a sin.''

''No, but lying to you is.''

''You didn't owe me any explanation for your name. I don't care who you were born as. I only care that you've been hurt.''

''You'll care who I was born as.''

She straightened. ''All right. What's your given name?''

''Jacob Steele.''

The entire universe stopped for Kate. Her eyes focused on the man before her. *You eat your hot dog just like Aunt Rachel…Ruth's fritatta?…And this time of the year, we used to take him on hayrides.* ''I don't understand. *You're* Ruth and Rachel's nephew?''

''Yes.''

''They can't possibly know you're here. They would have said something to me.''

''They don't know. Yet.''

Reality sneaked in around the wonder. Kate's stomach clenched. ''I don't understand,'' she repeated. ''You acted like you knew nothing about them.'' *The Steele family sounds like an institution.* ''You let me tell you about Jacob Steele.'' *He was a big basketball star for Riverbend High and went on to play at University of Indiana under Bobby Knight.* ''I gave you details about his life." *Apparently his books were his most precious possessions.*

"Yes, I know all that."

"Why?"

"Because…" He gripped the cup, turning his knuckles white, and stared at her bleakly. "Because I wanted to see what kind of person you really were."

"That doesn't make sense. We didn't know each other before you saved the twins."

"I knew who you were. I was on my way here to…confront you."

Her jaw dropped. For the very first time, she realized she'd never asked what he'd been doing on the side of the road across from her house. She'd been so upset and then grateful… "Confront me? Why?"

"Because of your relationship with my…with Abraham."

"Why, what about it?" When he didn't answer she said, "Jay, your father and I became friends the last few years of his life when he visited the bookstore almost daily. He was a lonely man who needed people."

"He was a monster."

"No. No, he wasn't."

"You'll never convince me of that."

"Why? What happened?"

"I won't discuss that."

"Is it why you didn't come home for his funeral?"

Raking a hand through his hair, he said, "I was vacationing on the French Riviera when he died. I didn't know until later."

She waited a moment. "Would you have come back?"

"I honestly don't know." He stared at her. "Let's table the issue for now, all right?"

"Fine. Tell me, why were you suspicious of my relationship with Abraham?"

"Because—" he drew in a breath "—you stand to inherit much of his wealth if...if I don't claim it."

Astonishment made her laugh. "Why on earth would he do that?"

"That's what I was coming here to find out."

"And why wouldn't you claim it?"

"It's complicated."

"I'm smart. Tell me."

He slammed the coffee cup on the counter, the sharp sound startling her. Then he turned to the window, as if he couldn't face her when he told her the rest. "Abraham left me Steele Books and this farmhouse on the condition that I return to Riverbend for eight weeks within the year and work in the bookstore for half that time. If I fail to meet the terms of the will, everything goes to you."

Something was wrong here. He must be confused. "But...but Abraham's *sisters* own the bookstore. And this house."

Jay looked at her again. "Did they ever tell you that directly, Kate?"

Fear stole through her. "No, not directly. But they lived in this house and ran the store from day one. *They* insisted I live here. *They* made me store manager."

"Abraham kept it all in his name."

"Why?"

"Because he was a manipulating bastard capable of anything." He watched her for a minute. "So is his son."

Kate leaned back in her chair and wrapped her arms around her waist. "I see."

"Do you?" He stalked toward her. She had to tilt her head to look at him. "Do you see what he's done to both of us? He's taken what you love most in the world, other than the girls and my aunts, away from you. Just like he took what *I* loved most away from me fifteen years ago."

She swallowed hard. "What did he do to you, Jay? What happened between you and your father to make you leave Riverbend?"

"I won't talk about it. I can't. I've never told another living soul."

She didn't know what to say. Finally, she asked the obvious. "Why didn't you just tell me all this two weeks ago? After you'd recovered from the shock of the accident?"

"Because you gave me a perfect opportunity to find out if you were what you appear to be."

"What else would I be?"

"It doesn't matter now."

"It does to me. What were you looking for?"

"I was worried that you'd talked my father into this little inheritance scheme. And that you were using my aunts, and maybe stealing from the store."

"*Me?*" This was insane. "I love your aunts more than I loved my own mother."

"I didn't know you then. Now I realize you'd never be capable of something like that."

Jay could see when reality began to sink in. He'd expected tears and recriminations. He should have known better. That solid strength that had gotten her through her disastrous marriage surfaced. "And that's why you decided to stay here," she said calmly. Her voice didn't even tremble, but there was an old and weary hurt in each word. "You were *spying* on us."

"Yes."

She shook her head, too untainted and innocent to believe what he'd done to her.

"I did spy on you. For a while. I discovered quickly I was wrong to suspect you of unethical behavior."

"It's why you wouldn't see anybody—Lynn and Tom, Mitch. You know them, don't you? They'd have recognized you."

Confirming her suspicions with a nod, he forced himself to endure the look of disappointment on her face. Briefly, she closed her eyes. "Oh, God, your aunts." She hit her forehead with her hand. "You even called her *Aunt* Ruth once."

"I'm sorry for my deception, Kate." He leaned over and brushed her face with his knuckles. "I care about you."

The chair scraped back, its sound like a gunshot. "I can't deal with that now. I have to think." She crossed to the window, her body tense underneath the soft robe. She looked small and fragile. As he'd thought before, she didn't stand a chance against him. "I have to plan."

He let her think, knowing the pain of all this was going to hit any minute. Witnessing it was the least he could do. She spun around. "All right, so this—" she waved her hand to encompass the house "—all belongs to you."

"I'm sorry, Kate."

She stared at him desolately. They both knew his apology was poor recompense for having just stolen her dreams. The hand-drawn sign in her Wish Folder flashed in front of his eyes. *McMann Books*. It sickened him.

Breathing deeply, she held up both hands, palms out. "Okay, I'll pack and get out of here," she said. "I'll take what we need for a few days, and you can move into the big bedroom. You won't want to stay in Jacob's room." Her voice cracked on the last two words, but she angled her chin determinedly. "I can get my stuff from the bookstore tomorrow."

"I don't want you to leave the farmhouse. Or the bookstore."

"Of course I'm leaving. They belong to you." Pushing away from the counter, she started to brush past him.

He grasped her arm. "Wait."

Her back to him, she halted.

"I want you to stay here. And at the store."

"Why?"

"A lot of reasons." When she remained silent, he struggled for the words. He hadn't planned this, but he knew it was right. "First, I know nothing about running a bookstore."

"You'll learn."

"I want you to manage it, at least until I sell it."

She whirled around. This was what he deserved. There was shock and deep loathing in every feature of her face. "You're *selling* the bookstore?"

"Yes, I need the capital."

"To buy into ComputerConcepts."

He should have known her quick brain would put it all together. He nodded.

Her shoulders sagged. "You're selling the farmhouse, too?"

Another nod.

"Do you have a buyer?"

"My associates have talked with Anderson Books about the store."

Her hand flew to her mouth, as if to keep the contempt from spewing out. "That will destroy Ruth and Rachel." Then as if something dawned on her, tears welled in her eyes. "This whole thing will. Do you have any idea how much those women *love* you? How much they've *missed* you?"

"I do now."

Visibly, she fought back tears. He didn't miss the fact that they were for his aunts' situation, not hers, which, in the space of an hour, had just become desperate. "You'll have to find a way to tell this to them gently."

"I think it will be easier if you don't abandon them now."

"Abandon them? What do you mean? I'd never abandon them." He heard the silent, *like you.*

"If you leave this house and the bookstore, it'll be harder for them."

"How?"

"They love you like a daughter. If you could just stay on until both places are sold, they'll have an easier time with the transition."

"Well, that's first-class manipulation if I've ever heard one."

"No, for once it's genuine concern for other people."

She sighed, obviously unsure of his motives, but worried about Ruth and Rachel.

He pushed ahead, an emotional marauder stealing all she had to give. "There's more to my concern. I need...I need you to help me break the news to them. They're old. I'm worried that the initial shock..."

"I see." She swallowed hard. "I'll do *that*, of course. I won't concede on the other." He didn't respond. "Do you want to tell them today?"

Waiting, probably deciding how much more to press her, he finally said, "Yes." He glanced at his watch. "Right after church if we can."

She checked the clock. "Then I have just enough time to shower and pack a few things." She rubbed her hands up and down her arms and shivered.

"Please, don't leave the farmhouse."

"I have to." She scanned the kitchen. Then the family room. When she glanced toward the bedroom, she flinched. The anguish in her voice hurt him. "I could never stay here now, not after last night."

"Kate, about that—"

She shook her head wildly. "No, please, I can't talk about last night." Taking a deep breath, she said, "I need to concentrate on one thing at a time."

Knowing she was right, he let her go. She needed all the strength she could garner to get through the next few days. She'd do it, too. Like everything else in her life, she'd take this on the chin, without a trace of self-pity or selfishness. She'd been concerned about Ruth and Rachel more than herself.

He looked around the farmhouse. He couldn't stay here, either. Last night had been— He cut off the thought.

And summoned the strength of Jay Lawrence. Because now he was about to break the hearts of the only *other* women in the world he cared about.

CHAPTER EIGHT

KATE'S TO-DO LIST for the day was simple. Drive to the bookstore. Let *Jacob* into the shop. Go to church as the service was ending. Ask Lynn to take the girls for an hour. Follow Ruth and Rachel back to their house. Tell them the prodigal son was back.

In the rearview mirror, she caught a glimpse of the green Volvo trailing her and fought the huge swell of emotion at seeing him sitting stiffly behind the wheel. *Don't think about his reaction,* she warned herself. *Concentrate on the list. The worst thing you can do is feel sorry for the man who just ripped your life apart.*

The man you slept with. The man who touched you, emotionally and physically, as no other man has done before.

Don't think about it.

Better to be the biblical brother, angry and upset at the return of the wayward child.

A little too fast, she drove into a parking space in front of Steele Books. She threw open the car door and climbed out. Looking down, she noticed the gray pin-striped slacks, baby-pink wool sweater and black blazer she'd put on this morning; she didn't even remember dressing. As she made her way to the front entrance, the Volvo pulled in behind her Jeep. At the shop door, she saw in her peripheral vision that Jay didn't exit his car immediately. Head bent, he gripped the steering wheel. It was clearly hurting him to come here for the first time in so long.

Just as it had probably hurt him to enter the farmhouse...walk into his old room...see his trophies and things.

Kate leaned her forehead against the door. And she hadn't even known. He'd been dealing with his emotions for more than two weeks and he'd kept it from her.

What's your best trait? she'd asked him.

I'm shrewd.

"Are you all right?" His voice was hoarse from behind her, where he stood close. But he didn't touch her. Thank God.

Straightening, she fit the key into the lock. "I'm fine."

The door swung open. On the threshold, she glanced around, refusing to acknowledge the sense of loss she felt when she stepped into the store that would never be hers now. The evidence of her efforts over the past several years mocked her: the wallpaper she'd put up herself, the desk and shelves she'd painted with loving care, the café area she'd designed and furnished. All so he could sell it to Anderson Books. Best to keep that fact in her mind, instead of feeling sorry for him.

"You don't have a security alarm?" he asked from outside.

She shook her head and stepped into the shop. Its familiar scent—the smell of new and old books, the faint aroma of coffee—made her stomach clench today. "No. It'll be one of the changes made, I'm sure."

Frowning, he followed her inside and surveyed the area. "It looks so different."

"A lot can change in fifteen years."

Casually, he crossed to the café area and ran his hand over the smooth surface of one of the tables, then slowly moved to the coffee server. His gaze rested on the wall above it, and he didn't move.

"What is it?" she asked.

For long moments, he didn't answer. Finally, he said, "The painting in the middle. It's…it's the Sycamore River and a tree where I used to play." He hesitated. "I jumped off that very limb a million times. I'd recognize it anywhere." His hands fisted, but he concealed them in the pockets of his sport coat and just stared at the painting. Then he bent over and read the signature. "Lily Bennett."

"Did you know her?"

"Yes, and her mother and…father." His reference to Julian Bennett, the revered town doctor, sounded chilly and resentful.

"You don't like him?"

Jay shot her a quick glance. His eyes were bleak. "He…I…" He turned back to the painting. "I liked his daughter. She was one of the River Rats. I remember the summer she fell off that limb and broke her ankle. Our parents forbade us to go back, but we snuck out there, anyway. Lily, too, riding on the handlebars of someone's bike." He faced Kate. "Is she still living in town?"

Kate didn't know what to say. Lily Bennett Holden was now Lily Mazerik. She'd married the half brother Jay didn't even know he had. He was going to be stunned by the revelation.

Not your problem, Kate. On her Things to Block Out list, she mentally underlined, *Don't feel sorry for this guy.* "Um, yes, she's living in town. She moved away, got married, but was widowed and came back to Riverbend this past year.'' Hesitating, Kate added, ''She just got remarried.''

Jay studied the painting.

''I'm going to the church,'' she said.

At that, he whirled around. He looked as if someone had gouged grooves of pain in his forehead and around his mouth. ''All right.''

She reached for the door but couldn't keep from glancing over her shoulder. ''Will you be okay here?''

He dug his hands deeper into his pockets and shook his head. ''You're something else, you know that?''

Her failure list came to mind. Had he ever really wanted her, or was it all part of the ploy? ''Yeah, sure.'' She battled back the hurt and left Jacob Steele alone with his ghosts.

RACHEL STRUGGLED for breath as she bustled into the front parlor ahead of Ruth and Katie. Something was dreadfully wrong, she thought as she removed her light wool wrap and hung it up on the coat tree. The girl had missed church, which was rare, only to show up as everyone was leaving and ask Lynn and Tom to take the twins for an hour. Then she'd told Rachel and her sister that she needed to talk to them privately. Even Ruth was worried; she'd asked Katie point-blank if something was wrong, but Kate had said no, that it was a good surprise. Ruth had sent Rachel a there's-a-problem look. Rachel had nodded in agreement.

Now, inside the house, Rachel switched on the small Tiffany lamp she'd bought in Chicago, brightening up the early-afternoon gloom, then went to stand next to Ruth. Neither asked if Kate wanted coffee. Sliding her hand into Rachel's, Ruth faced Kate. ''All right. What's happened?''

"Will you sit down?" Kate's voice was raw, her pretty hazel eyes filled with concern. For some reason she looked...torn.

"No," Rachel said. "We prefer to stand."

"Out with it, Katie girl."

Kate smiled. Rachel remembered that was Abraham's name for her. "I have some good news for both of you."

"You look like you're going to the guillotine, dear," Rachel tried to joke. "Are you sure it's good news?"

"It is." She cleared her throat. "It *is.*"

Rachel's pulse began to race. "Just tell us, dear."

With a phony smile like the one she donned for Hope and Hannah's sake when Billy hadn't shown up, Kate said, "Your nephew Jacob is back in town."

Ruth's free hand clapped up over her heart. Rachel felt the blood rush to her head and blinked rapidly. Both women stared at Kate. Rachel recovered first. "Jacob's back? Here? In Riverbend?"

The smile slipped a bit. "Yes, isn't that wonderful?"

Feeling Ruth's hand tighten, Rachel spared her sister's face a glance. It was stark white. "Come, sit down Ruthie." Carefully, Rachel led Ruth to the divan. Hands still clasped, they sank down onto the firm cushions. "Wh-where? H-how?" Rachel flushed at her stuttering.

Stiffly, Kate knelt and took each of their free hands in hers. Her fingers were icy, like the river in January. "Jay...Jacob came back to Riverbend at the beginning of November. He's been staying out at the farmhouse. He's the man who saved the twins' lives."

Ruth drew back. "I don't understand." Her voice was old and raw. And a little piqued. "He's been back for two weeks and you didn't tell us?"

"I, um, I didn't know who he was, Ruth." The girl blushed. "He didn't tell me his real identity until this morning."

"Why?" Rachel asked. Alarm tingled along her spine.

Again, Kate faked a smile. "He'll have to explain that. I just wanted to break the news to you that he's here. He was afraid it would shock you too much if he just showed up on your doorstep."

"Where is he?" Ruth asked.

"He's waiting in the bookstore."

"Next door?" Ruth's voice was incredulous. "Jacob's right next door?"

Kate's lips trembled. Throwing her shoulders back, she straightened. "Yes. I'll bring him over." She smiled down at the women. "Can I get you something first? Some tea? You both look a little pale."

Rachel said, "No..."

Ruth finished for her, "Go get our boy."

HER FACE WAS WHITE and her shoulders slumped as she walked into the bookstore. Jay battled back the urge to go to her and hold her close; he wanted, ludicrously, to make everything all right.

Now that's what they call irony, Lawrence.

"They didn't take it well?" His voice was gritty, like a smoker's.

As she watched him, he prepared himself for the knife she should rightfully twist in his heart. His aunts weren't the only ones he'd hurt by his disappearance and his return. "Actually, they're all right. A little shaken." She smiled. "They just want to see you."

Terror shot through him. He'd bought and sold companies, fired high-level executives and risked fortunes on the stock market, all without a trace of anxiety. Now stark fear gripped him with strong talons. He sought out Kate's eyes to steady himself. "Would you...I know I have no right to...would you come over with me?"

Her eyes told him he'd asked for too much. He felt the sting of his own selfishness. No longer was thinking only of himself acceptable. She mattered, too.

"Yes." She sighed. "Ruth and Rachel may need me."

I need you. No, no, that couldn't be. He had no right to need her. Didn't want the right. But an image of her beneath him, stroking his back after they'd made love, giving him a sense of peace he hadn't known in fifteen years, made a liar of him.

"Jay?" She was poised at the entrance. "Are you coming?"

He shook off the memory. "I'm ready."

She preceded him out of the bookstore and walked over to the house next door, never once looking back. Since she was first through his aunts' door, she blocked his view. Once he was inside, she stepped away.

And there they were. Like two jewels nestled in a bed of green satin, framed by ornate wood tables and an oak archway, they sat on the couch, shoulders touching, hands clasped. He remembered that tableau—when he'd been hurt on the basketball court, after they'd fought with his father. He'd also seen Hope and Hannah do the same thing.

No one moved. He just stared at them. After a long moment, he felt Kate's hand on his arm; it drew him from immobility as well as shamed him that she could be so generous. Still, he leaned into her for strength and cleared his throat. "Hello, Aunt Ruth. Aunt Rachel."

Their gazes locked on him unwaveringly as they rose slowly, warily. He shrugged like a little boy caught in some mischievous act. Then he felt Kate nudge him forward. Unsure of his welcome, he crossed to the two women who had once been a major part of his life. When he reached them, they craned their necks to look up at him. They'd gotten smaller. Older. "I don't know what to say," he whispered.

Tears appeared in Ruth's eyes, their clear brown a little duller than when he'd last seen them, but still lively. Then his aunts opened their arms and he stepped into their hug.

They smelled the same, like the lavender water that used to sit on their bureau. They felt frail though, underscoring just how many years he'd missed.

"I'm so sorry," he murmured against the smooth skin of Rachel's cheek.

They held on tight. Said nothing.

Until Rachel drew back.

Ruth disentangled herself, too. "'Sorry' doesn't cut it in this household, young man."

The corners of his mouth turned up. It was what they'd always told him when he did something wrong. "I know," he admitted. "It's important to make up for what I did." He searched his aunts' expressions, stunned, and monumentally humbled, by the unconditional love on their faces. "Is it possible to do that?" He cleared his throat. "To make up for leaving?"

They both smiled. "Of course it is, dear." Rachel reached up and brushed his face with her fingers. Only then did he realize his cheeks were wet.

"Now, sit down, I'll make some tea and we'll talk."

She stepped aside. "Katie, would you—" Rachel stopped midsentence.

Jay looked behind him.

Kate was gone.

"AREN'T YOU COMING to bed?" Lynn stood in the doorway of her kitchen in a soft green robe that highlighted the emerald flecks in her eyes. She glanced at the clock. "It's almost eleven."

Kate smiled at her friend's solicitousness. "In a bit. I want to finish reading the classified ads."

Lynn walked into the room to look over Kate's shoulder. "I thought you found a couple of apartments. Over on Third Street, off West Hickory, where you used to live."

Kate sipped her decaf and ordered herself not to shudder as she pictured the cracked shingles, peeling paint and filmy windows of the duplex where she'd grown up. Evie Mazerik lived in the neighborhood, too, a few houses down. "I have. I'm going to check them out tomorrow." She tapped her pencil on the newspaper. "Looks like I've come full circle." She stared at the newsprint. "I have nothing to show for the twelve years since I left there."

Settling into a chair opposite her, Lynn grasped her hand. "You have the girls. You have friends who adore you." A spark of anger flared in eyes usually filled with compassion. "And you built a thriving business even if that…man is going to take it away from you."

Kate grinned at Lynn's uncharacteristic lack of charity. Her friend had been stunned when Kate had returned from the Steeles and told her what had happened. Tom had taken the girls outside to give them privacy, and Kate had confessed everything. She hadn't meant to tell Lynn about sleeping with Jay, but her friend had invited the confidence, and quite frankly Kate had needed to talk about it.

"Oh, honey, I'm sorry," Lynn had said.

"How could I be so wrong about someone, Lynn?"

"He deliberately deceived you."

"And used me."

Lynn had sighed. "I'm really angry at him, Kate, but I'm not ready to condemn him for that. It sounds as if you were very close last night. You don't know that was faked."

"It was a sham. All of it."

Tom Baines hadn't been nearly as kind as Lynn. He'd become a surrogate brother to Kate, just like Mitch and Charlie, and he'd been infuriated at his cousin's deception, though Kate had only given him an edited version of the story. "That son of a bitch." He'd thrown his fiancée an apologetic look. "I knew I should've checked this out as soon as I heard, that a stranger was staying with her."

"It appears as if I should have let you," Lynn had said. "But things happen for a reason." She'd turned to Kate. "We don't always know why..."

Kate had taken no comfort in that sentiment nine hours ago, and she still didn't.

"Kate, I asked what you were looking for now." She pointed to the *Riverbend Courier*.

"Jobs."

Frowning, Lynn asked, "Do you think it's a good idea to quit the store immediately?"

"I don't want to work there." Kate swallowed hard at the thought of seeing Jay every day. "I can't work there."

"It's not wise to rush into anything."

Lifting her eyes from the paper, Kate stared at her friend. "I...I'm scared, Lynn. I thought I had everything in place, you know. That if I just worked hard enough, I could take care of the girls and still fulfill some of my dreams. When I was given the opportunity to run the store and live at the farmhouse, I thought I could really do this right."

"You did do it right."

"I know. And I don't regret that." She stood, straightened the lapels of her plaid robe and crossed to the counter. Absently she poured more coffee. "But it's time to move on. And the sooner I start making the changes I need to make, the better I'll feel."

"You can do—" A knock at the back door interrupted Lynn.

Kate frowned. "Was Tom coming back?"

Lynn shook her head. "Maybe it's a parishioner."

"I'll go into the living room."

"Wait till I look." Lynn went to the back door, brushed aside the curtains and sighed. "Now why am I not surprised?"

"I should go," Kate repeated.

"Katie, it's Jay. At least I think it is. He fits your description."

Deep fear assaulted her. She couldn't face him. Learning the truth about Jay, then witnessing his painful reunion with his aunts was about all the emotional upheaval she could handle in one day. She put down her cup and gripped the counter tightly. "I can't see him, Lynn."

"Are you sure?"

"Yes. I know it's cowardly, but..." In the semidark kitchen, out of view of the door, she threw up her hands. "I can't."

"All right." Lynn opened the door. "Hello, I'm Lynn Kendall."

Although Kate couldn't see Jay, she could hear him. "I know who you are. I'm sure you know who I am. I need to see Kate."

Lynn didn't say anything.

"I went out to the farmhouse. She isn't there. Then I called Tom. He said she was staying with you."

"Tom told you to come here?"

"No. He said he wanted to beat the..." A pause. "He's not very pleased with me right now."

"None of us is. It shouldn't take a rocket scientist to figure out why."

"Please let me see her."

"She doesn't want to see you."

"Of course she doesn't." Another pause. Kate felt like a kid hiding under the covers. "But I'm not leaving until I talk to her."

With weary resignation, Kate stepped out of the shadows. "It's all right, Lynn. He's a very single-minded man. I'll talk to him."

Lynn shifted her gaze from Jay to Kate. Then, as if she'd decided something, she stepped back. "All right. Come in."

Kate watched the man who entered the kitchen. His skin was drawn, and his jaw was like granite. His line-backer shoulders sagged and his whole body radiated weariness. Today had obviously been hell for him.

Lynn was at her side. "Shall I stay, Katie?" she asked softly.

"No, go to bed. Check on the girls, though, will you?"

"Of course." Lynn squeezed her arm, then whis-

pered, "Come to my room if you want. Afterward."
And she was gone.

Crossing her arms, Kate focused on Jay. She tried to
ignore the depth of sadness in his dark eyes. Abraham's
eyes. Ruth and Rachel's eyes. Why hadn't she seen
that? "Sit down, Jay." She blinked hard. "I mean...
Jacob."

"Jay, please." Wearily, he sank onto a chair.

Without thinking, she walked to the coffeepot and
poured him a mug. When she set it in front of him, she
chided herself for still taking care of him. He was transfixed by the red circles she'd drawn on the newspaper.
Looking up at her, he asked, "How are the girls?"

"Fine."

"Did you tell them about me?"

"No, not yet." *I couldn't do that today.* "They love
staying overnight at someone else's home, so I just told
them we'd be sleeping here tonight."

"You should go back to the farmhouse."

She sat across from him and shook her head. "I told
you I couldn't stay out there."

"I wish you'd reconsider."

"Your wishes aren't the issue, now. I've got to take
care of my children first."

In a quick move, motivated by anger, she guessed,
he snatched up the paper and read the circled ads. "A
tiny two-bedroom duplex over on Third Street is best
for the girls? I've lived in Riverbend. I know that section of town. It's not fit for little girls to live in."

I did. But then, she wouldn't wish that on anyone,
so the accusation pierced her already bruised heart.
And soul. And ego. "That's the best I can do at this
point. Until I get a couple of jobs, I need to be con-
scious of money."

"A couple of jobs?" He frowned down at the paper, then turned it over. "Cocktail waitress at Charter's? Foundry work at..." He raised disbelieving eyes to Kate. "Where in hell would you get time to do two jobs?"

Her chin lifted. "It wouldn't be the first time I've done it. Before I managed the store and while I was pregnant, I worked days at Steele Books and nights at Charter's."

"Ruth and Rachel let you do that?"

"No, as a matter of fact, they had a fit." She wasn't sure why she was defending her actions; all she knew was that she needed to stand up for herself. "Look, it's not any of your concern. I can take care of my family." When he just stared at her, she said, "And a little hard work never hurt anybody."

Anger shone in his eyes. "Billy should be paying child support."

The remark made her uneasy. "How do you know he's not?"

He hesitated a split second. "It's obvious, or you wouldn't scrimp like you do."

"Most of the world scrimps, Jay. It's not a tragedy."

He shook his head. "Of course it's not. I didn't mean it that way. It's just that you'll be better off all around at the farmhouse, and at the bookstore, until the first of the year."

"So I can manage it until your sentence is up?"

He flushed. "Until after I've fulfilled the terms of the will, yes. But not just so you can manage it for me. So you can save your money—"

"*Scrimp*—" she interrupted nastily.

Temper flared in his eyes. "If you stayed on in both places, you could look for a decent place to live and better jobs than—'' he rapped his knuckles on the paper ''—this.''

She bit her tongue to keep from telling him that there were no better jobs than this, no better places to live, for a high school graduate without many skills or much training beyond selling books.

''Think of the girls, Kate, and not yourself.''

Anger of her own sparked. ''You have some gall calling me selfish.''

He cursed heatedly. ''You're the most unselfish person I know. But you're reacting out of pride, instead of common sense. What possible benefit will there be for the girls if you disrupt their whole lives before the holidays? Especially since you can wait until after?''

Tears threatened. Because he was right. She could make this transition easier for them if she let go of her pride and her fear.

''Not to mention what it would do to Ruth and Rachel,'' he added meaningfully.

Ah, a trump card. He'd probably had a lot of practice in high-stake games. Though she knew she was being played, Kate's concern for her girls and for the beloved Steele sisters wouldn't allow her to hurt them. She was ashamed of not having thought about all of them first. ''How are your aunts?''

He shook his head, and a ghost of a smile came to his lips. ''They're good, believe it or not. After the initial shock, they bombarded me with questions. We talked through the afternoon, then they made me my favorite meal.''

''Fritatta.''

He nodded guiltily, then rushed on to describe their day. ''We drank more tea and talked until they got tired.''

"So you left?"

"Not exactly. We went to the apartment over the bookstore, spruced it up a bit, and I got my things from the car. I'll be staying there. After they went home, I went looking for you."

"Didn't they wonder why you weren't staying at your farmhouse?"

He cringed slightly at the pronoun but didn't reply.

"Or didn't they know you'd inherited it—and the store? I've been wondering about that. What they know about all this."

"Until I told them, my aunts only knew their inheritance didn't include either the store or the house. They didn't know who Abraham had left the property to. Nick Harrison told them everything would come out eventually. Abraham willed them a huge sum of money, and they had large trust funds of their own from my grandmother's side of the family, so finances aren't an issue."

"But didn't it did seem unusual to them? The store was their baby." *And mine.*

"Apparently Abraham left many unusual bequests. I guess they've just been waiting out this one."

"I see."

"I, um…" Guilt bloomed on his face, bringing color to his pale cheeks. He stood and began to pace the small kitchen. Then he pushed a restless hand through his hair. "I didn't tell them about selling the store and the farmhouse, and I wish you wouldn't, either, for a while."

"What?"

"I couldn't, Kate. It was hard enough dealing with having abandoned them fifteen years ago, although they handled that oddly, too." Nonplussed, he shook his head. "Ruth wanted to know why I left. But Rachel cut her off, said it didn't matter now. Let the past lie."

"That sounds like Rachel. So did you tell them why you left?"

He shook his head and leaned against the counter by the sink. "I still have no intention of doing that."

"Why not?"

"It would destroy their love for Abraham. I can't do that." As if to himself, he muttered, "It was one of the reasons I left."

She wouldn't feel sorry for him, damn it. She didn't care if his face got so stiff she thought it might crack. If his eyes turned bleaker than a February dawn. She averted her gaze to stop the rush of sympathy. "It's your business, I guess. I'm only concerned with what I can control."

He cocked his head. "Control's important to you, isn't it?"

"Right now, it's the most important thing in my life."

"Other than the girls and my aunts."

And you. No, no she wouldn't let herself think that. "Yes."

Pushing away from the counter, he crossed the kitchen to tower over her. She stood, too, but came only to his shoulder; she felt like David before Goliath, small and terribly unarmed.

"Please, Kate. Stay at the house. At the store. For all our sakes."

Her eyes closed briefly and she swayed toward him. She wanted him to draw her close, so she could weep in the arms of the man who had caused her pain. It was when his hands rested on her shoulders and he breathed out the endearment, "Honey, please..." that she realized what she was doing.

She jerked back; her hands clapped over her mouth. Pure humiliation overwhelmed her. She'd been ready to let the man who'd used her, who'd deceived her, comfort her. She couldn't think of anything more obscene.

Gathering her wits, she finally said, "All right. For the girls' sake, and for Ruth and Rachel, I'll stay at the store and live at the farmhouse for a while."

He breathed a sigh of relief.

Her eyes narrowed on him. "Not for you, Jay. You're done manipulating me."

A muscle leaped in his jaw, but he said nothing.

She held up two fingers. "And I have two conditions."

He arched a brow, a gesture so reminiscent of Abraham it made her sad. He'd thrown away so much. "What?"

"First, I'll only keep the sale information to myself for a few days. Till after Thanksgiving. Not telling something is tantamount to lying, and I won't lie to Ruth and Rachel any longer than necessary. So find a way to tell them."

"I will. What else?"

"That you promise never to touch me again."

The pain in his expression, the fact that her words had caused it, took her breath away. But in a moment, his face had become impassive. "Okay, I promise. I won't touch you ever again."

The words she wanted to hear hurt more than the crippling labor she'd had with the twins. She pivoted to hide her reaction. With her back to him she said, "Fine. Please leave now."

An eternity passed before she heard his heavy footsteps on Lynn's floor. She felt cold air on her feet when the door opened and closed.

Even after finding Billy with his girlfriend, even after delivering the twins early, she hadn't felt this scared and this alone. "Please," she whispered into the darkness of the kitchen. "Please let me be able to handle this."

CHAPTER NINE

WHEN KATE ENTERED the bookstore Monday morning, Ruth turned from one of Lily Mazerik's paintings to greet her. "Good morning." Quickly, she frowned. "You look tired, dear. Didn't you sleep well?"

Smoothing her hands down her plain navy slacks and tugging at the matching sweater, Kate offered a slight smile. "Yes, of course I slept."

The girl was a terrible liar. Even yesterday, she and Rachel had known something was bothering Katie. And Ruth was sure their long-lost nephew was responsible.

Shrugging out of her coat, Kate walked toward Ruth. Up close, her pretty hazel eyes were bloodshot, her face was pale and her freckles stood out in stark relief. "Did *you* sleep well?"

"Oh, no, Rachel and I were too excited to sleep. We talked all night."

As if on cue, Rachel bustled into the store, her step light, her eyes sparkling. Like Ruth, she'd dressed in a smart Chanel suit, hers of green wool, Ruth's dark rose. They had much to celebrate today.

"Good morning, Katie," Rachel said. "My dear, are you all right?"

"Yes, of course." Again, Kate struggled to smile. "Especially if you two are."

"Oh, we're wonderful." As she reached Kate and Ruth, Rachel asked, "Shall I pour you some coffee?"

Kate looked around the store. "Is, um, is Jacob here?"

"No, he's still asleep. And we're glad." Rachel set down the mugs of coffee she'd poured for them and reached out to squeeze Kate's arm. "We need to talk to you before he gets up."

Kate swallowed hard and sank onto an overstuffed chair.

Ruth and Rachel exchanged a quick look, then Ruth spoke. "We know it must be a shock to discover that Abraham owned the bookstore." She hesitated. "We never told you."

"You didn't owe me an explanation like that, Ruth. The store wasn't mine." Her voice trembled at the admission. "It doesn't matter who it belonged to."

A quick flash of temper came and went in Rachel's eyes. "In every way that mattered this store was yours, Katie. You should expect more in life."

"It's not good to expect too much," Kate said, averting her gaze.

"In any case," Ruth went on, "we didn't tell you about the store and the farmhouse because Abraham asked us not to. We never knew why."

"Truthfully," Rachel added, "we just assumed he'd left it to you when he died."

Kate didn't comment, just sipped from her mug. Ruth was alarmed by her docility.

"And in a way, he did," Rachel said gently. "If Jacob hadn't returned to claim it, the store would have gone to you."

Color suffused her cheeks. "Jay told you that?"

"Yes. Why wouldn't he?"

Sinking back into the chair, Kate shrugged. "Why did Abraham do that, do you think?"

A motherly gentleness was evident Rachel's face. "He loved you, dear."

"I cared about him, too."

"He loved you like a daughter, Katie." Ruth's tone was impassioned. "As do we. And now we're worried about you financially, even more than we were before. We're hoping, of course, that you'll stay on at the store, but we don't know Jacob's plans, and we don't want to pressure him when we've just gotten him back. But we thought we should discuss our concerns for you openly."

Kate's face flushed. And her shoulders stiffened. "I can take care of myself, Ruth. I always have."

"I know you can. It's just that we have so much. And we want you to know that we'll always be there for you, to help you if—"

Abruptly, Kate stood. "I don't want to discuss this. You have no obligation to help me." Her gaze strayed out the front windows. "No one does. I'll be fine."

She'd overstepped her bounds again, Ruth realized a bit too late. She hadn't meant to offend the girl. Katie had always had a mountain of pride that had been almost impossible to scale. Ruth admired her for it, but as a result, the sisters had had a devil of a time helping the McManns out over the years. Best to let the matter drop for the time being, though.

Rachel knew that, too. "All right dear, just so you know we're here if you need us. Now, we have a favor to ask of you."

Kate became visibly composed. She was more used to meeting others' needs than vice versa. Damned if that didn't annoy Ruth more than a poorly written book she'd paid good money for.

"Anything," Kate said, giving them her first genuine smile of the day.

"Jacob won't be starting work at the store until after Thanksgiving, which is time enough to get in his required month. We're going to spend this week with him, getting reacquainted, showing him off around town."

Kate said, "I can handle the store, though Friday may be a problem." It was the biggest shopping day of the year. "I'll see if Izzy, Simon and Joan can help out, too."

"That's not the favor we're asking for."

"What, then?"

Rachel sighed. "We have to tell Jacob about Aaron Mazerik."

"Before anyone else in town lets it slip," Ruth added.

"Yes, of course."

"We'd like you to be there when we do."

"Why?" Kate looked surprised. Ruth shook her head. For such a bright girl, she could be dense where men were concerned.

"It was obvious yesterday that he's gotten close to you. Saving the girls. Staying out at your place all that time. You formed a bond."

Kate paled, but averted her face. She only nodded.

"And this will be a shock to him." Ruth frowned. "Unless…"

Cocking her head, Kate waited.

Ruth finished, "Oh, hells bells, we don't know why Jacob left town years ago, but we know he had a falling-out with his father. It might be because he found out he had an illegitimate brother.''

''I'm sure it's not that,'' Rachel said. ''But it doesn't matter. This will be a blow to him, even if it's just because the whole town knows. We think it would help if you were there for support, like you were yesterday.''

Bleak eyes stared at them. ''I...'' She seemed to struggle.

''Katie, is there something you're not telling us?'' Ruth asked.

''No, no.''

''Did Jacob do something to offend you?''

She waited a bit too long to answer. ''Truthfully, I didn't like that he kept his identity from me.''

''Why *did* he do that?'' Rachel asked. ''He hasn't said.''

''He'll have to discuss that with you two. I'm sure once he settles in, he'll tell you everything.''

Shrewdly, Rachel watched her. ''Well, then, dear, will you help us out when we tell him about Aaron?''

Ruth noted the grim resignation on Kate's face. She'd seen it often enough.

''Yes, of course. I'll be there.''

The sisters rose, then walked over to Kate and hugged her. Ruth felt her tremble and held on extra tight. After they moved apart, Ruth smiled. ''We're fixing a special lunch at noon. We'll see you then.''

She bustled out ahead of Rachel, but Kate's bleak expression stayed in her mind. Ruth would just have to get to the bottom of this.

''STEELE BOOKS. Kate McMann speaking.''

''Hello, Katie.'' Ruth's voice bubbled with joy.

"Lunch will be ready in fifteen minutes. Do you think you could run up and fetch Jacob, then come over?"

She counted to ten before she answered. "I'll just call him to meet us there."

"The apartment phone's not hooked up yet."

"He has a cell phone."

A pause. "Do you know the number?"

"Yes." Kate glanced around the store, noting to herself that the carpet needed vacuuming. "Don't worry. I'll call him."

"See you in a bit, then. The meal's all ready."

No doubt a fatted calf, Kate thought unkindly as she ended the call. Staring at nothing, she bit her lip and told herself to shape up. Ruth and Rachel knew her well. They already sensed something was wrong. And she'd be damned if *she'd* be the one to spoil this reunion for them.

Pulling out her directory, she found Jay's cell-phone number and punched it in. *Busy.* Damn. She glanced at the clock. With a heavy heart and even heavier steps—she *hadn't* slept, of course—Kate headed to the back of the store. As she passed the office, she stopped. "I'm going to lunch, Simon. Are you sure you can handle this alone?"

From the computer, where he was updating their rare-book listing on the American Book Exchange, Simon grinned mischievously at her. "Only if Mrs. Keller stops flirting with me. My Annie said the woman's got the hots for me."

Kate smiled back. The levity felt good. Life would work out, because Lynn was right. Kate had the girls, the Steele sisters and her friends. No one, not even the fair-haired boy of Riverbend, could take that away from her.

There were two staircases to the apartment above. Because the temperature had dropped, Kate climbed the inside one. Even here she'd paid attention to details. She'd painted the walls and the high ceiling—which had been a pain to reach—and put up posters of authors. At the top of the stairs, she smoothed the edge of Jack Kerouac's and thought of Ruth. Taking in a deep breath, she faced the door and knocked.

"It's open."

At his invitation, Kate turned the knob and pushed the heavy wood-paneled door. This entrance led into the living room. All the furniture in the large space had belonged to the Steeles' grandparents, which Rachel had saved. An old but sturdy tapestry couch, two accent chairs and several tables graced the hardwood floors, covered partly by a braided rug. Kate had refinished some of the pieces herself. She loved the polished oak of the archways and baseboards, and had matched the stain on the end tables and the desk to it.

He was at that very desk on the phone. Over his shoulder, he called out, "Let me just finish this up, Aunt Ruth, and I'll be right with you." Then into the phone he said, "No, I don't think that's a good idea."

Against her will, Kate studied him; covered in a bulky brown sweater, the broad expanse of his back, which she knew had a few freckles, was muscular and sturdy. She remembered the feel of those shoulders from when he'd playfully hoisted her over them in a fanciful moment late Saturday night. The memories hurt her heart.

"I said no, Mallory. I'm not going to discuss this further. I have to go. Goodbye." And he closed the cell phone.

Surprised at his curt tone, Kate cleared her throat. "It's not Ruth."

He spun around in the ornate wooden chair. "Kate." He breathed the word reverently. Warily. And he had a strange look on his face. "I was expecting Ruth."

"She asked me to fetch you. Lunch—" Kate broke off when she noticed what his body had blocked. Adrenaline rushed through her veins as if she was walking at night and had sensed something was about to strike. Her eyes were riveted on the sleek, expensive laptop in front of him.

All I need is a cell phone and a computer.

You can use mine.

"You have a computer." The inane remark was about all she could manage.

He glanced at it, then back to her. "Yes."

"You've had it all the time."

"Yes."

She folded her arms across her chest to ward off the blows she knew were coming. "Let me guess," she said, raising her eyes to the ceiling where Charlie and Mitch had put up a fan for the summer months. "You used mine to spy on me."

"I...I didn't know you then, Kate. I had to find out what was going on with Steele Books."

"So you hacked into my store accounts."

He could have corrected her—they were *his* accounts—but he didn't. That small courtesy prompted her to admit he had the right. "Oh, hell. They're really yours, anyway, so it doesn't matter." She tossed her head. "After all, that's what this is about, isn't it? Money?"

"It was in the beginning."

She let that odd remark pass, because the mention

of money tapped into a memory. *Billy should be paying child support...I know how you scrimp...*

Her stomach roiled as she pieced it together, a macabre puzzle she didn't want to assemble. "My personal accounts are on my computer, too. Tell me you didn't break into those."

He stared at her, his look hard. His face revealed the truth.

"Oh, no, please. You spied on me *personally?*"

Gravely, he nodded.

She threw up her hands. "Next, you're going to tell me you searched the house." He didn't say a word. "Oh, God. You did."

"I'm sorry."

She blinked several times, then turned away from him. After a long moment, she said, "'Sorry' doesn't cut it in my household, either." She reached for the door.

"Wait."

She did, if only because she was afraid she might trip and fall down the stairs. And she didn't want to end up like the crippled Maddie in *Ethan Frome* with nothing but a broken body because of some man.

"I tried to tell you this on Sunday. I didn't know you when I began it all. After the first week, I knew you were on the up-and-up and I stopped—"

"Spying? You stopped *spying* on me after seven days? Is that supposed to make me feel better?"

"It was before I came to care for you. And the girls."

She whirled around. "You don't care about anyone but yourself, *Jacob.*" She raised her chin. "But don your good-boy mask for a while, will you? For some reason Ruth and Rachel love you and think you're a good man.''

"I told you I wasn't.''

"My mistake for not listening. People have always warned me about being a Pollyanna. I guess they were right.'' She glanced at her watch. "We need to leave. I don't want Ruth and Rachel to have to wait for you.'' She regarded him coldly. "I think fifteen years was enough.''

HE WAS TRYING hard to keep it all contained, but the feelings kept surfacing, like a geyser, buried too long. As he seated Ruth, then Rachel, he was overcome by a swell of warmth.

Always pull out a female companion's chair before you seat yourself, dear, Rachel had told him.

You'll have them swooning at your feet, boy, Ruth had added with a wink.

He stole a quick glance at Kate, rocked by the knowledge that nothing he could do would ever get her to swoon at his feet. She sat stiffly, as he took his place beside her, across from his aunts. Casually, she inched away, but still his shoulder brushed hers. Her flowery scent assaulted him, piercing the armor he'd been trying to erect since yesterday.

He was losing the battle to stay distant, big time, with her and with his aunts. "This looks wonderful,'' he told them as he eyed the cheesy quiche, hot rolls and salad.

Ruth reached over and squeezed his arm. "Nothing but the best for our boy.''

"I don't deserve this,'' he blurted, not intending to say it, but somehow the confession felt right, necessary.

"Of course you do, dear." This from Rachel. "Now bow your head and let's thank God for your return."

He tried to block out the blessing. Kate's hands were clasped so tightly the knuckles had become white. And her head was bent, but she was probably cursing him, not thanking God he'd come back.

"...and mostly, thank you for returning Jacob to us."

The meal progressed with remarkable ease, right into coffee and dessert. Though Jay was aware of the tension in every familiar curve of Kate's body, the aunts seemed oblivious to it. They chatted on about the weather and the store. It was only when he accidentally bumped Kate's leg, and they heard the small intake of breath, quickly disguised as a cough, that they noticed something was amiss.

"Oh, dear, Kate. I hope you're not getting a cold."

She cleared her throat. "No, Rachel, don't worry. I'm fine."

"We wouldn't want you ill for Thanksgiving." Ruth smiled with such innocent delight Jay's heart tripped in his chest. "Just think, Jacob will be joining us at the farmhouse this year. Like old times."

Kate's fork clattered to her plate.

"Is there a problem with that, Katie?"

"No, of course not," she lied.

"Who else is coming?" Jay asked her.

"Lynn and Tom and his two children. I asked Mitch and Tessa, but something's going on there. They said they were staying in town." For some reason, her eyes darted to both Ruth and Rachel. "Lily and Aaron said yes, by the way."

Jay cocked his head. "Lily and Aaron?"

It was like the beginning of a funeral, where everyone falls silent for the service. Slowly and deliberately, Ruth and Rachel set down their forks. They glanced at Kate, who smiled in what looked like encouragement.

Rachel began. "Jacob, we have something to tell you. Something you need to hear from us before you go out about town."

He braced his elbows on the table, aware of an ominous feeling sweeping through the dining room. "What is it?" He frowned. "Is it about Lily Bennett? And Aaron who?"

Ruth's eyes were sad. "Lily Bennett married Aaron Mazerik last month."

"Aaron Mazerik? Maz?" Jay had an image of a lanky, dark-haired boy with bleak eyes. Coach Drummer had asked Jay to befriend him, and back then, Jay would have cut off his right hand for his basketball coach. But something about Aaron had always drawn him, anyway.

"Yes." Rachel smiled like a proud mother.

"You have contact with him?" Jay remembered that Aaron had been the closest thing to a juvenile delinquent that Riverbend had had. He'd both intrigued and frightened most of the other kids.

"Yes. He moved back to Riverbend a few years ago to take care of his mother after she had a stroke. Wally Drummer talked him into staying. He's a guidance counselor at the school, and he coaches the basketball team now."

Ruth jumped in. "We've been seeing him regularly since your father's bequests were revealed."

He recalled Harrison's words. *Your father left several unusual bequests. To people you wouldn't expect.*

"Aaron got one of the bequests?"

"A sizable one."

"Why?"

Ruth hesitated. Rachel's hand went to her sister's arm. "Jacob," Rachel said, "Aaron Mazerik is your father's son."

It took him a minute. *Your father's son.* That meant…that made him… Jay couldn't sort it out. "I don't understand. Aaron's father was…" Then he remembered. Aaron's mother had never married, and sometimes, the kids had speculated nastily about who his father was. But Jay had never heard…never considered… Oh, God, *his* father had had an illegitimate son. *His* father had never claimed the boy, dooming Aaron to a lifetime of taunting and cruel remarks. Children, teenagers and small-town minds could be brutal.

Jay tried to harden his heart. This just took the cake. It was so typical, so keeping in character of the man who had raised him.

"We take it you didn't know," Ruth said.

He finally found his voice. "Know? Of course not. Why would you think that?"

Ruth's eyes were bleak. "We thought maybe that was why you left."

"No, Aunt Ruth. It's not why I left." But it fit well into the picture that had been painted for him that one dreary Christmas Eve when his life had fallen apart.

Jay put his hands over his face and blocked out the sight of the women before him. He remained that way for a long time, struggling for control. Then, like yesterday, he felt a hand squeeze his arm. When he looked over at Kate, there was a compassion he didn't deserve on her face. "This must be such a blow," she said softly.

He cocked his head. "I…I have a brother. At least

a half brother.'' He shook his head. ''And I never knew.''

''Aaron's told us how nice you always were to him,'' Rachel said.

Jay remembered things. *Wanna shoot baskets after practice, Aaron? I'll help you with your layups... Come on, it's cold out. I'll drive you home.* Home had been a seedy little apartment on Third Street that made the farmhouse look like a mansion.

Jay had played basketball with his brother. He'd driven his brother home—and hadn't even known it. The notion sickened him. But anger was easier, so he let it erupt.

''I hope Abraham's burning in hell for this,'' Jay spit out. ''He had no right to do that to a young boy. To his *son.*''

''Jacob, your father was—''

Jay shoved back his chair and stood. ''My father was a monster, Ruth.'' Wildly, he looked around the room, feeling like a tiger thrown into a cage after a good romp in a field. All the old resentment and rage returned. ''Listen, I'm sorry...but I have to go out for a while. I need to think about this. I need to...deal with it.'' His gaze settled on Ruth and Rachel. ''Is it all right? I don't want to leave if you're upset, but I need to...think.''

''Of course it's all right. Just be careful if you drive.'' Rachel's voice was hoarse.

Ruth asked quietly, ''You'll come back this time, though, won't you, Jacob?''

His heart, already maimed, broke into fragments at their wariness. ''Of course I'll come back.'' He went to them, hugged them and said, ''I promise. I just need a few hours.''

He stopped before he brushed by Kate. She gave him a sympathetic smile, then squeezed his arm again.

Even her comfort didn't help. He left the room quickly.

THE SYCAMORE RIVER was turbulent, its muddy brown water swirling lustily, waves crashing against the bank, its scent earthy and a little menacing. A cold breeze blew off the water, playing hide-and-seek with Kate's hair, ripping the heavy mass from its loose tie. She zipped up her jacket, but still shivered. Clutching the fine wool scarf and gloves she carried, she picked her way down to the big sycamore tree with its famous limb where Jay was standing, a solitary silhouette against the late-afternoon dimness.

Please, Katie, go find him. It's been two hours. We're sure he's at the river, by the tree probably. He always went there when he was upset.

She shook her head as she walked lightly through the twigs and small rocks to the riverbank. After finding out about his snooping, she'd decided to have nothing further to do with him. But she couldn't ignore Ruth and Rachel's concern.

Or your own. Admit it, Katie girl.

Despite everything, she *did* care. It was impossible to witness what she just had and not respond. She wouldn't have sought him out, though, if it hadn't been for the aunts. *Please, Katie, we're so worried.*

Six feet away, she stopped. He stood on the riverbank, feet apart, hands jammed into the pockets of his leather coat, his back stiff, the wind ruffling his hair.

She said simply, "Jay."

He gave a start at the sound, but didn't look at her. After a long moment, he said, "You shouldn't have come. Especially after..." He trailed off, not needing to list his offenses against her. Both knew every rotten thing he'd done.

"Ruth and Rachel are worried."

He spun around. "I said I'd be back." His face was wind-whipped and ravaged. His hollow eyes came straight out of a Van Gogh painting.

She stepped closer. "They believe you." She held out the scarf and gloves. "They said to bring you these. It's cold."

A grim smile claimed his lips. "They're still taking care of me." Like a dutiful son, he donned the fine leather gloves and wool plaid scarf. "Where did they get these?"

"You don't want to know."

"What's one more blow?"

Shrugging, she said as kindly as she could, "They bought you these the last Christmas you were home. Rachel saved them in her hope chest after you left on Christmas Eve."

One more blow was obviously too much. His bleak eyes became bleaker. Because she hated to see people suffer, and because, despite everything, she cared for the man before her, Kate said, "What's important is *now,* Jay. You've hurt them, but you have a chance to make it up to them."

He arched a brow. "By selling the store and moving back to New York in January?"

Stark reality stung more than the raw wind. She hadn't even known where he'd lived. But this was her chance to really help Ruth and Rachel after all they'd done for her. So she squelched her own devastation and concentrated on them. "You have choices. You can visit here. They can visit you. New York isn't that far away.''

"With the life I live, I may as well be on another planet," he mumbled, turning back to the river.

She didn't speak, just listened to the caw of a bird and the rush of the water. "Do you want to talk about Aaron?" she finally asked.

"I don't know."

"Tell me what you're thinking."

"Mostly about the irony of life. Abraham Steele had two sons. Because of his stubborn pride, or whatever it was that kept him from claiming Aaron, he wound up with none." An ugly laugh escaped him. "He could have had Aaron when I left fifteen years ago, and then when Aaron came back here— What was it? Two years ago?"

"Yes," was all she said. She'd liked Abraham but couldn't condone what he'd done. It was repugnant to her, especially when she remembered all the cruel things kids had said about and to Aaron. "Abraham was very wrong, Jay. There's no getting around it."

Unexpectedly, Jay kicked a loose stone near his booted foot. It flew into the water and splashed. "I don't want to get around it. It's good to know he's done such a despicable thing."

"Does it make it easier...that you left?"

His shoulders sagged. "Yes. It does."

"What will you do now?"

He faced her. His cheeks had reddened in the wind; even his ears were rosy. "Go see Aaron, of course."

"That's the right thing to do."

"Surprised I have some integrity, Kate?"

His bitter tone gave her pause. "You saved my children's lives. Regardless of everything else you did, I'll always be grateful for that.''

Jay watched her for a few moments, forcefully quelling the burning anger that surfaced inside him at her comment. "I don't want your gratitude."

Her face drained of color. "What do you want?" she asked, as if she was driven against her will to say the words. Her innocence, her lack of guile, could destroy her.

I want your love.

As soon as the thought surfaced, he banished it. He didn't want her love. Long ago, he'd trained himself to stop wanting the things he knew he'd never have. "I want you to help Ruth and Rachel through this."

"I told you I'd do that."

"I don't expect you to help *me*." He waved his hand at the river. "Coming here, talking to me..."

"I came here for your aunts, Jay, not you."

Her words stung. "I understand. So go back to the store. Tell my aunts I'm fine. I'll be home after I see Aaron." He glanced at his watch. "He's working as a guidance counselor at the school, right?"

"Yes."

Jay checked his watch. "He should be done, then?"

"He's probably holding a basketball practice, though."

"I see. Tell Ruth and Rachel I'll be back to take them out to dinner, as I promised."

"They'd like that."

Staring at the river he once loved, at the river that used to soothe his childhood pain, he heard her footsteps crunch on the twigs behind him. He had the urgent and absurd need to beg her to stay with him, to help him deal with this newest revelation.

But he only glanced over his shoulder and watched her go. The wind rippled through her hair, making it fly around her shoulders. She was hunched against the cold, and he worried again that the jacket she wore wasn't warm enough. She didn't take nearly as good care of herself as she did others. As she disappeared into the trees, he felt a longing so intense it startled him.

And scared him to death. The man he'd become did not know how to deal with the emotion. At one time, as a young boy, he'd reveled in these feelings. But he'd killed that trait with quiet determination. He couldn't understand why it had returned now.

Damn Riverbend, Indiana, for doing this to him.

CHAPTER TEN

HE SHOULDN'T HAVE come here. He hadn't realized what the sight and smell of the gym would do to him. Twenty years had passed, but everything had remained the same—the pungent odor of sweat, the squeaking of sneakers on the court and the trill of the whistle, the heavy air that was only minimally dispersed by the big ceiling fans.

Late-afternoon light filtered in through the gym windows as Jay stood in the shadows and watched his half brother run up and down the court with boys who looked impossibly young. Jay remembered vividly the time he'd spent on this court, the sneaky layups he got in around Sterling and Callahan during scrimmages, the "Hail Mary" shot from center court during the championship game his junior year and searching out Abraham's eyes when the ball had hit nothing but net.

Unfortunately, the sweat-soaked, flushed man out there now had had no father to look for, no one to nod approvingly when he scored. Had Evie Mazerik even attended the games? Unnoticed, Jay watched Aaron and studied him for family resemblances. He was tall—not as tall as Jay—but they had the same broad shoulders. Aaron's damp hair looked darker than it had as a teenager. When he turned, Jay noticed his chest had filled out. Would they have shared sweaters if they'd been raised together? Fought over the bathroom? Consulted each other about girls?

The movement of a man sitting on the bleachers drew Jay's attention. Mesmerized, Jay watched as Riverbend's revered old basketball coach, tall, tan and still burly, rose and approached him. Wally Drummer's hair had turned mostly silver now, and although his blunt features had softened somewhat, he still had a determined jaw, big shoulders and beefy hands.

When he reached Jay, Coach Drummer studied him, but said nothing. For much of his time in Riverbend, Jay had adored this man. Remnants of those feelings surfaced, despite Jay's determination to remain distant. "Hi, Coach," he said, unable to bite back the slight smile that crept over his face.

"Hello, Jacob." Again, the stare, the one that had seen through the fibs Mitch, Charlie and Jacob had told about not attending that wild party over in Graysberg and about having kept their curfew during vacation. Before Jay could dredge up any more memories, the older man extended his hand. "Good to see you."

Jay clasped the proffered hand, held on. Coach raised his other arm and clapped Jay on the shoulder. Jay savored the contact.

"Welcome home." Coach's voice was gruff.

Somehow Jay managed, "Thank you." He looked around the gym. "You're not still coaching, are you?"

"No, I dropped in to help Aaron out with some drills." Bushy silver eyebrows knitted. "You know about Aaron and...your father?"

"I just found out." He glanced toward the court. "That's why I'm here."

"I see."

"I didn't mean to interrupt practice. I'll wait."

Just then all action on the floor ceased. Several pairs of eyes watched Jay and the old coach. Surrounded by the team, Aaron stood in the middle of the court, feet apart, cradling the ball under his arm. Jay recognized the stance as one of his own.

Drummer squeezed Jay's shoulder. "Don't think this will wait, boy." He turned and, heading toward Aaron, called over his shoulder, "Come see Mary, she'd love it."

"I will."

Coach spoke to Aaron, touched his shoulder, left his hand there, too, for a minute. Little emotion passed over Aaron's face, reminding Jay of the cold look of indifference Aaron had always worn. Even then, Jay suspected it was for self-protection. Staring at Jay, Aaron handed the ball to Coach Drummer, then jogged to the sidelines. Dimly, Jay heard play resume. But he focused only on Aaron. On his brother.

Up close, Aaron was bigger than Jay remembered. And the perpetual sneer was gone, replaced by something mature and...satisfied. The underlying restlessness that had always simmered beneath his skin was absent, too. "Hello, Aaron."

Aaron nodded. "Jacob." His voice was deeper, like Jay's.

Raising his chin, Jay fought back the impact of too-intense emotions. He'd always wanted a brother. "I just found out."

Again, a silent nod from Aaron.

Jay indicated the court with a toss of his head. "I didn't mean to stop practice." Suddenly he was thirteen and wanting desperately to make friends. "But I couldn't wait. I thought we could set up a time to talk."

Aaron shrugged. "Now's good. Wally can run the drills."

Jay smiled. "It's a lot to take in, you as the new coach of the Rivermen."

"Yeah, things change. People change." Both silently acknowledged the understatement. "Let's go back to my office."

As they entered Wally Drummer's old office, Jay was again assailed by memories, but along with them he experienced the contentment that comes from being in a safe and familiar place. The small space was cramped as always, especially now with the addition of a computer and the small table it sat on. Jay ignored the old team photos, not yet ready to face that part of his past.

"Have a seat." Aaron donned a sweatshirt that sported the Rivermen logo. When he sat, the swivel chair creaked just as it always had. "Want some water?"

"No thanks." Knees spread apart, hands linked between them, Jay watched as Aaron fished out a bottle from a tiny fridge under his desk and took a long swallow.

After draining half of it, he set the bottle down. Then leaned back. "So, big news, huh?"

Jay struggled to find words, didn't even know what he wanted to say. All he knew for sure was that he was determined, in some small way, to make up for his father's negligence.

"What do you think, Jacob?" The confidence of a grown man who'd faced demons of his own was there, but Aaron's voice wavered a little bit. Jay realized his opinion mattered to Aaron. From somewhere, he recalled a conversation.

Why are you bein' so nice to me?

Why not?

You're the town's fair-haired boy. I'm the town screwup.

Not anymore. You're all right, Aaron. Accept it.

Jay cleared his throat, straightened and took a steadying breath. "I think having you as a brother is one of the best things that's ever happened to me. I'd like to have known twenty years ago." He swallowed hard. "I'm sorry I didn't. I'm sorry Abraham did what he did." Jay's tone hardened. "He was a real son of a bitch."

Aaron appeared to be suppressing some strong emotion. Anger probably. "He was." He shook his head. "He had two sides to him, that's for sure."

"Yeah, well, you got hit with his bad side."

"And you got his good side."

"It isn't fair, Aaron. How can you not be furious?"

A smile claimed Aaron's face, and he looked so wise, so settled, that Jay yearned for some of that peace.

"I was, but it's calmed to a slow burn," Aaron told him. "I lost it when I found out in July. And I took some of my anger out on your cousin Tom when he first got back here." Aaron shrugged. "But I'm better now. Lily helped me deal with it."

Jay smiled, too. "You married Lily Bennett. That's great."

"It couldn't get any better."

Jay's smile turned to a scowl. "You should have had *better* all your life. I'm sorry you didn't."

"Yeah, well, you had better," Aaron said, "and look what happened to you."

Jay didn't miss the irony. It was clear who in this

room was happier. Growing up had been hell for Aaron, but Jay knew, even in his own hardened heart, that in the intervening years, the other man had found contentment in a way Jay never had.

"I didn't mean to offend you," Aaron added when Jay remained silent.

"No offense taken."

Aaron glanced at the clock. "I'd better get back. Wally's getting up there in age. He's in good shape, but the kids'll run him ragged."

"I always thought maybe *he* was your father, the way he took you in." Jay stared at his brother. "I wish he was."

Aaron stood, as did Jay. He extended his hand, and Jay clasped it. Neither man let go and their eyes locked. "You know, I always wished Coach was my father, too, but right now, Jacob, I'm glad he isn't." He smiled. So did Jay. "Let's get together, bro."

"You can count on it," was all Jay could manage around the golf ball of emotion in his throat.

"I THOUGHT YOU'D BE GONE by now." Jay stood in the doorway of Kate's office, his hair disheveled, his face etched with strain. Despite that, he looked good in his leather jacket, tailored tan wool trousers and brown sweater. Kate chastized herself for noticing.

"I was waiting to talk to you." Seated at her desk, she was tallying the monthly income on the computer. "How'd it go with Aaron?"

Digging his hands in his pockets, he leaned against the doorjamb. "Fine. He's sure different now."

"Marriage has been good for him. He and Lily are happy."

"I can tell." Jay focused on her with dark eyes that

pierced her heart. "Is my meeting with Aaron what you wanted to talk to me about?"

Pushing back the chair, Kate said, "No. The girls are next door with Ruth and Rachel. I've told them who you really are and they asked if they could talk to you before we go home."

"What was their reaction?"

"Confusion."

His jaw was tight. "Any suggestions on how to handle this?"

Kate stood and brushed imaginary lint off her navy pants. "Just be honest with them." She shrugged. "As honest as you can."

"Kate I—"

"Let's go," she interrupted, checking the clock. She wouldn't feel sorry for him. Wouldn't comfort him. Wouldn't listen to any excuses. Damn it all, she *wouldn't*. Brushing past him, she made her way to the aunts' house. Jay followed.

Two sets of twins sat on the couch. They were even dressed in similar shades of blue, Ruth and Rachel now wearing teal pantsuits, the girls in light- and dark-blue sweaters. Each pair shared a book, the third Harry Potter Kate recognized. All action stopped when Jay came into view, and for a minute, Kate was resentful of the power he had over the people she loved. Her heart ached for all of them. "Hi, look who I've brought."

"Jacob," Ruth said first. "Are you all right?"

"I'm fine, Ruth." He approached the couch and kissed her cheek.

"How did it go with..." Rachel's question trailed off.

Giving her a poignant smile, he brushed his lips over her forehead. The gentle gesture got to Kate, and she closed her eyes against it. "It went fine. Better than I imagined." He glanced down at the girls. "We can talk about it later."

Hope sidled in close to Rachel, but Hannah sprang to her feet, St. George ready to do battle with the dragon. She jammed her hands onto her hips and glared at him. "How come you lied to us?"

Kate put *Be respectful of adults* on her Twins' Manners list, but kept quiet. Every female in this room had a right to be angry at the man who stood before them.

Jay's eyes narrowed. Kate wondered how corporate executive Jay Lawrence, used to commanding men who made six-figure salaries, was going to deal with such impertinence. She moved behind him, ready to interfere if necessary. *Please, God, let him be nice.*

Squatting in front of Hannah, Jay faced the little girl squarely. "I didn't tell you who I was, Hannah, because when I came back here, I was confused about a lot of things. I was trying to figure them out."

"Not telling is the same as lying, Mommy says." Hannah's blue eyes were wide. "You lied."

He took a deep breath, stood, then made his way to a chair and sat. "Come over here, okay?"

Hannah marched over and stood before him. Jay said, "Hope, will you come here, too?"

Mutely, Hope shook her head, her fingers buried deep in her mouth, and inched even closer to Rachel. Kate didn't blame her for staying where she was safe.

"All right, then, just listen, honey." He looked at Hannah. "I did lie. And it was wrong. As I said, I was confused about a lot of things when I came back to Riverbend. I didn't want anyone to know who I was until I wasn't so confused anymore. Then, when I hurt my knee, it wasn't the right time to tell the truth."

No, it was the right time to spy on us. But Kate held her tongue.

His explanation was vague and imprecise, yet Hannah seemed to accept it. Hope still looked wary, though.

But it was Ruth and Rachel's reaction that concerned Kate. They were obviously very confused themselves, now. Probably because a big piece of the puzzle was missing. Jay had withheld from them his suspicions of Kate. She wondered again how he had explained his secrecy.

"Do you understand that, Hannah?" Jay asked.

"I guess. Mommy says when you lie it hurts God's heart."

Jay looked at his aunts. "I've hurt a lot of hearts by my actions. And I'm sorry."

Hannah's eyes sparkled. *This* she could relate to. "I do that, too. But I'm good after."

"Then I'll try to be good from now on, all right?" He ruffled her hair, and Hannah threw herself into his arms for a hug. Kate's throat tightened, and she saw tears brim in Ruth and Rachel's eyes. When Hannah stepped back, Jay stood, and holding her daughter's hand, crossed to the couch. He knelt in front of Hope, Hannah right beside him. "Hope, did you hear what I said?"

She nodded.

"Can you forgive me for tricking you?"

She mumbled something unintelligible.

"Take your fingers out of your mouth, love," Rachel scolded gently.

Hope did. "Mommy cries sometimes when Daddy lies to us. Did you make Mommy cry?"

Oh, God, Kate hadn't known the girls heard her cry

when Billy dumped them at the last minute for some football game or a new girlfriend.

Jay bent his head. He seemed to be struggling for control. Rachel placed a hand on his shoulder. After a moment, he faced Hope again. "I know I hurt Mommy, Hope. And I'm very sorry for that, too."

"Promise you won't hurt her again."

Kate couldn't look anymore. She heard Jay murmur something, saw in her peripheral vision that Hope finally let go of Rachel to hug Jay. She faced them then, and caught Jay's eye.

Both knew that he would hurt Mommy a lot more before the next four weeks were over.

ON TUESDAY, while he waited in the bustling Sunnyside Café at lunchtime for Tom Baines, Jay was still trying to deal with being back in Riverbend. First, he'd taken a walk around town and been flooded by memories of the time he spent in the places he'd passed: sharing a soda with Sarah at Jones' Drugstore, buying his aunts flowers at the Elm Street Florist and renting his first tux with Mitch and Charlie at Killian's department store. Jay thought about Aaron, who hadn't attended the proms, probably because he was an outsider, and because he couldn't afford a tux. Then Jay arrived at the café and found Evie Mazerik sitting at the cashier counter. Evie Mazerik—his father's mistress. Perched on a stool, she nodded nervously to him. She was small and flashy, like a piece of costume jewelry. He remembered the quiet beauty of his mother, who was more like a rare sapphire. He'd nodded back to Aaron's mother, but seated himself so she was out of his line of vision. Lucy Garvey, Charlie Callahan's sister, had served him coffee. He'd been surprised to see her. Younger than Jay, she'd been an up-and-coming basketball player. She'd told him a knee injury had ended that. He didn't reveal why he'd given up his own dream of succeeding in professional basketball.

Now as Jay waited for Tom, he sipped his coffee and could no longer keep thoughts of Kate at bay, as he'd done all day. He'd dreamed about her for two nights; one was stunningly erotic, one sweet and tender.

Thoughts of Kate led to thoughts of the girls. Hope's innocent request had shamed him. *Promise you won't hurt Mommy again.* Jay had feared he might lose it then, overcome by the realization of just how much pain he'd already brought to all the women in his life, and how much more was in store for them. For the first time, he was beginning to doubt his ability to fulfill his plan to come back to Riverbend and sell the store and the farmhouse.

"Jacob?"

He glanced up to see Lily Bennett—no, Lily Mazerik—standing by his booth. She smiled. "Hi." He remembered that sweet smile, and how she'd been like a sister to him growing up. Now, she *was* his sister, of sorts.

"Hello, Lily." It seemed right to stand and give her a hug. She was still slender, and very pretty, he noticed when he pulled back. Her posture was regal; her silvery blond hair hung loosely to her shoulders, and her blue eyes shone with the same contentment he'd seen in Aaron's.

"It's good to have you back," she told him.

Jay didn't say it was good to be back. "Congratulations on your marriage."

Lily gave him a knowing smile. "Thank you for visiting Aaron. It meant a lot to him."

"It's the least I can do." He heard his voice harden. "I wish…"

"I know." She put her hand on his arm. "But we all have to start from *now*." Her face clouded. "We can't let the past interfere with the present."

Though Jay didn't believe that for a second, he sensed Lily needed to believe that, so he said nothing.

She gestured to a booth across the room. "I'm having lunch with Lynn Kendall, our minister. She's getting married to your cousin—did you know that?"

Lynn acknowledged Jay with a nod, but her look was anything but friendly. He didn't blame her. "Yes, I know. Ruth and Rachel told me. As a matter of fact, I'm meeting Tom here."

Just then his cousin entered the diner. Tom had aged more than Lily and Jay. His hair was shot through with silver, and there were deep creases around his eyes and mouth. He'd been a hotshot reporter and had quit abruptly for unknown reasons, according to media gossip. Jay wondered what had happened to him. He remembered Tom as a carefree, handsome devil who caused the girls of Riverbend to trip over themselves every summer when he came here.

Now he only had eyes for one woman. Jay watched the smile come to his cousin's face as he walked over Lynn. Ignoring all sense of decorum, he kissed his fiancée on the mouth. Lynn's expression—one of pure adoration—made something twist in Jay's gut; suddenly he wished more than anything that Kate would look at him that way. Never before had he wanted this from a woman. Not Mallory. Not anyone.

"I'll be going," Lily said after a moment. "Lynn

and I are discussing wedding plans. She wants me to make the banner to hang in the church when they're married."

Jay nodded and watched her join the happy couple. Tom's head snapped up as soon as Lily spoke to him. His smile died as quickly as the sun setting over the river, and his laughing eyes narrowed. Then he headed toward Jay.

"You gonna punch me out?" Jay asked, sticking his hands in his pockets when Tom reached him. "Because I remember that right of yours. And if we're going to have a barroom brawl, we should go outside so we don't ruin the café."

Tom cocked his head. "I'm reserving judgment." His fist flexed. "For now."

"Yeah, sure." Jay slid into a booth and his cousin did the same. "You sounded pissed as hell on the phone the other night."

Tom's gaze strayed to the side of the diner where Lynn sat, and his expression turned sappy. "Can't be hooked up with a minister and not learn a few things. She says you deserve a chance."

Jay's eyebrows arched. "She acted like she'd take a punch at me herself the other night."

"Nah, Lynn's smarter than that. She'll get to you without physical violence, help you to see how stupid you're behaving, teach you the error of your ways and even make you like it."

Though a kernel of envy formed within him, Jay smiled. His cousin was in love, big time. "Is that what she did to you?"

Tom nodded. "Yeah."

"Wanna tell me about it? I...thought about you over

the years. Read your articles. It was top-notch reporting.''

"It almost destroyed me. I traveled all over the world, lived a life as exciting as James Bond. But after I watched my cameraman get blown to pieces, I threw it all away within six months." Tom looked intently at Jay. Jay was reminded of the time he and Sarah had finally "gone all the way" and he'd confided in Tom only because he needed advice about birth control. "A lot like you threw everything away fifteen years ago, Jacob."

Jaw hard, Jay picked up the menu.

Tom grabbed the top of the laminated folder and slammed it down on the table. "I loved you like a brother, and I never heard from you after the Christmas we both turned twenty. What the hell happened?"

Saved from answering by Lucy's appearance, Tom ordered the diner special without even looking at the menu. Jay followed suit, not caring what it was. When Lucy left, Tom speared him with a demanding glare. What the hell, he'd tell him some of it.

Jay said, "I found out something about my father...something that my father did..." God, this was hard. He'd never once discussed any of it with anybody. "The Christmas of my senior year in college. I was destroyed by it. I had to leave Riverbend, and everything and everyone associated with it." Jay felt his throat tighten. "I had to. It was the only way I could deal with it."

Tom's expression softened. "I know how it is, to have to get away." His look was thoughtful. "Was it about Aaron Mazerik?"

Jay shook his head. "I didn't discover that until I

came back. Tom, I realize I hurt a lot of people. I was…selfish. I know that now.''

Sighing, Tom stared over Jay's shoulder. ''Yeah, I learned that lesson, too. I have two kids I let get away from me.'' Again his gaze strayed to Lynn. ''She helped me find my way back to them.''

''Two kids?'' Jay smiled genuinely. ''Really? Boys or girls?''

''One of each.'' As Tom delved into his pocket for his wallet, Jay thought of Hope and Hannah, who were now out of his life.

After looking at the pictures of Pete and Libby, Jay said, ''I envy you.''

''It isn't too late, buddy.''

Just as their meals arrived—the special was meat loaf, gravy and mashed potatoes—the door to the diner opened and two men strode in. Both were tall and lean. They reminded Jay of cowboys walking into a saloon. He recognized Mitch Sterling first, probably because they'd been such good friends. Dark hair that needed a trim fell over his forehead and into eyes that seemed to survey the Sunnyside but not really see it. The other was slighter than Mitch with an innocent smile that triggered a memory. *Come on, Jacob. Your old man won't know if we use the houseboat. It'll be cool.*

Charlie Callahan, the Huck Finn of the group. When he caught sight of Jay and Tom, he nudged Mitch. Sterling's scowl became fiercer. Jay felt like one of ''America's Most Wanted.''

After exchanging a few words, the men made their way to Jay and Tom's booth. Furthering the gunslinger image, they pulled straight chairs up to the end of the table and straddled them. All their attention was focused on Jay. Charlie looked the friendlier of the two.

Mitch seemed about ready to spit nails. Jay thought of several tactics he could use to defuse the situation, ones he'd honed in the corporate world. Not the least of which was leaving. But something told him to stay and take it on the chin. "Uh, even outlaws get a trial before the hanging."

Charlie's mouth quirked into that same old smile.

Mitch's frown remained in place. He said in a low, gravelly voice worthy of Judge Roy Bean, "What are you doing to Katie, Steele?"

Jay raised his chin. If he could face his aunts and the twins, he could do this. "I withheld my identity from her because I thought she'd been milking my aunts and had duped my father."

Three jaws dropped. It would have been funny if the stakes weren't so high, the situation so desperate.

"I know, I know. She's as innocent as a newborn calf. I found that out fast."

"Word has it you inherited the store and the farmhouse."

"Yes, I did."

Mitch straightened. "It's Katie's livelihood you're screwin' around with."

"I know that now, but I didn't when I first came back."

Charlie raised innocent brows. "I got a million questions, Jacob. You answer them okay, we'll deliver the verdict at the end of the meal." He signaled Lucy Garvey over. "Bring two more specials and coffee for us both, sis."

"I'm not hungry," Mitch growled.

"Tough. I dragged you away from the store for some chow."

"You're not my mother."

"Your mother wouldn't put up with this crap, either." Then he clapped a hand on Mitch's back. "Come on buddy, you gotta *eat.*"

Jay was transported back twenty years. Tom, Mitch, Charlie and he had camped out on the bank of the river. Charlie was moping about his newfound feelings for Beth Pennington, another River Rat they'd all considered a sister. "I'm just not sure it's right," Charlie had told them. Mitch had been goofy over a new cheerleader who had legs to die for. Jay'd been mad at Sarah for flirting with Nick Harrison, who consequently had not been invited to boys-night-out. Tom had been giving them all advice.

Mitch interrupted his reminiscence. "Out with it, Steele. Why'd you leave and what're you gonna do about Katie's situation now that you're back?"

"KATIE, THERE'S A MAN from—" Ruth stood in the doorway of the bookstore office and put her glasses on to read the card she held in her hand "—the Allen and Young Agency. He'd like to see you."

Rubbing her temples, Kate willed the headache away and put ibuprofen on her Shopping list and neck exercises on her Relaxation list. The name of the firm sounded familiar, but she couldn't place it; her head pounded too hard to think clearly. "Is he a salesman?"

"No, dear. He looks very official." She giggled girlishly. "Actually, he looks like Ichabod Crane."

Kate stood. "I'll come right out."

Ruth opened her mouth to speak, but instead, preceded Kate into the bookstore. At the front of the shop she could see the man talking to Rachel. He was tall and thin, with a small head, huge ears and large eyes. Ruth was right. Except for the dark-rimmed glasses, he did look like Ichabod Crane.

"May I help you?" she asked.

"Are you Mary Katherine McMann?"

She nodded. Butterflies danced in her stomach. Something about this man…

"I'm James Porter from Allen and Young. I'm here to audit your books. It should take about three days. I wouldn't have come so close to Thanksgiving, but there was a rush order on this job." At her blank look, he added, "We sent you a letter regarding this matter. You were to respond if this date wasn't convenient."

Vaguely, she remembered a letter and being unable to reach the sender by phone. "Audit?" The butterflies were frenzied now, and Kate clasped her hand over her middle to still them. "You must be mistaken, Mr. Porter. I didn't order an audit."

"The owner of Steele Books ordered it."

Kate faced Ruth, then Rachel. At their pained look, she remembered.

She didn't need to hear Mr. Porter say, "A Jay Lawrence."

The room tilted a bit, but Kate forced it steady. "I see. Why don't we…" Her voice trailed off as the bell over the front door tinkled merrily.

Through it came Jay Lawrence. He appeared…happy for the first time since he'd told her the truth. His eyes had brightened and his jaw was relaxed. The meeting with his cousin must have gone well. He was whistling softly—until he saw all four of them staring at him.

His hands jammed in his pockets, he said, "Hi, everybody.'' Resting his gaze on Kate, he cocked his head. ''What's going on?''

Standing stiffly, she said simply, ''Your auditor's here.''

CHAPTER ELEVEN

"Who brought the minestrone soup?" Lynn called over her shoulder from her position at the sink. She was peeling potatoes in the huge fellowship-hall kitchen of the church because a sleet storm had hit Riverbend the day before and knocked out the town's electricity. Thanks to a generator Mitch had brought from the store, the church was the only place other than the hospital that had heat and electricity on Thanksgiving Day.

"Kate brought it." This from Lily Mazerik, who looked like a fashion model, though she was dressed casually in soft beige slacks and a sweater to match.

"Who brought the homemade applesauce?" Lucy Garvey asked, directing the action in the kitchen like the good waitress she was.

"Kate did," Beth Pennington said. Her long, curly, black hair was pulled back in a ponytail, accenting her strong features. Both she and Lily beamed with new-found happiness, Lily from her recent marriage, Beth from her engagement to Charlie Callahan.

"Who brought the cranberries?" Lily's mother wanted to know. Still striking at sixty, Eleanor's pretty face glowed from the heat of the stove, where she stirred the gravy.

There were five other women in the kitchen—including Wally Drummer's wife, Mary—and they were all watching Kate. She felt their gazes, though she didn't look up from the butcher block in the center of the room. "I, um, had a lot time on my hands this week," she mumbled defensively.

Lynn asked dryly, "Was that before or after you ran the bookstore single-handedly so the Steele sisters could show off their nephew?"

Their nephew. Who'd turned into a bully.

"All right, so I had trouble sleeping these past few nights." She blew a strand of hair out of her eyes and pushed up the sleeves of the frost-green fleece sweater she wore with jeans and boots.

As if on some silent signal, the five women crowded around her. Mary Drummer began the interrogation. "Did Jacob really drive out to your farmhouse in the middle of the storm to see if you and the girls were all right?"

Kate sighed. "Yes, though we were fine." She caught Lynn's minister look that said it wasn't nice to lie on Thanksgiving Day.

In truth, she'd been scared and the girls had been petrified when they'd all awakened at three in the morning to the howl of the wind and the total absence of electrical power. The twins had climbed into her bed and slept restlessly until the storm abated. Kate had gotten up about five and had just entered the chilly porch to get firewood when headlights pierced the darkness outside. In seconds, a wet Jay Lawrence was pounding on her door. She'd had no choice but to let him in.

"I heard you had a whale of a fight about his coming out there," Beth put in.

"Who told you that?"

"The girls told Allison."

Kate frowned. "We had words." A whole dictionary full, some of which she hoped the kids hadn't overheard…

Facing Jay, Kate had shaken back her tousled hair and stared him down. "What the hell are you doing here?"

"I was worried about you being this far out of town alone. So were Ruth and Rachel. I drove out to make sure you were okay." His stance was as belligerent as hers.

"How did you get here? The roads must be caked with ice."

"I followed a sand truck. I got him to do your driveway, too." He'd glanced over his shoulder and said, "The weather's better now, though the power's out everywhere."

Furious about the audit he'd ordered, she hadn't been about to play nicely with him. "Fine, then you can go back to town. The girls and I don't need you."

"The hell I will. I'm staying until daylight, then you're coming back to town with me."

"In your dreams, pal."

Before he could speak, the girls were throwing themselves into his arms, saying, "We were scared. You came to save us just like the woodsman in 'Little Red Riding Hood.'"

"More like the wolf," she'd mumbled, but just like poor misguided Red, she let the enemy into the house…

Lucy chuckled, bringing her back to reality. "I think it's so romantic."

Scowling, Kate wiped her hands on the towel wrapped around her waist. "It's irritating." She glanced out toward the fellowship hall. "*He's* irritating."

"Who is?" Tom asked as he came through the kitchen door. Like most of the other men, he was dressed for a day of roughing it in jeans, a flannel shirt, leather boots.

"Your cousin," Mary Drummer told him from the stove. Cooking up the combined turkeys and trimmings of several Riverbend Community Church members had started early this morning, and getting such a large quantity of food ready would delay dinner for some time. "You know, Wally's thrilled to have him back."

Kate watched as Tom crossed to Lynn, put his arm around her and nuzzled her ear. Lynn leaned into him for a second. The intimate gesture made Kate's heart lurch.

After a futile effort at helping, Tom made a beeline for the door just as two other men entered—Charlie, who started cutting vegetables with Beth, and Paul Flannigan, who remained just inside the kitchen doorway.

Paul was a nice-looking man, and though not as tall as Jay, he had world-class muscles from working out and a smile that was sincere. His sandy-brown hair and brown eyes were pleasant. "What can I do?" he asked, his gaze on Kate.

"Come over here and help me peel these onions," she said on a whim.

"Only for you, sweetheart." When he reached her, he placed a hand familiarly on her neck and gave a gentle squeeze.

She thought about leaning into him, but just couldn't summon the interest. Damn it!

JAY STARED at the door to the kitchen, then glanced at his watch. Flannigan had gone in there thirty minutes ago. Jay had thought about finding an excuse to visit the kitchen himself, but he'd been afraid to face a knife-wielding Kate, so he'd taken a seat at an empty table with a bird's-eye view of the door.

He'd been introduced to the pharmacist as soon as they'd arrived at the church. Flannigan was good-looking and in great shape, making Jay think about not having visited a gym in five weeks.

Is he a boyfriend? Jay had asked Kate the night she'd listened to Flannigan's message on the tape.

He'd like to be.

Jay sighed. Kate had remained livid even after he'd explained why he'd ordered the audit. Though he'd discovered early on that the suspicious account she kept had been legitimate savings from her salary, deferred for tax purposes, he'd thought the audit would be a smart idea. Then he'd forgotten about it. She'd been good and angry when the auditor had arrived, and Jay's heavy-handedness this morning hadn't done anything to change her feelings. Used to women capitulating, he'd all but ordered her to pack her Thanksgiving food and get in his car. The girls had clamored to go with him to town, so Kate had given in.

Just then she and Flannigan came through the swinging door and headed toward the table where the girls sat with his aunts. Her pale-green sweater reminded him of cotton candy and made his mouth water. It draped softly over her curves, a fact that Flannigan sure as hell noticed. With her hair piled on top of her head like that, her neck looked graceful and inviting. Flannigan's hand rested intimately at her back. Jay gripped his soda can, making it crunch, and scowled at them.

"What's the matter, Jakey boy?" Tom asked, plopping down into a chair beside him. "The green-eyed monster bite you?"

Jay refused to take the bait, but admitted to himself that for the first time in his life, he did feel jealous. "What do you know about him?" Jay didn't even try to disguise his interest in the pharmacist.

"He's a nice guy. Divorced. Lynn says he has a daughter who lives with her mom on River Road. He runs a good business." Tom took a sip of his drink and stretched out his legs. "And he has the hots for Katie."

Jay cursed.

Tom laughed. "I knew you were lying at lunch when you said you weren't involved with her." Another swig. "Just like I knew you were hedging when you said your plans for the store were up in the air."

Jay said nothing, but recalled how he'd danced around his old buddies' questions, suddenly confused about what he really wanted to do. Only Mitch Sterling had pushed; he'd made him swear he wasn't going to hurt Kate. Brushing aside the thought, Jay watched Flannigan again. Had Kate slept with this guy? Would she again when Jay left?

The idea caused his stomach to sour. For a minute, he visualized her all warm and flushed from his lovemaking. She said she hadn't responded to anyone else as she had to him. Still, Flannigan's attention irked him. And that was the reason he got to his feet. Maybe he'd run a little interference.

RUTH WATCHED her scowling nephew cross the room toward them, as she cuddled a drowsy Hope on her lap. She caught her sister's eye, and Rachel arched an eyebrow in acknowledgment. When Jacob arrived at the table, he stopped behind Kate, who jumped when he spoke. Ruth couldn't help but notice that Kate also moved away from Paul Flannigan. Hmm.

Bending down, Jacob lifted Hope out of Ruth's arms as naturally as any father would. He sat down in a vacant chair and soothed Katie's little girl, who cuddled right into his chest; all the while, Jacob stared aggressively at the pharmacist. In minutes, Kate excused herself to go back to the kitchen, and Paul left to talk to Dr. Julian Bennett.

When Ruth turned to say something to Jacob, she saw he was still watching Paul. "Jacob, is something wrong?"

Taking a breath, he was about to comment, when Hope raised her head and said, "Daddy won't come now."

"What, sweetheart?" Jacob asked.

"Mommy said Daddy won't come to get us because of the ice."

Ruth explained. "Billy was planning to take the girls for the weekend."

Jacob gave the child a hug. "I'm sorry, Hope. Would you like to do something with me and your aunts Ruth and Rachel this weekend?"

She lay her head back down on his chest. "Go to Disney World." Sleepily, she stuck her fingers in her mouth and closed her eyes.

Jacob smiled. "Well, I don't think that's in the cards this weekend, but I'm sure we can find something to do, can't we, Aunt Ruth?"

"I'm sure we can," Ruth said, basking in the joy of having her beloved nephew home again. Her gaze traveled from him back to little Hope. Maybe, just maybe, he was back for good.

KATE CONSIDERED throwing a tantrum, but instead, she prowled the apartment over the bookstore, where she'd been coerced to stay for the night...

Ruth had been the most vocal. "Katie, love," she said, "you can't go home tonight. There's still no power out on River Road. You and the girls take the apartment, and Jacob can bunk in our spare room."

Rachel had added her opinion, Jay had said he wouldn't even consider driving her back out to the farmhouse, and even Lynn had sided with them.

The day had been physically and emotionally draining. More had happened on this one Thanksgiving Day than had happened on all the Thanksgiving Days in the past ten years put together. Gathering all the food cooked for everyone who'd shown up at the church hall. Feeling Jay's eyes on her every time she turned around. Trying to warm up to Paul's overtures. And then she'd found out that Tessa had gone into labor and Mitch had had to rush her to the hospital, where she'd given birth to a baby girl.

The grandfather clock in the corner chimed ten times. She hoped it didn't wake the girls. Twenty minutes ago, dressed in *Mr. Lawrence's* T-shirts, they'd collapsed into *Mr. Lawrence's* bed, snuggled into his pillows and fallen promptly to sleep. Kate had dragged blankets out of the linen closet and made up the couch for herself.

She'd refused to sleep with the girls because the room smelled like Jay. Even the bathroom did, where she'd changed out of her clothes and put on one of Rachel's pink flannel nightgowns.

There was a knock on the apartment door, and even as she swung it open, she knew who it was.

"I came to get my shaving kit and some sweats to sleep in." Jay nodded to the closed bedroom door. "I left them in the bathroom, so I won't wake the girls."

She turned her back on him and strode to the window. "Fine."

Heavy footsteps fell on the hardwood floor. She heard him rummaging in the bathroom, then footsteps again. From the corner of her eye, she saw him stop halfway across the room. "What's all this?" he asked. When she turned, he was standing by the couch she'd made up. "I'm sleeping there tonight," she said.

"Why? There's a queen-size bed in the bedroom. Big enough for all three of you."

"I can't sleep in your bed."

"Why?"

She shook her head, presented him with her back again. There was a soft thud, then footsteps behind her. He didn't touch her, but he was close. *"Why?"*

Closing her eyes, she whispered, "The room smells like you. I can't bear it."

She heard his quick curse. Then there was a pause before he said, "Is what we did together that repulsive to you?"

She shook her head.

"What is it, then?"

"Nothing. Go away."

He stepped closer. In a gravelly voice he murmured, "I hated seeing you with Flannigan today. Every time he touched you, I wanted to deck him."

"Please don't tell me that."

"Every single night this week, I've wanted you with me here."

Kate swallowed hard. "Why are you telling me this? Don't you know it only hurts me to hear it?" She cleared her throat. "Or don't you care?"

He said simply, "I care."

Angry, she spun around. "What are you trying to do, Jay? Convince me to be your playmate these four weeks? You already got me to run the store and stay at the house. Do you want me to warm your bed until you fulfill your prison term here in Riverbend and then take off for the city lights and all your glamorous women?"

He jerked back as if she'd slapped him. "Is that what you think of me?"

"What else am I supposed to think? You lied to me, you invaded my privacy, you're forcing me to watch while you take away everything I love in the world." She battled back the tears that brimmed in her eyes. "What else am I supposed to think about you?"

"Yes, I've done all those things. But my relationship with you, that last night, and in the days before, was real."

"Was it? Why should I believe that? And even if it was, what difference does it make?"

"None, I guess. It's just important to me that you believe that."

"You don't get it, do you? I don't *want* to believe that. It makes the whole thing that much harder." This time she didn't turn her back. She faced him squarely. "Now please go. And stay away from me. If you do care for me, just stay away."

"All right. As much as possible, I'll stay away."

HE DID STAY AWAY, too. At the end of the first week of working in the store, Jay was proud of his restraint.

The town's power had been restored, Kate and the girls moved back to the farmhouse and things were calm.

He'd just finished cleaning the shelves in the collectible-books section, a filthy task that Kate had assigned him with obvious glee. She must have made a list of the Worst Jobs in the Store and given them to him. It made him smile because it showed she was human. As he left the rare-book room and made his way to the front of the store to get coffee, he caught a glimpse of red in one of the aisles. Kate was working in the art-books section, finishing some inventory. He knew it was her because he'd been thinking all morning about the way that sweater had hugged her curves. Yesterday she'd worn a green blouse, the day before a burgundy tunic with matching leggings. Damn, he could barely remember what Mallory looked like, but he'd managed to memorize the contents of Kate's closet.

Pouring coffee, he heard behind him, "Hello, Jacob."

The voice was low, cultured and one he'd never forget as long as he lived. The last time he'd heard it, it had been full of pleading. *Don't do this, please. I'm so sorry.*

Slowly he turned to face Sarah Smith. She held herself like a queen, as she always had. The bow mouth was the same, but her blond hair seemed lighter. Expecting to feel rage well within him, he waited for a nasty remark to come to his lips. He said only, "Hello, Sarah." His tone was stiff but not unkind.

She unbuttoned her cashmere coat. "I heard you were back. You look…good."

"So do you." Actually, she looked old and worn.

"I was wondering if we could talk."

He sipped his coffee. "I don't think so."

"I see." She fiddled with the strap of her purse. "Did you bring your family to Riverbend with you?"

How like Sarah. Tell her no, and she'd find a way to get what she wanted, anyway. As a teenager, he'd had no idea how to deal with her. "I'm not married."

"Never?"

"No." He didn't ask if she was. Truthfully, he didn't care.

"I'm widowed."

He nodded politely.

"No children."

He would *not* react to that, allowing himself to be distracted by Simon coming out of the office. "Well, duty calls," Jay said, stepping away.

"Jacob I…"

But he was already heading to the back of the store, and the rest of her comment drifted off to nowhere.

He was vacuuming the rug at noon when the girls burst through the door. He had just enough time to let go of the vacuum and catch the twins as they leaped into his arms. "Hey, are you guys playing hooky?"

Hannah tugged on his shirt. "You got dirt on your face." She sniffed. "And you smell."

"Your mommy gave me the grunt jobs to do."

Hope slid down and stood demurely by his side. "You musta been a bad boy. Mommy makes us clean out the basement when we're bad."

"I done a lot of that." Hannah's head bobbed with her words.

"I'll bet." Jay ruffled her hair. "Why are you out of school, ladies?"

"We had a half-day." Hannah eyed the cookies on the sidebar. "And Daddy's coming to get us."

"He wants us for the whole weekend." Hope's face was filled with pleasure.

Jay said a silent prayer of thanks for their father's attention.

Until Billy McMann walked into the store—an hour late. Jay had expected him to be larger-than-life, the way the girls talked about him. The way he'd affected Kate. Instead, he was a rather small guy with light-blond hair and tired blue eyes. He was dressed well, though—in hand-tooled boots and an expensive-looking jacket.

Not bad for a man who wasn't paying child support.

The girls jumped out of the chairs where they'd been keeping watch and flung themselves at McMann, much as they'd done with Jay minutes earlier. Watching from the stacks, Jay found he didn't like sharing their affection with their father.

"How are my little angels?" McMann hugged them with genuine warmth.

Jay realized he was eavesdropping but couldn't tear himself away. Nor did he understand the negative emotion that welled up inside him as he watched McMann with the twins.

Kate came into view, carrying their backpacks. "Hi." Jay listened for any affection in her voice. He heard none.

"Hi, doll. You look great." McMann's gaze swept over her. "Nice sweater."

A twinge of anger shot through Jay. He studied Kate to see if she liked the compliment. Her face was blank.

"Here's all the stuff the girls'll need. When will you bring them back Sunday?"

"Uh, I..." McMann ran a hand through his hair. "Listen, something's come up. I can take them tonight, but I got a job that starts tomorrow over in Lynchberg, so I'll be dropping them off tomorrow morning.''

Hannah's eyes widened. "But you said you'd take us to Chicago to see Santa's train. Like the one in *The Polar Express*."

"I know, sweetheart, but Daddy's got to work."

Kate's expression said, *You liar. You don't start a job on a Saturday.*

Hope's eyes filled with tears and she clutched Kate's pants.

Hannah stared him down with very adult contempt. "Then I don't wanna go with you." Without another word, she took off for the back of the store.

Jay was startled by how much he wanted to punch McMann. But he held himself back and watched as Kate cut him to slivers with a look of pure loathing. Then she did what was best for the girls: she suppressed her own feelings, talked Hannah into spending at least one night with her father and, with a brave front, ushered the three of them out the door.

Jay had never respected her more. Stepping out of the stacks, he studied her as she watched them through the window. Her back was hunched, her head was down.

"Kate, I'm sorry."

Hastily, she swiped at her cheeks. "You know, all I want is for him to spend a little time with his children. I don't ask for child support. I don't make him pay medical bills or buy their clothes. I just wish…"

Jay didn't know what to say. He was shocked by his reactions. First he wanted to beat Billy McMann to a pulp. Then he wanted to comfort Kate. But it was the third reaction that really floored him. He wanted badly to replace that man in the twins' lives, to fulfill all their wishes and dreams and make sure McMann never hurt them again.

BY FIVE O'CLOCK that afternoon, Kate had calmed down enough to think about where she could find the money to take the girls to Chicago. She calculated the amount in her Emergency Fund list. The total was too low to dip into. And it would be irresponsible to charge anything when she didn't know how long she'd have a job. Maybe she could cancel her order for a new winter jacket. Exasperated, she sighed and behind the locked door of the store's office, finished washing up in the small bathroom. She changed into an old but still nice black cocktail dress that she'd brought from home and decided to put on a little makeup.

Sick of thinking about Billy and his negligence, she eyed herself critically in the mirror. Her cheeks were really too full. Should she pluck her eyebrows? The mascara she applied made her lashes thicker, sexier, and she fluttered them whimsically. Lipstick helped and thank God her freckles were almost gone. Some light foundation covered the remnants. Maybe she should get her hair cut.

She wondered what kind of women Jay Lawrence dated. She'd asked, but he'd never said.

How about you? Are there women who are missing you?

Scores, I'm sure.

Sighing, she shut off the bathroom light, slid into heels and resisted the urge to dart back and look at herself in the mirror again. She grabbed the vintage wrap she'd picked up secondhand and headed for the front of the store. Paul should be here any minute. Paul, whose invitation she'd accepted because she needed adult company.

And because you need to get your mind off Jay Lawrence.

When she reached the desk area, she found Jay in the café leaning against the counter sipping a cup of coffee. Which he promptly dropped when she came into view.

"Oh, shit," he said, grabbing some napkins and wiping at his pants.

"Blot it up from the carpet so it doesn't stain."

She watched him follow her directions. Finally, he stood and, holding a handful of soiled napkins, gave her a very male once-over. "Where the hell are you going all dressed up like that?"

Arching an eyebrow, she said, "I have a date."

Hot emotion flared in his eyes. "A date? With who?"

"Not that it's your business, but with Paul."

He clenched his hand, crushing the napkins. Rivulets of coffee seeped out.

"Watch out, you're dripping."

"Huh?"

"The napkins."

"Oh." He deposited them in the trash, then turned back to her. "Where are you going?"

She didn't answer.

"It's Friday night. I thought you always went to the basketball game."

"Not tonight."

"Why are you all dressed up?"

"It's none of—"

"Isn't it?"

Had he been demanding or yelled, she would have

told him off. But his softly uttered words were a plea she couldn't ignore. "He's taking me to dinner at Charter's, then we're going to a play in Cleesberg."

"That's pretty far to drive."

"It's why we're going early."

Jay gritted his teeth, she suspected to keep from asking something. It didn't work. "You're not staying overnight there, are you?"

She thought about not answering. About taunting him. But at the top of her Morals list was *Never Hurt Anyone on Purpose.* And no matter why he was acting the way he was—probably some male territorial gene surfacing because they'd slept together—she wouldn't lie or intentionally cause him pain.

"No, we're not staying overnight."

He blew out a heavy breath. "You look beautiful."

She felt her face flush. "Thank you."

"Kate, I—"

The door to the store opened, interrupting him. Paul entered, dressed in a conservative navy suit and tie.

The two men nodded to each other, and Kate said goodbye before preceding Paul out the door. But she couldn't leave behind the look on Jay's face. She prayed it didn't stay with her all night.

AT ONE O'CLOCK in the morning, Jay sipped his drink and stared out the apartment's front window. Where was she? He'd started this vigil about midnight, and she still wasn't back. Damn it, if she'd stayed in Cleesberg with Flannigan after all...

He pounded his fist on the window sill. What the *hell* was he doing mooning over a woman? Just because she had a date. He hadn't seen Mallory in weeks, and it had never crossed his mind to wonder if she was spending time with anyone else.

But the vision of Kate dressed up for another man was still imprinted on his mind. When he forced himself to stop thinking about her, he'd remembered the twins' reaction to McMann's news. Both visions had driven him crazy. Jay wasn't used to standing idly by, but what action could he take here?

He couldn't leave Riverbend, get back to his old life, his old self. Not if he wanted the money to buy into ComputerConcepts.

You could stay here. For good.

He banished the ridiculous idea.

Headlights broke the darkness, and a moderate-size sedan pulled up next to Kate's Jeep. With the streetlights on, Jay could see the car, but not inside.

He waited.

She didn't get out.

He pictured Flannigan's hands on her, and he clenched his own. They were kissing, he knew it. She was letting another man touch her. He remembered the feel of her, soft yet supple, smooth yet strong. She smelled like bubble bath and flowers. His imagination ran wild for the ten minutes that passed until a car door opened. Flannigan exited and circled the car. He took Kate's hand and helped her out. From this angle, Jay could see her hair was mussed. Damn it.

Flannigan didn't let go of her as he escorted her to the car. She handed Flannigan the keys; he unlocked and opened her door. Good, he'd leave now. Instead, the other man pulled Kate close, and Jay's chest hurt. Flannigan cradled the back of her neck, and Jay's throat got tight. When Flannigan took her in his arms, aligning her whole body to his, Jay closed his eyes. He couldn't take this. Another man was touching her. A better man was touching her. Flannigan was even able to be the father McMann wasn't.

Jay stepped away from the window.

It's good she has someone else, he told himself. *This way you can leave and not worry that you hurt her too much by making love to her.* From what he'd seen, she'd only been singed.

It's good. It is!

Swearing, he strode across the room to his cell phone. Flipping it open, he punched the speed dial for his attorney in New York. He didn't care about the time, that it was an hour later there. He paid his lawyer a retainer that warranted late-night phone calls.

Martin Jones answered on the fifth ring.

"Jones?" Jay said in a clipped voice, shooting a glance at the window. "It's Jay Lawrence." He pictured the girls' faces, and Kate's. "Stop negotiations with Anderson Books immediately."

A muffled sound, one of surprise being covered up, Jay guessed. "May I ask why?" Jones asked. "Have you decided not to sell?"

Jay stared at the window. "I'm not sure anymore what I want to do."

CHAPTER TWELVE

LYNN KENDALL looked like an angel, dressed in white lace and satin; she practically floated down the Riverbend Community Church aisle on her wedding day. The sanctuary, redolent with Christmas greenery and poinsettias and dimmed for the candlelight service, shimmered around the bride. As one of the honor attendants, Kate felt her eyes mist with tears, as she thought about all Lynn and Tom had been through and thanked God for the happiness they'd found.

Next to Kate at the altar, Libby Baines, Tom's teenage daughter, beamed as her stepmother-to-be smiled at her father. The thirteen-year-old girl was the second honor attendant, dressed in a shade of light pink that set off her auburn hair and eyes. Tom stood next to his son, Pete, and Jay, who both served as best men. The groom looked a little as if he couldn't quite believe his luck.

As Rachel played Beethoven's "Ode to Joy" on the organ, Lynn made her way down the aisle on the arm of her uncle Will, a minister who would also perform the service. When she reached the altar, she took Tom's hand.

"Ready, love?" Tom asked huskily.

The emotion-filled words and the devotion they represented made Kate's throat tighten. The bride and groom took their places in front of Lynn's uncle, who began the ceremony with the traditional, "We are gathered here together…"

Kate's gaze shifted to Jay, who wasn't watching the couple, hadn't been watching them since the ceremony began. Dressed in a perfectly fitting tux and pristine white shirt, he was so handsome it made her heart hurt. That he was staring at her with the same knowing half smile he'd been giving her all week made her nervous.

The minister's words registered. "First we'll have a reading, one Lynn and Tom have chosen, that has relevance to their life together."

As Lily Mazerik, dressed in a delicate winter-white suit, rose and approached the podium, Kate studied Aaron, seated in the second pew. He was totally enraptured by his wife. Behind him, Mitch and Tessa sat holding hands. Next to them, Charlie kept Beth close with his arm across the back of the pew. Everybody was happy. Except… Shaking off the introspection, Kate listened to the tribute to love Lily gave. The words from "Song of Solomon" suggested rebirth and new beginnings.

When Lily finished, the minister rose and faced Tom and Lynn. "It's time to speak your vows." He made a few comments to the congregation. Then he smiled at the couple. "I'd like you to repeat after me. Do you, Tom…"

Kate smiled as Lynn and Tom committed themselves to each other in specially written words, then exchanged rings. When the minister declared, "I now pronounce you husband and wife," he winked at his niece. "You may kiss the bride."

Taking advantage of the situation, Tom kissed Lynn lustily, drawing a huge chuckle from the congregation, before escorting his wife down the aisle with a flourish.

As they'd practiced in the rehearsal, Kate met Jay in the middle of the altar; he took her arm and entwined it with his.

I have one condition. That you promise not to touch me.

As if he'd heard her earlier admonishment, Jay whispered, "This doesn't count because it's in church."

There it was again, the teasing, the mischief. Something was gone, some cloud that had been hanging over his head. She couldn't figure it out.

He touched her during the picture-taking, too, at the front of the sanctuary after the wedding party had greeted everyone. They were, after all, still in church, Jay told her. During the long but somewhat entertaining photo shoot—Damon Hudson, a local teenager whom Lynn and Tom had helped straighten out and who'd been hired to take pictures—Kate thought back to the week before.

First Jay had insisted he take the girls to Chicago on Sunday afternoon. He'd heard Billy cop out on them on the Friday, and Kate's heart warmed at Jay's thoughtfulness. She tried to beg off going along, but the twins wouldn't hear of it. So Ruth, Rachel and the twins had scrunched into the back of Jay's Volvo, and she had taken the front seat.

Later this week, she'd given him the tedious and once again dirty job of inventorying the old books up in the attic, which he'd done without complaint. He'd teased her about it, though, and told her to call him Cinderfella. When the afternoon mail arrived, and in it was the audit report, he'd whipped the document out of her hands and thrown it in the trash. He'd said only that he'd been stupid to order it the first place, and he didn't need it anymore. He wouldn't say why.

After a good half hour, the photo session ended. As they headed for the church fellowship hall, she wondered if the hall was considered part of *church*. On her Be Sensible list, she mentally entered *Stay Away from Jay Lawrence*.

JAY SMILED at the transformation of the fellowship hall. The church women had turned it into a "chic restaurant" for Tom and Lynn's reception. As he followed Kate inside, with Mitch and Tessa behind him, he heard her exclaim, "Oh, this is lovely!"

Dark-pink tablecloths covered several round tables, each sporting a long white candle in the center. The lights were dimmed, and a refreshment area was to the left, the head table to the right. The smell of roasting meat and cooking vegetables permeated the air.

Though she'd given birth only a few weeks ago, Tessa looked remarkably slim. "It's beautiful," she said, holding on to her husband's arm. Surprising everyone, Mitch and Tessa had been married minutes before her baby was born. "So is your dress, Kate. Did you make it?"

"Uh-huh."

Beautiful was an understatement. The green satin dress had a strapless top under a pretty, long-sleeved jacket. Though the hem touched the floor, its side slit revealed way too much leg. Jay groaned when he saw the dance floor and heard the DJ start a song. Though he relished the idea of holding Kate close, he wasn't looking forward to watching her dance in that dress with anybody else.

He felt a tug on his jacket and looked down. "You wanna get some punch with me, Mr. Lawrence?" Hannah stood before him, looking like a little princess in a taffeta dress with puffy sleeves and a wide skirt, the same color as Kate's. Hope's matching dress was pink, like Libby's. Ruth had told him Kate had made all four outfits. Jeez, didn't the woman ever sleep?

"Why, darlin', I'd love to." He took Hannah's hand. "You gonna save a dance for me?"

The little girl nodded vigorously and led him to the punch table. As they walked through the crowd, Jay held on tight to her hand and wondered how he was ever going to live without the twins in his life. He'd sat with both of them on the train in Chicago, screeched as it climbed its steep slope, cheered when they passed Rudolf and Santa, then shared hot chocolate with them afterward. They'd been so grateful they hadn't stopped hugging him the entire day.

Jay poured two glasses of punch, though he didn't quite fill Hannah's. "Be careful, sweetheart. This will stain that pretty dress of yours if it spills."

"'Kay," she said around a long sip. Her eyes wandered to the corner of the room where three boys kicked around a hackeysack ball. Sam Sterling, Mitch's hearing-impaired son, was one of them.

"Can I go watch them play?" she asked Jay. As if he was her father.

His heart lurched at the innocent question. "Sure, but give me—"

She darted off before he could confiscate the punch. Weaving through the crowd, she was almost to the boys when a woman stepped in her path and Hannah ran right into her.

The cup flew out of Hannah's hand.

And onto Sarah Smith's elegant silk dress.

Sarah stared down at the girl in shock. "Look what you've done!"

Hannah froze and her face reddened. Jay reached her just as tears welled in her eyes. Scooping her up, he cradled her to his chest, his hand on her neck. "Shh, Hannah, it's all right. It was an accident."

Mumbling something, Hannah snuggled closer to his chest. But Jay was watching Sarah, who looked at him with myriad emotions crossing her face. The primary one was regret.

He knew why.

"I'll pay for the cleaning, or the dress itself," Jay told Sarah coolly. "Hannah didn't mean to ruin it."

Sarah shook her head. "Of course not. The dress doesn't matter." Her sad eyes told him what *did* matter.

"Hannah." Jay kissed her hair. "Did you hear Mrs...." He cocked his head.

"Cole."

"Did you hear Mrs. Cole? She said she knows it was an accident."

Big blue eyes peeked out at Sarah.

"Really, Hannah, it's not important." Sarah straightened. "I'll just go home and change."

Jay whispered to Hannah, who was holding on to his neck for dear life, "You should say you're sorry, even if it was an accident, honey."

"Sorry," Hannah told Sarah.

As Sarah walked away, Jay pivoted to find Kate standing behind them. On her face was a look so tender it made his chest ache. "Thank you," she whispered.

And this time, Jay wondered how he was going to live without *her*.

DANCING STARTED about nine. By ten-thirty Jay was leaning against one of the church pillars and glaring out at the floor.

The groom came up behind him and handed him a flute of champagne. They clinked glasses.

"Thanks." Jay sipped the wine and returned his gaze to Nick Harrison's hands—which were way too low on Kate's back, Kate's *half-naked* back. She'd taken off the damn jacket at about ten.

"Hmm, pretty dress," Tom said.

"Can it, Baines."

"I hear Nick's good with kids, too. Katie could sure use some help with her two. They're a handful."

Jay fumed silently.

"Bet Nick would volunteer for the job." He glanced around the room. "I *know* Flannigan would."

"Not funny." If Harrison's hands moved one inch lower...

A new song started, and somebody cut in. Mitch Sterling. Now that was safe. He was happily married. But the slow song gave way to a catchy dance number, and Kate didn't miss a beat. The slit in her skirt revealed all female leg as she "rocked around the clock" with his former best buddy.

When the macarena blared out over the speakers, Charlie Callahan stole Kate away from Mitch, who joined Tom and Jay on the sidelines. The material of Kate's dress strained dangerously across her breasts as she executed the fluid arm movements.

Aaron ambled up to them.

Tom clapped him on the back. "How ya doin', cuz?"

Aaron smiled. "Just waitin' my turn to dance with Kate."

Suspicious, Jay studied the three of them. "All right, wise guys. What's going on?"

"Nothing." Aaron's face was as innocent as a choir-boy's. No one said any more until the DJ played a twist, and Aaron said, "Hot damn, my turn!"

Jeez, she's gonna bust right out of that dress if she tries...

She tried. She matched all of Aaron's slick moves. Who would have guessed the town's bad boy could dance like that?

Winded, but smiling, she clasped Aaron's hand when the dance ended. To their left, Jay caught a glimpse of Paul Flannigan scanning the floor, probably for Kate. "Not on your life, mister," he mumbled, and straightened up from his slouch. Around him, his buddies chuckled.

"Better go get her," Charlie suggested.

Mitch added, "Flannigan's closin' in."

"She sure can dance," Aaron quipped coming off the floor, where Kate remained, talking to Lily.

When Nick Harrison joined them and added, "You know, that dress fits her..." Jay handed his glass to Tom and strode away to the sound of mocking male laughter.

He caught Kate's arm just before Flannigan reached her. "This is my dance," he said roughly as he dragged her into his arms.

Her eyes sparked some fire, but he noticed she went to him willingly.

As they glided over the floor, she pulled back a bit. "Thanks for taking care of Hannah earlier. Most people would have yelled at her."

"It was an accident."

"Sarah looked as if she'd seen a ghost, she got so

white. I know the dress was silk, but to care that much about clothes..." Kate looked around the hall. "She hasn't come back."

"Sarah can take care of herself," he said coldly. Only he knew it wasn't ruined clothes that had gotten to his old girlfriend. He felt a spurt of sympathy for the woman, and then was unable to believe he could experience that emotion for her. He quelled it immediately and held Kate closer. "You can show me how grateful you are by letting me take you home."

She hesitated. "I drove."

"Please."

"I'll think about it." She rested her head on his shoulder. His hand went to her hair. Nothing had ever felt so right in his life.

Unfortunately, the feeling evaporated an hour later at the party's end. All the over-sixty and under-ten crowd had left—Ruth and Rachel had taken home a tired Hope and Hannah—and Jay was helping Kate on with her coat when a uniformed policeman burst through the fellowship-hall door. Mayor Baden was also leaving the reception, and she was stopped by the cop. "Is Police Chief Garvey still here, ma'am?" he asked.

"Yes, John. Why? Has something happened?"

"Yeah. Sarah Cole just wrapped her car around a telephone pole. I'm afraid she didn't make it."

RACHEL CLIMBED the stairs to Jacob's apartment with a heavy heart. Though she had reason to dislike the woman, she mourned the death of Sarah Cole. So young. So unhappy. But right now, Rachel was worried about Jacob. It was time to do something with the painful secret she'd carried with her since her nephew had left Riverbend fifteen years ago. Not only because Sarah was dead, but because Rachel knew in her heart that Jacob was on the brink of some big decisions and that he needed guidance. She knocked lightly on the door.

A gravelly voice answered. "Come in."

As she opened the door, he glanced over from the window where he stood, and she saw the hope on his face fade when she stepped inside.

"You thought it was Katie, didn't you?"

Grimly he nodded.

"Well, then, young man, your disappointment should tell you something."

Again he faced the window and sipped his drink. "I don't know what you mean."

She came fully into the room and stood a few feet away from him. Clad only in his tuxedo pants and white shirt, now rolled up at the sleeves, he resembled Abraham so much it hurt Rachel to look at him. "You feel bad about Sarah, don't you?"

He nodded.

"Everyone in town will. Even though she was almost a recluse, her death will be mourned."

Jacob didn't respond.

"Even by you." Still no answer. Rachel tightened her robe around her waist and came close enough to place a hand on his arm. "Even after what she did to you."

Slowly, Jacob turned his head toward her; his look was questioning—and sad.

"I know, dear."

The mask slipped back into place. He was summoning Jay Lawrence, the man he'd become. Well, Rachel wasn't going to let that happen. She'd like to bury Jay

Lawrence right along with Sarah Cole. After all, the
latter had brought about the former.

"You know *what*, Rachel?" Even his voice was too
controlled.

"I know what happened with your father. And how
it involved Sarah."

The poor boy's face paled. "How...why haven't
you..."

"How do I know?" He nodded. "When you left, I
confronted your father. I was certain you wouldn't
abandon us without good reason. I insisted he tell me."

"And he did?"

"Yes, of course." She straightened her shoulders
and patted her hair. "Everyone thinks I'm a marsh-
mallow, Jacob, but I assure you I'm not."

"I can see that." There was a trace of amusement
in his voice.

Rachel scowled. "I didn't tell Ruthie about this."

"Why?"

"Because there was no need to. It would have hurt
her more than your leaving. She was very close to
Abraham, though they sparred like cats and dogs. I saw
no sense in it. Until now."

"She still doesn't need to know."

"Yes, she does. It's time to reveal this infectious
secret. I'll tell her tomorrow." Rachel hesitated. For a
moment, she wondered about interfering. But, God be
praised, she wasn't going to let this beloved boy go
again. "And Katie needs to know."

"Kate? Why?"

"Because you're in love with her."

Jacob's face turned even paler. "No, you misunder-
stand what's between us."

"Of course I don't. I've seen the way you look at

her. The way you can't take your eyes off her. And tonight, at the wedding, I watched you with her. It's time to risk again, Jacob.''

"I can't."

Tall and handsome though he was, he was still her boy. Lightly she caressed his cheek. "Yes, you can, son. Go after what you want."

He closed his eyes and shook his head. "You don't know what I've done. I hurt her too much."

"A woman can forgive a man anything if she loves him."

"You don't understand."

"I understand more than you think." Again the silence. "Go out to the farmhouse tonight, Jacob. Tell her you've changed your mind about selling the store."

His doubt turned to surprise. She shook her head. Did everybody think age meant senility? Rachel was no fool. "I figured out your plans right away. But plans can change, Jacob."

"She won't forgive me."

Rachel smiled knowingly. "If you grovel enough she will." He returned the smile weakly. "It's what you want, isn't it?"

Conflicting emotions were reflected in his eyes. "All I know for sure," he admitted, "is that I want Kate in my life."

Rachel rose on tiptoes and kissed his cheek. "Then go get her, dear."

FOR THE MILLIONTH TIME, Kate turned over in her bed and sighed. The clock told her it was 3 a.m. She'd been watching the red numbers flip over for two hours. But sleep remained elusive, like a name you couldn't remember or a smell you couldn't place.

She kept seeing Jay's face when the policeman announced that Sarah Cole was dead. He'd gripped Kate's shoulders so hard it had hurt, and then they'd left the reception in stunned silence. She tried to talk to him about it on the way to the car, but he wouldn't discuss it. He'd insisted on driving her home—the aunts had taken the girls, so they were doubtless fast asleep there and spending the night—and although she'd denied him before, she couldn't bring herself to fight him on it then. He'd left her concerned and confused and alone at the farmhouse door.

Though they didn't have a future together, Kate couldn't turn off her feelings for him. Three weeks ago, she'd cared enough to sleep with him; that hadn't changed, though she'd never get over that his using her.

You don't know that he did.

"Of course I do." And she could never trust him again, even if he wanted her to. Even if *she* wanted to. It was just like with Billy. Once she'd caught him with his girlfriend, their relationship was over.

Flipping to her other side, she wrestled with the bed covers and mentally summoned her How to Get to Sleep list—pleasant things that calmed her and made her drowsy—and tried to lose herself in them. She was still awake a half hour later when a light pierced the early-morning darkness. Intuitively she knew it was Jay. She sprang out of bed and, in her flannel pajamas and wool socks, hurried to the back of the farmhouse. She opened the porch door just as he was about to knock.

At his stunned expression, she said, "I saw your headlights."

He stared at her. "I have to talk to you."

Taking him by the hand, she drew him into the living room and switched on a lamp. In the dim light, she could see his face was ravaged. Shrugging out of his coat, he tossed it on the chair; he was still wearing his dress pants and shirt.

He swallowed hard and clenched his fists at his sides. "I'm not sure I can do this."

"Do what?"

"Tell you what I have to."

Somewhere inside her, fear flickered, a spark ready to ignite. But she sensed this wasn't like his other revelations. This wasn't about her. "Do you want a minute? I can make coffee and you could start a fire."

Mutely he nodded. They went about their respective tasks. When she returned to the living room, he had a blaze burning, but the look in his eyes chilled her.

She handed him his coffee and took a seat on the couch. He sipped from his mug, but didn't join her. After more silence, she coaxed, "Is this about Sarah's death?"

"In a way."

This time she waited.

Finally, in a hoarse, pain-filled voice, he said, "You know Sarah and I went together all during high school. I was crazy about her, and I thought she felt the same about me. We had our differences, mostly about me spending so much time with the River Rats."

"Sarah wasn't a River Rat, was she?"

"No." He shook his head, the firelight accenting the harsh planes of his face. "Sarah was a snob, really. The River Rats were beneath her." He shrugged. "But I loved her. When we graduated, I headed for the University of Indiana and she went to the junior college over in Cleesberg. We…we planned to get married at the end of my senior year.'' Staring into the fire, he was obviously years away. "I was hoping to play pro basketball. When I got hurt in my sophomore year, I was afraid my career was over. But I could have handled that, as long as I had Sarah. She didn't want to spend her life in basketball stadiums, anyway. She hoped to live in Riverbend. She urged me to come back and run the bank, be just like my father.'' His last words were bitter.

"But you played again, didn't you?''

"Yes, my knee healed. I started on first string my junior year and half of my senior year. Scouts were swarming all over me.''

Kate knew the story. "Why didn't you finish college, Jay? What happened?''

He closed his eyes briefly. "I...I've never told anybody this.''

"Tell me. I want to know.'' And he seemed to need to say it.

He gripped the mantel of the fireplace with one hand. "I gave Sarah a ring just before Christmas that year. I remember I was so happy. She was pouty, though, and I thought it was because I was going to play pro ball. On Christmas Eve, we had dinner at the house on East Poplar Street with my father, and we were just about to come out here to tell Ruth and Rachel about our engagement.'' He scrubbed a hand over his face. "I remember it as if it was yesterday. I came down the back staircase that led into the kitchen. My father and Sarah were at the table, talking.''

"About what?''

"About their *secret*.''

"What secret?''

"He said they had to be careful I didn't find out.

That I didn't need to know. It should remain between them.''

Fear skittered down Kate's spine. Oh, God, Abraham and Sarah hadn't… Oh, Lord, he *had* with Evie Mazerik. But surely not with his son's girlfriend. ''What was the secret, Jay?''

Placing his mug on the mantel, he gripped the oak with both hands and leaned into it. ''She said she felt guilty for not telling me. He said I couldn't know.'' Jay paused. ''And that abortion was legal now, not a crime. Not even a sin.''

''Abortion?''

He nodded. ''Sarah had been pregnant with my child. She found out after Thanksgiving break. Between Thanksgiving and Christmas, she…she told my father. He was upset. He said this could ruin my basketball career, not to mention my reputation in town. He convinced her to have an abortion.'' Raggedly Jay added, ''She did. Julian Bennett arranged it. They killed my baby because of some stupid career and our standing in the town.'' An ugly laugh escaped his lips. ''The man who fathered a bastard son and didn't have the guts to claim him was concerned about reputation. How ironic.''

Tears leaked from Kate's eyes. Putting the mug down, she stood and went to him. From behind, she slid her arms around his waist. ''Jay, I'm so sorry.''

For a moment, he stood rigidly. Then he turned and wrapped her loosely in his embrace. His beautiful face was wet. She wiped away the tears with her hand. ''I wanted a whole basketball team, Kate. I love kids.''

''I know you do.''

''Two people I trusted took my child away from me, made this obscene decision for me.''

"I'm so sorry."

He straightened. "I left Jacob Steele in Riverbend, Indiana, that night and became Jay Lawrence."

"I can see why."

"Can you?" Her gripped her shoulders. "Can you understand why I became the man I am?"

"Who are you now, Jay?"

"I'm the man who abandoned two old women who loved me because I couldn't handle bad news."

"First, an abortion is more than bad news. Second, you told me yourself you couldn't stay in Riverbend because you didn't want your aunts' view of Abraham tainted."

"They loved him so much. Everybody thought he was a dedicated family man. I knew he could be harsh. Demanding. But I still thought he was a good man. He wasn't."

"No, he wasn't. Not to do what he did to you."

"And to Aaron." Again he paused. "Anyway, I started to contact my aunts several times, but I was afraid they'd get me to tell them why I had to leave." He smiled grimly. "They could always make me talk. Eventually, I decided it was best for everybody if I just dropped out of sight. I became Jay Lawrence. It was the only way I could leave everything behind."

Kate nodded, picturing the young boy she'd come to know through his books and the stories his aunts told, finding out his father was flawed, his girlfriend weak, and giving up a life he'd dreamed of. Her heart broke for him.

He straightened and stuck his hands in his pockets. "Rachel knew, anyway."

"*What?*"

"She came to see me tonight. She told me she's

known all these years. She confronted Abraham and forced him to tell her.''

Kate smiled, though the situation was grim. ''She's no cream puff, is she?''

''No.'' His gaze flicked to the ceiling. ''For fifteen years, I've been carrying that secret around with me.''

''You never told anyone?''

''No. Just you.'' He stared at her. ''It's important to me that you know why I'm like I am.''

''I'm not sure I really understand who you are.'' She cocked her head. ''I'm not sure *you* understand who you are.''

''Maybe you're right. I've changed since I came back to Riverbend. I have to figure out just who I am and what I want now.''

She smiled, hurting inside. She wanted to be part of that change, but that was impossible now. As Jay had discovered when he was twenty, without trust, a relationship couldn't work.

That didn't mean she couldn't help him through this, though. Couldn't be his friend. Reaching for his hand, she tugged him to the couch. ''Sit down and tell me what happened to you before you came back here.''

He looked torn, as if he didn't want to say. ''All right.''

They sat in front of the fire and talked. He held her hand as he told her about bumming around for years, taking odd jobs, drinking to forget. He drew her to his side and talked of how his pain had turned to bitterness, then to determination. Stretching out on the couch, he pulled her down beside him and absently stroked her arm as he told her about going back to finish college and grad school, starting his own company, making a lot of money, but never being truly content. As her eyes closed, the last thing she heard him say was, "I'm not happy, Kate. I know that now. I'm just not sure what to do about it."

JAY AWOKE to bright light and a crick in his neck. It took him a moment before he realized Kate was nestled in his arms. They were cuddled on her living-room couch. Luxuriating in the feel of her body next to his, he reviewed the events of the night before.

Sarah was dead.

Rachel knew why he left Riverbend fifteen years ago.

And he'd finally told someone. What's more, he was glad Kate knew. Now he needed to plan.

What would he do? He wouldn't sell the store and this house. And he knew he couldn't let Kate go. Was he willing to give up his life in New York? Everything he'd ever wanted was there. No, that wasn't true. The woman in his arms had changed that. He wanted her now, and the girls.

Rachel had told him to grovel. All right, so he'd grovel. He'd never done that with women before, but...*women!* Oh, God, how could he have forgotten? Mallory was still in his life. Though he talked to her weekly, he pretty much forgot about her in between. That told him something, since he couldn't stop thinking about Kate for five seconds, let alone seven days.

All right, he'd have to break it off with Mallory. The man he'd been for fifteen years would have done it by phone, but he couldn't do that now. It wouldn't be fair to Mallory. He held Kate closer and she burrowed into him. He'd have to wait, then, because he couldn't leave Riverbend for a few more weeks without giving up his inheritance.

For now, he'd start gaining back Kate's trust. Then, after he broke it off with Mallory, he'd ask Kate to marry him.

She stirred in his arms. Smiled when her eyes opened. He kissed her nose. "Good morning."

"Good morning."

He waited a few moments. "Are you awake now?"

"Mmm." She snuggled closer.

"I have something else to tell you."

She looked up at him. "There's more?"

"Just a bit."

"What?"

"I'm not going to sell the bookstore or the farmhouse, Kate."

"Why?"

"I want to show you I've changed, and that I can be the man I was when I lived here. I want another chance with you."

She was so still it frightened him. He was even more concerned when she slid out of his arms and crossed to the fireplace, where red embers glowed softly.

He was devastated when she said, "I don't think so, Jay."

CHAPTER THIRTEEN

ON DECEMBER 12, the day after Sarah Cole's funeral and three days after Jay had asked for another chance with Kate, she entered the bookstore and found a large crystal vase full of sunny daisies on the cash counter. It was thirteen days before Christmas, and she'd been concentrating on her Gifts to Buy list, struggling not to think about Jay. The flowers made it impossible.

Her mind shot right back to Sunday morning, after his big disclosure...

"I care about you," he'd said achingly.

"I care about you, too." She couldn't face him. "But it's too much of a risk."

"I'll prove it's worth the risk. I'll show you I've changed."

"Billy tried that and it didn't work."

"I'm not Billy."

She turned to him. "Who are you?"

"I'm not sure anymore."

At a stalemate, she'd left him in the living room while she showered and, together, they drove back into town so Kate could retrieve her car and pick up the girls. The last thing he'd said to her when he left her at his aunts' door was, "I mean it, Kate. I'm not giving up."

He'd begun wearing down her resistance that day. At Sarah's funeral, Kate had been moved by the directive Lynn gave the congregation—to live life to the fullest. Jay had caught her eye and, though his were sad, he nodded to the altar, indicating his agreement with her words.

"Who are those from?" a male voice asked.

Turning, she saw Simon had come into the store.

She picked up the card. "I don't really know. The card says, 'On the first day of Christmas, my true love gave to me—bright sunny daisies...'"

"'And a partri-idge in a pear tree.'" Simon sung the words and his blue eyes twinkled. "But those twelve days are after Christmas, not before."

Kate rolled her eyes. "The card says, 'Pardon the before/after discrepancy.' And that they start early because Christmas is on a Monday this year."

"Ah, a literate man. Is he a new beau?"

"Nope."

"Interesting," was all Simon said as he walked to the office.

The aunts were pushier. They bustled in with Jay after a late breakfast at the Sunnyside Café. Rachel was very impressed. "Oh, my, look at the lovely flowers, Ruthie." She winked at Kate. "Didn't Jack Kerouac send you some spring flowers in the middle of winter once, sister?"

"Maybe," Ruth said, hedging. "I wonder where someone would get daisies this time of year."

Bundled up in his leather jacket, scarf and gloves, Jay smiled at Kate over the aunts' heads. It was a sexy, I-want-you smile.

Kate scowled at him. "I have no idea."

"Are they from Paul?" Ruth asked.

Jay's smile faded, replaced by a look so blatantly possessive it made Kate's blood warm.

Turning to the desk, she simply said, "No, I don't think so."

The girls whooped when they tore into the store after school and saw the flowers. "Mommy never got flowers from anybody before," Hannah announced to Jay, who was fiddling with the front-desk computer.

Kate added *Respect people's privacy* to her twins' Manners list.

"Never?" he asked incredulously.

Hannah climbed onto Jay's lap. "Nope. We read *Ramona Gets Roses* once, and Mommy told us she loved flowers, but nobody had ever sent her any."

Jay rested his chin on Hannah's head and captured Kate's gaze. "Mommy should have flowers every day."

"Don't you dare!" Kate whispered after the twins scampered away.

His look was ludicrously innocent. "Don't what?"

"Send me flowers every day."

"I wouldn't dream of it." His dark eyes glinted devilishly, and Kate was drawn to this new, lighter side of the sober man she'd known for weeks. It chipped away more of the wall she'd built between them.

"Promise?"

"I promise I won't send you flowers every day."

There was something about his tone…but the phone rang and she didn't question him further.

Each morning that week she found a beautifully wrapped gift on the counter when she came into the store. The second day, it was the expensive Paloma Picasso bath oil she'd coveted after smelling a tester in Killian's. On the third day, an electric sander. Following that was a beautiful leather-bound edition of *Romeo and Juliet.* On Friday, the fifth day, an electric drill was the prize. It was then that she caught on.

Her Wish Folder. Jay had found her Wish Folder and was seducing her with her own fantasies. *Damn it.* She'd arrived early at work today and, new drill in hand, marched up the back stairs cloaked in righteous indignation. She pounded on the apartment door. He didn't answer right away. When he did open the door, she wished he hadn't.

Obviously he'd been asleep. He stood before her bare-chested, wearing only fleece shorts. His hair was mussed and his eyes were slumberous. Her gaze traveled from his face to his muscled chest to a washboard flat stomach to...

"You'd better stop looking at me like that, Kate. Or I can't be held accountable for my actions." His voice was husky. Like it had been when they'd made love.

Rattled, she held up the drill. "You found my Wish Folder."

"I did?"

"Yes. When you *spied* on me." She brushed past him into the room and then spun around. "I won't let you do this."

He closed the door and leaned against it in an arrogant slouch. "Do what?"

"Grant all my wishes."

A sexy glint sparked in his eyes. Again, she was mesmerized by this new, happier Jay. Gone was the brooding Heathcliff. He'd never be Don Quixote, but this side of him was...endearing.

And dangerous.

"You pried into my most personal things."

"I already confessed to that."

"Do you think it's okay to use them against me?"

"I plead the Fifth."

She sputtered.

"Though I will say, all's fair in love and war."

Her voice rose a notch. "Jay! You're not listening."

"You know, your eyes sparkle like polished jade when you're angry." He raked looked at her with blatant sexual intent. "Or when you're aroused."

"I've never seen polished jade."

Again, Satan's grin. "Would you like to?"

She felt her face flush. "Don't you dare."

He laughed and her pulse started to race. Never before had she heard that uninhibited, pure sound come from his lips. For the first time, she wished she'd known him as Jacob Steele.

"Sweetheart," he finally said, "women are supposed to love jewels."

Shaking herself out of her trance, she took an exasperated breath. "Not this woman."

He crossed to her and broke his promise not to touch her by tipping her chin up, then caressing her throat. "No, this woman doesn't need jewels." He kissed her nose. "Because she's one herself." Her eyes closed when his lips brushed her forehead. "Very rare. And very precious."

"Jay, don't, please."

"Don't what?"

"Pursue me like this."

He whispered in her ear, "Oh, darlin', I've just begun."

JAY REALIZED Kate wasn't about to make things easy for him when he showed up at the farmhouse at noon on Saturday.

"What are you doing here?" she asked. "It's bad

enough that I had to accept the Godiva chocolates you had the girls sneak in to give me this morning."

He grinned and ignored the jibe. "Didn't the girls tell you about today?"

"What about today?"

"I'm taking them to see Santa. Every year jolly old St. Nick commandeers an entire section of Killian's department store."

"I know. I always take them."

He rubbed his hands up and down his arms. "Do you think I could come in? It's damn cold out here." Dressed in a black sweater woven with thin red squares, under which he wore a red shirt, he'd left his coat in the car so she'd take pity on him and let him in. After she saw him shiver, she allowed him through the door.

Once inside, she put her hands on her hips. "*I* always take them to see Santa."

He said in his most convincing voice, "Come with us, then."

She grumbled, but she was no match for the twins' stamina when it came to pleading.

To Jay, the afternoon was magical. He loved watching the girls sit on Santa's lap, giggle when they talked to him, smile up at Jay as they wandered, holding his hand, through the winter wonderland the store had set up. Never in his life had he been so content. Over hot chocolate, they asked him what he wanted for Christmas.

His gaze leveled soberly on Kate, who sat across the table next to Hannah. "Forgiveness," he said simply.

Hope's eyes rounded. "Mommy said forgiveness is the best gift you can give."

Sipping his cocoa, he locked his gaze with Kate's. "Mommy said that, huh?"

"There's Mr. and Mrs. Sterling with Sam and Laura Marie, the new baby." Hannah jumped out of her seat. "Can we go see her?"

"Yes, but stay in sight," Kate said.

When the girls scampered over to Mitch and Tessa, Jay reached across the small table she'd made sure was between them and brushed a speck of whipped cream off the corner of her mouth. "Didn't Lynn ever tell you to practice what you preach?"

"I do." She looked at a passing customer, then back to him. "I forgive you, Jay. I just can't trust you."

"Because of what Billy did?"

"Partly."

"Why else?" He picked up her hand and held it in his, loving the feel of her. "Tell me."

"I'm afraid." She raised her chin. "I care about you, Jay. Too much. I can't give you the power to hurt me again." Her eyes were sad. "You're not the kind of man I can depend on."

Her softly uttered words cut into his soul like a surgeon's well-placed knife. In spite of that, he said earnestly, "I haven't been trustworthy, I admit that. But I've changed."

"Have you?"

"What do you mean?"

"How do I know that after your eight weeks are up, you won't run back to New York and leave us all again?" She glanced at the twins, who were fawning over Tessa and the baby. "I'm already worried they're too attached to you."

"What if I promise to stay in Riverbend?"

She shook her head. "That won't work, either."

"Why?"

"Because you'll get bored. The girls and I could never be enough for you."

The objection came quickly to his lips. However, he wasn't able to voice it because the Sterlings were headed for their table.

"Hi, guys," Mitch said, leaning over to kiss Kate's cheek.

"Hi." Jay watched Kate smile at Mitch and greet Tessa. But mostly she had eyes only for the new baby. "Can I hold her?"

"Of course," Tessa said.

Gently, Kate took the child. Jay was mesmerized by the sight. She cooed delightedly at the little girl. A sudden flash of Kate, big with his child, poleaxed Jay. Bored? With her? Never.

"Jacob?"

"Huh?"

"I asked why you weren't at the basketball game last night."

"I, um, was busy."

"Well, how about playing some ball with us? We have weekly pickup games at the gym, and this one's Wednesday afternoon."

Dragging his gaze from Kate, he looked up at Mitch. "I don't think so." He hadn't touched a basketball in fifteen years and had refused to go to the high-school games.

"Won't the slave driver let you out of work?" Mitch's eyes glimmered with mischief as he gestured toward Kate.

"It's fine by me," Kate said. "He's supposed to get a day off per week, but he never takes it." Her voice was still soft and gushy, and she hadn't taken her eyes off the baby. "What time?"

"Around three."

"I don't know." Jay was surprised to find that his palms were sweaty.

"A lot of the River Rats come—Tom, Charlie, Nick Harrison, Ed Pennington. And Wally's coming to watch." He grinned. "It'd be just like old times."

That was what Jay was afraid of. Could he face *that* ghost, too?

"Maybe," he said. Glancing around, he searched desperately for a change of subject. "Where are the girls?"

LYNN KENDALL increased her stride to keep pace with Kate, who was power walking around the gym floor red-faced and sweaty.

"It's infuriating," Kate said, pumping her arms furiously. "I can't believe he'd do this to me."

"Make all your dreams come true?" Lynn asked dryly. "How dare he?"

Kate eyed her friend. "Well, marriage has certainly made you spunky."

Lynn giggled. "It has."

Kate slowed down. "Sorry. I'm happy for you, Lynn, really I am." And jealous. Because deep in her heart she wanted what Lynn and Tom had. What the Sterlings had. What Aaron and Lily had. And Beth and Charlie. "You and Tom deserve it."

They walked a few more yards. "So do you and Jay."

"*Don't* mention his name."

"All right. What color is the outfit, anyway? You didn't say."

Kate rolled her eyes, picturing the burgundy cashmere dress he'd given her the day before, the ninth day. He'd told her, when she'd stormed up the stairs to his apartment again, that the color would bring out the highlights in her hair.

"It doesn't matter because I'm taking it back." Along with the shoes and Coach bag he sent for the eighth day. Her pace quickened again. "The grocery shopping was bad enough."

Kate could still see his face, about as guileless as the snake in Eden, on the seventh day as he'd said, "Well, if you want to be responsible for Joan Kemp *not* having extra money to buy her kids Christmas presents, call her and tell her the deal's off."

"It was nice of him to give Joan a way to earn some money," Lynn said.

Kate bit her tongue. It *was* nice. But it was also manipulative. He *knew* she wouldn't tell her part-time helper, who had three kids under four, that she couldn't grocery shop for Kate for the next two months.

She groaned and walked faster.

After a few moments, Lynn stopped, dropped to the floor and leaned against the bleachers. She patted the space next to her. "Come sit a minute."

Kate did, and Lynn took her hand. "Why are you doing this to yourself?"

"What?"

"Fighting him so hard."

"Because he's wearing me down. Not so much with the gifts, but with the consideration behind them. Add that to what he's done for his aunts and my girls..." She gripped her friend's hand. "I'm afraid, Lynn."

Lynn studied her carefully. "Are you going to let Billy McMann ruin you for all other men?"

"No, just for Jay Lawrence, or Jacob Steele, or whatever the hell his name is."

Chuckling at her uncustomary curse, Lynn remained silent.

"I've been seeing Paul. And Nick Harrison's shown some interest lately. He's a doll."

"Methinks the lady doth protest too much."

"Don't quote Shakespeare to me."

"All right, I'll say it straight. You aren't interested in either one of them, and you know it. If you were, your radar would have picked up on *their* interest long before this."

"Maybe I can be."

"No, you can't." Again, Lynn gave her a smile. "Put this on your New Year's Resolution list, Kate—take risks."

"How do I know he'll be here after New Year's?"

Lynn raised her chin. "That's easy. Make it impossible for him to leave you." They stood and started walking again. "My guess is he's almost there, anyway."

JAY GLANCED at the clock as Kate came through the office door after her walk with Lynn. She was sweaty, and her braided hair was coming undone, but she looked beautiful—and sexy. She looked calmer, too, much different from when she'd gone after him about the cashmere outfit. He'd never seen her so livid. Just wait!

She checked the clock. "It's two-thirty," she said, stopping at the desk. "The guys are meeting at the gym at three."

"I'm not going." He shifted his gaze from her to

the computer screen. "There's a book for sale I think you should look at."

"I will. After you go play ball."

"I'm not going."

"Why?"

He sat back in the chair and linked his hands behind his neck. "I'm not ready to face those ghosts."

Her expression softened, but damn it, he didn't want her feeling sorry for him.

"Don't look at me that way. I don't want your pity."

"I don't pity you. I'm just surprised you're such a coward."

"Coward?"

"Yeah. You don't even go to the high-school games, and now you're saying you can't face a little pickup game?"

His eyes narrowed on her. "As my aunts used to say, isn't that the pot calling the kettle black?"

The question erased her smirk. "What do you mean?"

"I mean, if I'm a coward, so are you. You're letting *your* ghosts affect the present. Affect *us*."

"I don't want to talk about this."

"Fine." He sat up straighter. "I don't want to talk about the basketball game."

She stormed back to the office and he returned to the computer. Five minutes later, she stood before him, glowering. "Lynn said that, too."

"What?"

"That I'm a coward."

"The good reverend knows best. She's got an in with You-Know-Who."

"Go to the game. It'll be good for you."

"Go out to dinner with me afterward, and I will."

He hadn't planned on saying that, but now that it was out, he was glad. So he pushed. "Since the girls are staying over at Allison's to go on the field trip Grace is chaperoning tomorrow and you have the afternoon off, you can go home to change." He gave her his best smile. "Into the cashmere dress."

"No."

He shrugged. "See, you are a coward."

Her eyes narrowed. "You're manipulating me again."

"At least I'm being open about it." He checked the clock. "You'd better decide. Pretty soon it will be too late to go to the game."

Taking a deep breath, she said, "All right. I'll go."

Forcing himself not to get down on his knees and thank her, he stood. "I'll pick you up at six."

"No, I'll meet you here. I have some work I want to do before we go."

"Fine." Leaning over her, he grasped her chin and planted a solid kiss on her mouth. Then he headed to the back of the store and took the stairs to his apartment two at a time, happier than he ever believed he could be again.

KATE TRIED HARD to summon her Reasons Not to Let Jay Lawrence Back into Your Life list, but it kept coming up blank. As she drove home, then drew a bath, all she could picture was the sparkling challenge in Jay's dark eyes when he said he'd play ball if she went out with him. As she donned the damn cashmere dress, all she could hear was that beautiful laugh of his.

On the drive back to town, honesty asserted itself. She wasn't doing this because of his teasing, or his laughter or challenge. Quite simply, he'd worn her down. With the most intangible of presents—first, his devotion to his aunts and, next, his kindness toward the girls. In truth, he'd been gradually working his way into her heart since the day he got here. She was ready to admit that.

If he could face his ghosts, she could, too.

She arrived at the store at five-thirty, shooed Izzy and Joan out early to do some Christmas shopping and headed to the back of the shop. She'd hear if anyone came in because they'd rigged a bell to sound in the office. At exactly six o'clock, she finished her paperwork and Jay appeared at the door.

Her jaw dropped. He looked as handsome as Rhett Butler in his finely woven blue sports coat, pristine white shirt, striped tie and gray wool slacks. His hair was combed back and his eyes were glistening with…joy. She started to ask him about the game when he commanded softly, "Stand up."

Just his tone sent shivers down her spine. She stood and faced him.

He sucked in his breath. "You're stunning."

Normally, she'd object to the exaggeration. But she'd applied makeup and curled her hair to elicit this reaction from him. And she'd noticed how every curve she had was nicely outlined in the clingy dress. "Thank you."

He crossed to her. The top of the dress fell into an alluring scoop. Lifting his hand, he ran his knuckles along her collarbone. His eyes glimmered with intensity as he bent his head and brushed his lips over her bare skin. Kate felt the touch in every nerve ending. One hand slid to her waist, rested for a moment, then traveled to her thigh. His forehead met hers and he closed his eyes. "I can't touch you much longer or we'll never make it to dinner."

Her laugh was sultry.

"Don't do that, love, please."

Love.

"Kiss me," she said.

He shook his head. "I can't. I'll never—"

She brushed his lips with hers. "I want this, Jay. I want you. I want another chance to see if we can make it." She hesitated, then finished, "I'm ready to risk."

His mouth closed over hers with unleashed passion. "Oh, Katie..."

"Jay..."

The sound of the bell ringing in the office was like a gunshot, bringing Kate back to reality. Not Jay. He pressed her against him.

"Jay, that's the bell over the front door."

"Don't care." He was taking tiny nibbles out of her neck.

Someone called from the store. "...body here?"

"Jay, there's a customer."

"It's after six."

"I didn't lock up." She eased his hands from her. "I have to go out there."

Sanity returned by degrees and he stepped back. She was shocked to see his tie askew, his belt undone. Had she done that? She giggled. Smoothing down her hair, she said, "Stay here. I'll get rid of whoever's out there."

He kissed her quickly. "Good idea."

She swiped once more at her hair as she left the office. Her mind on how he looked and felt and smelled, Kate practically floated to the front of the store. At the desk, a woman waited. As Kate drew closer, she took in the customer's long leather coat, trimmed in fur. Her stance, as well as her dress, shouted wealth and confidence. When Kate reached the desk, the woman turned to her. "Well, it's about time."

Kate said, "I'm sorry, but it's after closing time. I didn't expect anyone."

Exquisitely made-up eyes surveyed her critically. Kate wondered what remnants of Jay's touch were evident. The woman tossed back sleek blond hair and, from a very red mouth, said, "I'm not a customer."

Kate cocked her head.

"I've come to…" Her words faded off as her attention was caught by something behind Kate. "Jay! There you are." She stepped around Kate, who turned to see the woman run straight to Jay and throw herself into his arms. "I missed you so much."

Dying inside, Kate watched the woman kiss lips that had, only moments before, kissed hers. She closed her eyes when she saw Jay's arms go around the woman's waist to draw her close.

MALLORY FLEW at him so fast Jay had to grab and hold onto her to keep his balance. Shocked to see her, he was immobilized from the moment she kissed him. It took a few seconds to get his body to respond to his brain. "Mallory, wait. Stop."

When he finally peeled her off him, he looked at Kate. For as long as he lived, he'd never forget the emotions on her face—confusion, shock, then awareness and pain.

"Oh, dear, I forgot myself." Mallory turned to Kate. "You'll have to excuse me. I haven't seen Jay in weeks. We've never been apart this long."

"Apart?" Kate's voice was husky.

Mallory entwined her arm with Jay's and leaned into him. Her pert breast pressed into his biceps. He felt his stomach roil.

"Yes," Mallory replied. "We haven't seen each other since he left for Riverbend." Her tone was possessive, as if she'd sensed what had happened moments ago in the office. Before he could speak, she added, "I'm Mallory Claybourne, Jay's fiancée."

Jay watched as Kate's eyes dropped to Mallory's hand, where a three-carat diamond rested. He remembered blithely telling Mallory he wasn't good with gifts and to pick it out herself.

"And you are…?" Mallory asked.

Kate's chin came up. "I'm Kate McMann. I manage the bookstore."

"Oh, how nice of you to have kept this place going for us."

Kate blanched, and that finally dragged him from his stupor. "Kate, you don't—"

"Excuse me," she said, cutting him off. "I have… some…calls to make."

"Kate, wait." He reached for her as she brushed past him, but she eluded him. He started after her, but Mallory grabbed his arm.

"Jay, what's going on?"

He turned back to Mallory. Best to deal with this first. "What are you doing here?" he asked angrily.

She fluttered her lashes. "I missed you, darling. And you haven't returned my calls in a week. So I came to see you." She pressed her body against his. "I'm staying in this nice little inn on the outskirts of town. We can go there right now."

Feeling ill, Jay took a deep breath and disentangled

himself from her. "Listen to me carefully, Mallory. Go back to the inn. Now. I'll come out there in…" He glanced at the clock. "As soon as I can."

"Why on earth would I do that?"

"Because I'm asking you to," he said simply.

She stepped back. "Has something happened, Jay?"

He sighed. "I'm sorry. I'm…" He looked toward the back of the store, feeling the seconds tick off. Every one Kate was away from him could be disastrous. "Look, just go. I'll come as soon as I can."

Mallory followed his gaze. "All right. But I have to tell you, I don't like this."

"I know." He raked a hand through his hair. "I'll explain it all later."

Giving him a puzzled look, Mallory exited with a flourish.

Jay locked the door behind her, recalling the cliché about closing the barn door after the horse has gone.

Too late, it's too late.

"No, it can't be." He raced to the back of the store, his heart pounding. *Please don't let it be too late.*

When he reached the office, the door was closed. Breathing a short prayer, he grabbed the handle. It was locked. "Kate, open up. Let me in."

No answer.

"Kate, please."

Still no answer.

He banged on the door. "Kate, open up. *Please.*"

Silence.

"I'm not going away." He began to pace. "I'm not!" he yelled. When the silence stretched into minutes, he stood before the door. God, he *had* to see her.

So he raised his foot and kicked open the door.

The room was dim, but he could see her clearly. She sat on the floor, her back to the wall. It was as if she'd leaned against it and then slid down because she could no longer stand. Her arms wrapped around her knees, she stared at him with a tearstained face.

And said absolutely nothing.

He stood where he was for a few seconds, then crossed to squat down in front of her. "Sweetheart, are you all right?"

"Please, just leave me alone."

"Kate, I...you misunderstood."

The brief flare of hope that lit those eyes crushed him. "She's not your fiancée?"

He swallowed hard. "Yes, she is."

Kate closed her eyes but moisture leaked out. "I was right all along." She shook her head. "I was right about you."

"No, no baby, listen, it's not what you think."

Impatiently, she swiped at the tears and looked at him accusingly. "What were you doing? Luring me into your bed until you could go back to her?"

His hand went to her hair. It was a sign of her distress that she didn't push it away. "No." He searched for the words. "She *is* my fiancée. But that was before we..." Even to his own ears, his explanation was inadequate. Obscene, really.

Still crying, she said in a surprisingly strong voice, "It was before we *screwed*, Jay. Oh, God I was so easy." She closed her eyes. "And I was ready to do it again. Just a few minutes ago." Tears fell freely down her cheeks, and she buried her face in her hands.

"Please, let me explain." She wouldn't look at him. "I'm not in love with her."

Her head came up, then. "And that's supposed to make it okay? What kind of man *are* you?"

"I can explain," he repeated.

Wildly she shook her head. "No. No explanations this time." She pushed him away and scrambled to her feet. Shaking back her hair, she watched him stand, then said, "I can answer my own question. I know what kind of man you are. You're more of a bastard than your father ever was." She brushed past him, grabbed her purse and walked out the door.

He knew he should go after her. Knew he should try to explain. But her words bolted him to the floor. Because she was right. And he'd always known it.

He *was* a bastard.

CHAPTER FOURTEEN

MERCILESSLY, KATE YANKED OFF the cashmere dress and flung it to the floor. Tears welled in her eyes, but she battled them back. She would never cry over this man again. *Never.* Instead, she summoned anger; it gave her the strength to put on a sweatsuit and stalk to the kitchen. Retrieving a big garbage bag, she returned to the bedroom and stuffed the discarded dress and accessories into it. In the bathroom, she picked up the bubble bath—stupidly she'd used it this afternoon—and put that in the bag, too. The electric drill, the sander and the beautiful leather-bound edition of *Romeo and Juliet* that she'd kept by her bed followed. Then she tied up the bag and dragged it to the porch to put out with the trash. The cold air made her shiver, but it was nothing compared to the slap in the face she'd gotten earlier.

I'm Mallory Claybourne. Jay's fiancée.

How could she have been so stupid?

Of course a man like him would have women, or a particular woman. He was too good-looking, too suave and too sophisticated not to attract them in droves.

The ugly truth was clear—Kate had been a stopgap until he could get back to Mallory. The thought made her ill. She had to do something. Marching to the kitchen, she rummaged in the cupboards for cookie ingredients. It was important to keep busy and not think.

But as she assembled the chocolate chips and butter and sugar, her mind raced back to their many conversations.

I'm not a good man...I can't be trusted to do what's right for others.

She'd even overheard him on the phone. *I said no, Mallory. I won't discuss this further.*

When a car pulled into the driveway at about ten, Kate had flour in her hair and chocolate on her face, and four different kinds of cookies were stacked on the counter. The car door slammed and Kate prayed it wasn't him.

"Oh, stop being a wimp," she told herself disgustedly. "If it's him, don't answer the door. Better yet, answer it and punch him in the face." Head high, she strode to the porch and looked out.

Coming up the walk was Lynn Kendall.

Kate squeezed her eyes shut. There was no way Lynn could know so soon. Even the Riverbend grapevine wasn't that fast. So her friend must be here for some other reason.

Oh, God, the twins were at the Penningtons'.

Frantic, Kate whipped open the porch door just as Lynn reached it. She grabbed Lynn's arm. "Are the girls all right?"

"Yes, as far as I know. Where are they?"

"At Allison's. I talked to them at about four—" which seemed light-years ago "—but I thought maybe..."

Lynn squeezed her arm gently. "I'm sure they're fine."

"What are you doing here?"

"Can't a girl visit her best friend?"

"Oh, sure. Come in."

Lynn followed Kate into the kitchen. She unbuttoned her heavy winter jacket as she looked at the countertop. Kate acknowledged Lynn's perusal and sighed. "I'm upset about something. It's no big deal."

"I'm sure you are." Her friend drew in a breath. "And it *is* a big deal."

Her body tensing, Kate said, "I thought you were just here to visit your friend."

"I am. But I know what happened with Jay."

Kate swallowed hard. Felt the tears threaten again at just the mention of his name. "I don't want to talk about this, Lynn."

"Fine, then sit down and I'll talk."

"Listen," Kate went on as if Lynn hadn't spoken. "I tried some new cookies and I have some decaf…"

Lynn grabbed her arm as Kate tried to brush past. "Honey, don't."

Kate closed her eyes to block out Lynn's pity. "How do you know?"

"He's over at our place. With Tom."

Whirling around, Kate stared at her friend. "What?"

"He's beside himself, Kate. I think you should talk to him."

A huge swell of anger shattered Kate's composure. "No! No, I won't talk to him." She shook her head at Lynn. "Look, I know you're a minister and you have to listen to him, but I don't. I won't see him, now or ever."

To give herself time, Kate guessed, Lynn removed her coat and sat down at the table. "Ever?"

"I've made some decisions."

"Kate, it's not—"

"—a good idea to make decisions when I'm angry. Well, I'm done with being sensible, practical Kate. I've had it with being *good* about everything. Now I'm going to do what's best for me."

"And what is that?"

"I'm quitting the bookstore the day after Christmas and moving out of this place as soon as I can. I plan to make the arrangements tomorrow morning."

"I see. And you're just going to let the love of your life go without a fight."

Hurt, strong and vicious, surged inside her. "The love of my life is engaged to someone else, Lynn. Or did he keep that minor detail from you like he did me?"

"He told us. But he has an explanation you didn't give him a chance to tell."

"I don't want to hear it. What's more, I don't like that you're siding with him."

They faced each other across the kitchen table. Not even a flicker of resentment crossed Lynn's face. "You know in your heart I would never do anything to hurt you."

Kate braced her elbows on the table and bowed her head. "Of course, I know that. I'm sorry. I was out of line."

"Listen to me, Kate. Please."

"Oh, Lynn, I can't."

"I'm going to have to insist."

Kate crossed to the counter and poured them coffee. Then she reseated herself across from Lynn.

"He's overwrought, Kate."

"I'm sorry, Lynn, but that's hard for me to believe." She didn't take her eyes off the dark liquid in her mug. "Quite frankly, I'm surprised he isn't with Mallory."

"Mallory's on her way back to New York. *Without* the engagement ring."

"It doesn't matter."

"I think it does."

Kate looked into her friend's face. "Lynn, he spent an incredible night of lovemaking with me while he was engaged to someone else."

"And he was wrong."

She slapped her hand on the table. "Very wrong! What's more, he purposely set out to pursue me, to get me back in his bed, when he was still engaged to her." The smooth sophistication of Mallory Claybourne's face swam before Kate, fueling her fury.

"I know. He told Tom and me that he planned to break the engagement with Mallory when he saw her again and then ask you to marry him."

Marry him. At the words, her heart skipped a beat. But she was quick to stifle the joy she felt. "And you believed him?"

"Yes, I did. If you could see him, you would, too."

"I never want to see him again. And I don't believe what he told you." She scrutinized Lynn's face. "Don't you understand, Lynn? He'd say anything, do anything to get his way."

"That's your hurt talking."

"No, it's common sense. What he's done is detestable. He's a horrible person."

"Actually, I think he's a good person. It's what got him into this current misunderstanding."

Kate leaped up, causing her chair to fall over and clatter to the floor. "It's not a misunderstanding, Lynn. I saw the ring on her finger." The diamond winking in the store's overhead lights had been cold, hard proof.

Remaining calm, Lynn gazed up at her. "He told us he didn't want to break it off over the phone with Mallory. That he might have done something that cold and callous once, but now he knew he would do it face-to-face. As soon as he was able to leave Riverbend, he planned to go to New York and tell her in person that he couldn't marry her.''

Kate paced the kitchen. "Do you hear what you're saying? If he really cared about me, he would have been honest with me about this whole thing.''

"That was a mistake in judgment.''

"Well, it's a mistake I can't forgive.'' Kate avoided looking at her friend. "I'll never forgive him, Lynn. You can tell him that.''

After a long pause, Lynn said, "He's going to stay out at Tom's place. Tom's taking him there now. Jay said he thought you wouldn't want him staying in the apartment over the bookstore.''

"I don't.'' Kate stopped pacing. "And give him a message for me. Ask him not to come to work for a few days. He gets time off, which he's never taken, so assure him he won't lose his inheritance by staying away.''

"Kate—''

"No, Lynn. This conversation is over!'' Kate stared down at her friend implacably. "I won't talk about it again.''

THE FOLLOWING MORNING at eight o'clock, Kate sipped coffee in the kitchen of Jay's farmhouse, trying desperately to quell the headache that had begun last night and never really gone away, despite the painkiller she'd taken. Combined with the fact that she'd gotten almost no sleep, she was as jittery as a junkie needing a fix.

For most of the night, she'd prowled the house, thinking about Lynn's arguments, then juxtaposing them with the facts of Jay's deception right from the first morning she'd met him. She also remembered what he'd told her about his father and Sarah, but she refused to consider that. In the clear light of day, she refused to feel sorry for him. Instead, she got up, showered, dressed and was headed out the door when an express deliveryman ambled up the sidewalk. He held a large rectangular box.

"Are you Kate McMann?"

"Yes."

"Sign here, please."

Confused, she signed before realization hit her. This was probably Jay's tenth present.

Taking a deep breath, she marched back into the house, tore off the mailing paper and found a Neiman Marcus box. Inside was a beautiful brown suede coat with dark fur lining. She remembered trying on the coat when she'd been in Chicago once. The smooth lining had slid down her body, its warmth enveloping her. A picture of it, found in a magazine, was in her Wish Folder.

Her eyes stung. He'd been so solicitous. *That coat's not warm enough, Kate. You need something better.* She sagged against the table. Why had he pretended to worry about her? All along he'd been promised to someone else. Kate could hardly bear it.

Straightening, she breathed deeply again, crossed to the garbage bag that held his other gifts and stuffed the beautiful coat inside. Tying the bag up, she made a mental note on her Household Chores list to put the bag out for the trash that night. Then she left the house to run her errands.

She drove straight to the foundry on the outskirts of town. The beige building with few windows loomed before her, big and ugly and smelling of smoke. In no time, she'd gone inside the office, talked to Mr. Conklin, the manager, and secured the job she'd found in the paper the night before. Eight to five. Five days a week. Seven dollars an hour. All he'd said was, "Sure you can do this work, girl?"

"Yes, Mr. Conklin. I'm strong."

As she headed to her next stop, she repeated that mantra: *I'm strong. I can do this. I'm strong.*

Charter's, the restaurant where she'd worked years ago, was open for lunch. The big clapboard restaurant, a stately mansion right out of a Victorian novel, was situated about five miles out, on the other side of Riverbend. As she pulled into the parking lot and trekked up the steps, she recalled the last time she'd waitressed here, pregnant with the twins, heartbroken over Billy's infidelity.

Some things never change.

Inside, she talked to her old manager and told him that this time, she wanted a cocktail-waitress job that didn't start till nine. She knew a woman who did nighttime child care cheaply, and Kate planned to hire her to stay with the twins after they went to bed.

The manager assessed her with a critical eye. "Kate, you were a terrific worker. I'd hire you back in a second. But have you seen the new outfits the cocktail waitresses wear?"

She hadn't, and swallowed hard when he produced the tight black spandex pants and top with the plunging neckline. But she'd shrugged, cavalierly saying it was fine with her. She'd be okay. She would. All the way to Third Street, she had to force herself not to cringe at the clothes on the seat next to her.

But taking the foundry and waitress jobs were easy

compared to entering the "office" for the grungy little duplex she was about to rent. She knew Mrs. Valerio from when she lived there as a child. "Whatsa matter girl? Why you movin' out of the farmhouse and back in here?" Mrs. Valerio asked. There was concern in her tired brown eyes.

"It's being sold the first of the year."

"By that no-good Jacob Steele?"

Her throat tight, Kate answered, "Yes, by that no-good Jacob Steele."

Luckily, the duplex was empty now. Mrs. Valerio told Kate if she cleaned it up herself, she could have it free for the six days between Christmas and New Year's. Without hesitating, Kate signed the lease and took the keys.

She almost changed her mind when she stepped in the front door. It was as horrible as she remembered it. Crossing to a small window, she could barely see out through the grimy panes of glass. The carpet she walked over held stains from God knew what. As she wandered around the cramped space, she noted the living room wall was cracked, and the kitchen appliances were still greasy from the last tenant. Everything needed a new paint job.

Well, she could clean and patch and paint. She'd lovingly redone several rooms in the farmhouse. Though unable to face the two bedrooms upstairs, she told herself the place wouldn't be so bad once their things were here. But she couldn't let the twins see the duplex in this shape. Tonight, after work, she'd ask the aunts to watch the girls and she'd come over and start cleaning. Decision made, she locked up her new home. Head down against the wind, willing herself to be strong, she crossed the crumbling sidewalk and bumped right into someone.

"Oh, I'm sorry." She looked up into the face of Aaron Mazerik.

Aaron's big hands steadied her. "Kate? Hi."

"Hello, Aaron." She glanced at her watch. "Aren't you working today?"

"Yeah, last day before Christmas. I left on my break because my mother's faucet sprung a leak, and she didn't want to bother the superintendent."

Kate shook her head. Poor Aaron. Evie Mazerik still didn't appreciate him.

"What are you doing here?" Aaron asked.

"I, um, just rented a duplex."

He didn't seem surprised. "I'm sorry, Kate. About the whole mess with the will."

"I'll be fine." She wouldn't cry at his kindness. She wouldn't. Shifting from one foot to the other, she smiled tentatively at him.

"Jacob came over early this morning, before school. He had coffee with Lily and me."

Kate frowned.

Aaron studied her. "He was acting strangely. Said some funny things."

"Like what?" she asked, just to be polite.

"Oh, how glad he was we were brothers. How he hoped things between us were straight. How he wanted to stay in touch."

"It's hard not to stay in touch in Riverbend."

"I know." Aaron stuck his hands in his pockets. "It sounded almost as if he was saying goodbye."

Kate thought she'd better warn Aaron. "After he fulfills the terms of the will, I'm not sure he'll be staying here, Aaron. You should be prepared for that."

"Oh, I am. But I was under the impression that wasn't going to happen until January first."

"He's a complicated man." Kate shrugged. "Who knows why he does what he does."

"Yeah, I guess." Aaron peered at her closely. "You all right?"

She pulled her fleece coat around her, but the wind whipped right through it. "Yeah, I'm fine. Just cold. It was nice talking to you."

Turning away, she hesitated at his next words. "Kate, if you need to talk, I'm a pretty good listener." His gaze darted to the duplex. "I grew up here, too. I know what it's like."

Emotion threatened to overwhelm Kate. "Thanks, Aaron, I'll remember that."

AT FOUR O'CLOCK that afternoon, Kate was tallying up Christmas receipts in the office, fatigue heavy on her shoulders and neck, and vying for prominence with the headache. What a day. Ruth and Rachel had sensed something was wrong and had questioned her gently but firmly about why Jay was at Tom's and what she'd been doing in the neighborhood she'd grown up in— apparently a neighbor had seen her. Kate stalled them on both questions.

As soon as Izzy arrived, the aunts had left. To see Jay, Kate guessed. Kate was refilling coffee in the front when Mitch Sterling and Charlie Callahan strode through the door.

"Hi, guys. What's up?"

"We're looking for Jacob," Mitch said.

"He, um, has today off."

Mitch pulled a white envelope from his pocket.

"This is a letter from him. Do you know what it's all about?"

"No. Why would he write you a letter?"

Charlie shrugged. "Dunno. I got one, too. So did Wally Drummer."

"I don't understand."

"Neither do we. All three letters say—"

Kate held up her hand. "Stop, Charlie. It's none of my business what's in those letters."

Mitch stepped close and squeezed her arm. "Isn't it? I delivered some supplies to the foundry today. What's this about you taking a job there?"

Small towns. At times like these, Kate hated them. "I won't be working here after Christmas."

"Why?"

Anger came, quick and cutting. "It belongs to Jacob now."

"He fire you?" Charlie asked skeptically.

"No, I'm quitting."

Several customers came through the door, sparing Kate from further grilling. "Look, I've got to help out here. I'm sorry I can't talk any longer."

Making a beeline for the customers, she could see out of the corner of her eye both men stare at her, speak to each other and then finally leave.

She checked the clock. Wasn't this day ever going to end?

THE NEXT MORNING wasn't any better. Her head still hurt, and as she drove to the store, sleet pelted her windows. The twins sat sullenly in the back seat; all that could be heard was the soft swish of the windshield wipers.

Hannah's voice broke the silence. "We don't wanna go to day care today."

"We wanna see Mr. Lawrence," Hope added.

That refrain had frayed Kate's nerves for hours last night, until she lost her temper and told them curtly that talk of Mr. Lawrence was to cease.

"It'll be busy at the store today. Since school's closed, I can't watch you there."

"Mr. Lawrence would watch us," Hannah said, pouting.

"No, he's busy, too."

"He likes us. He'd watch us."

The pounding in her head escalating, Kate struggled for calm. "I told you both last night, you shouldn't count on Mr. Lawrence too much. He's only visiting Riverbend."

Tears welled up in Hope's eyes, just as they had when Kate had first broached the subject. She'd prayed the twins would bounce back today, but she'd apparently underestimated Jay's influence on them.

"Tell you what. You can come to the store until it opens at ten. We'll have some of that coffee cake I made last night, and hot chocolate. Then I'll take you to day care, okay?"

Somewhat mollified, they were quiet for the rest of the trip. When they reached Steele Books, she herded them inside and was surprised to find both Ruth and Rachel sitting on one of the couches. Their choice of cheery, holiday-red wool suits belied the somber looks on their faces. The twins, equally morose, ran right to them.

"Hi," Kate said, removing her coat. "Why are you here so early?"

"We must talk, dear." Rachel cuddled Hope on her lap but held Kate's gaze.

"I don't want to talk."

"We thought you wouldn't." Ruth stood and, gripping Hannah's hand, held out a big square manila envelope.

"What's that?"

"It's the eleventh Christmas gift for you. From Jacob."

Stepping back, Kate stared at the envelope. "I'm sorry, Ruth, I can't accept it. Give it back to him."

"That isn't possible now."

Kate frowned, not understanding.

"Actually, Katie, it's for all five of us." Rachel's smile was sad.

"Us, too?" Hannah asked.

"Yes, love."

"It doesn't matter." Kate tried to be firm. "We can't accept a gift from him."

"Yes, we can, Mommy." Hope began to plead.

"At least see what it is, Katie," Ruth said.

"No."

"I'll look." Before Kate could stop her, Hannah snatched the envelope out of Ruth's hand and tore it open. Brochures fell to the floor, along with airline tickets and a white sheet of paper. Hannah picked up the brochures. "Mommy, it's Disney World."

Hope joined Hannah on the floor. She grabbed the note.

Every ounce of fight drained out of Kate. How could he play so dirty? "What is this, Ruth?"

Before Ruth could answer, Hope held up the paper. "It's from Mr. Lawrence. It says, 'Dear Kate. Please accept this gift for you, the girls and my aunts. It's all a…ar… I don't know the word.''

"Hope, can you read that note?" Kate asked incredulously. Everyone else stared at the shy child on the floor.

"Uh-huh.''

"How long have you been able to read?"

"I dunno. A long time. Mr. Lawrence guessed. We were gonna surprise you Christmas morning.''

Stunned by the revelation, Kate watched openmouthed as Ruth took the paper from Hope. "I'll finish it. 'It's all arranged and paid for, starting December twenty-seventh. I've gotten coverage at the store—'''

"Stop!" Kate cried, grabbing the paper and ripping it to shreds. "This isn't fair. He can't do this. He can't—''

Loud banging at the back of the store stopped her tirade. After a few stunned, silent seconds, Rachel stood and smoothed down her skirt. Then she walked to the rear entrance. Hope, Hannah and Ruth all stared at Kate accusingly.

The tableau was broken by the reappearance of Rachel, followed by two men, who were carrying a huge, heavy piece of wood wrapped in plastic. "These are deliverymen, Kate. They say this was supposed to come tomorrow, but they got Saturday off, so they brought it today.''

Kate closed her eyes. Now what? She couldn't deal with this. "I don't want it, whatever it is.''

The eyebrows of the deliverymen skyrocketed. "What?"

"I don't want it.''

"Yes, you do, dear.'' Rachel's voice was firm as she put her arm around Kate. Kate leaned into her. "Set it right there," Rachel ordered. "Facing out, please." When they turned the thing around, Kate could see some black script through the plastic.

No one moved until the deliverymen left. Then Rachel crossed to the counter and found a pair of scissors. Kate wrapped her arms around her waist, summoning the courage to face this newest onslaught. When the plastic fell away, she stared at what was revealed.

It was a beautifully scripted sign. In calligraphy just like the one over the store. Except it read *McMann Books*.

This time Kate couldn't stop the tears. "I don't understand."

The bell tinkled over the door and Kate closed her eyes. She turned to find a tall, broad-shouldered man in a leather jacket poised in the entrance.

For a minute she thought it was Jay.

But it wasn't; it was Nick Harrison.

"Hi, Kate." He studied her before glancing around the room. "Is this a bad time?"

No one spoke. Spotting the sign, he said, "Oh, I see you know already."

"Know?"

He set his briefcase on the counter, opened it and withdrew a sheaf of papers. Then he looked at her.

"Know what, Nick?"

"That the store is yours." He held up the papers. "Here's the documentation."

"Mine? I don't understand."

Nick's eyes sought out Rachel's. She nodded to him and he continued. "Jacob left town last night, Kate."

"But that's crazy. He can't leave town. If he does, he won't fulfill the terms of the will."

"That's right, Katie," Ruth said. "Jacob didn't fulfill the terms of the will."

Everyone stared at Kate.

Rachel soft voice broke the charged silence. "He's given you the store and the farmhouse, dear. Legally, they're yours now."

CHAPTER FIFTEEN

THE WIND BLEW DOWN Fifth Avenue and bit Jay in the face, like an angry god demanding payback. Buttoning up his black cashmere coat and tightening Rachel's scarf around his neck, he ignored his raw cheeks and frozen lips. When the snow started to fall, in big fat flakes the size of fifty-cent pieces, he hunched his shoulders and kept walking. He deserved the physical pain. He deserved a whole lot more than that.

What kind of man are you?… You're more of a bastard than your father…

That Kate had been right had tortured him more than any physical punishment could. He was in agony over what he'd done to her. Picturing her tearstained face the last time he'd seen her, he quickened his pace. But in every store window he looked in he saw her. Every whistle of the wind carried the words she'd said when she thought he was someone else. *You're a good man…you're a lifesaver…I care about you, too.*

"Well, not anymore," he mumbled, crossing the street, heedless of the honking cabs and hurrying city dwellers anxious to get home for supper. The bustle of Christmas mocked him. It was five o'clock on December 23, and he had nowhere to go. His own fault. He could be at several parties. He'd found the invitations, neatly opened and stacked up by his housekeeper, who'd looked after his Park Avenue apartment while he was gone. He could have even been with Mallory. They lived in the same building, and he'd bumped into her on his way out this afternoon, when the walls of his own apartment closed in on him, and he couldn't stop thinking about how he'd bungled things.

"This is a surprise," Mallory had said with an astonishing lack of animosity.

"Hello, Mallory."

Her perfectly shaped brows arched. "Didn't it work out with the shopkeeper?"

His heart had lurched in his chest. "No, it didn't."

She seemed to sense his distress. "You really love her, don't you."

He could only nod.

Clearly, she was puzzled. Neither of them had experienced that depth of feeling for each other, and they both knew it. But they'd been good business partners. And friends.

"Then I'm sorry." She'd shrugged. "It's four. I could fix you an early cocktail."

"No, thanks."

"If you change your mind, I'll be in until six."

"Thanks, Mallory. I don't deserve your kindness."

Finally Jay stopped walking to take stock of where he was. Across the street, a crowded store beckoned. *Don't go there,* his inner self warned. But he went into F.A.O. Schwarz, anyway.

Of course, the famous toy store was mobbed with kids and harried parents; he threaded his way among them, wishing he was here with Hope and Hannah. When he passed a board game display, he stopped and stared at it...

Uncle Wiggly says go back three spaces. He wondered if Kate knew yet that Hope could read. It had been his and Hope's little secret, and they'd planned a big surprise Christmas morning for Kate. Swallowing hard, he continued through the store, his stomach clenching at every sight of a toy he knew the girls would like.

Damn, he could still feel their solid weight in his arms, recall their strong hugs, remember Hannah hiding her face against him when she spilled punch on Sarah's dress. He wanted so badly to be their father he almost couldn't stand it.

A display of Christmas books twisted the knife of regret in his gut. He gulped back the sense of loss. But when the strains of ''I'll Be Home for Christmas'' suddenly blared around him, he decided to leave. For fifteen years, he'd hated that song.

On his way out, he came upon a display of ornaments, and right in the center was an angel with cornsilk-blond hair and big blue eyes. She looked so much like the twins, he could hardly breathe. Unable to stop himself, he picked up the decoration and got in line at the cash register. Ordering himself to think about something else, he pictured Ruth and Rachel.

After paying for the decoration, he walked out into the cold again and headed down Fifth Avenue. He'd told his aunts how he'd ruined things when he went to say goodbye...

''I blew it with her.''

''No!'' Rachel had protested. ''Give her time.''

''I have to leave.''

Their panic-stricken looks shamed him.

''We'll make arrangement to see each other. But I can't stay and ruin her Christmas.''

''Jacob, you'll lose your inheritance.''

''I've already lost what matters most,'' he'd told

them. "I want her to have the store and the farm-house."

"If you love her so much, stay and work it out."

"I love her too much to stay." He'd hugged them tightly and said, "I promise we won't lose touch again…"

He was nearing his apartment building when a window display caught his eye. It was the suede coat he'd bought for Kate. He wondered what she thought of his gift. If she'd even wear it. Material possessions weren't important to her; she was more appreciative of little things, and it had made him angry that she'd never had more in her life. Cooking her dinner…*This is so sweet of you…* When he grocery shopped…*Nobody ever did anything like this for me before…* And he knew that she loved the thought behind the gifts from her Wish Folder more than the gifts themselves. Damn, she didn't deserve the life she'd had. Maybe her future would be better. Who would she share it with?

Is Flannigan a boyfriend?…Nick Harrison sure seems interested…

The thought of another man touching her was almost enough to drive him into the bar adjacent to his build-ing. But he'd promised to call Ruth and Rachel tonight. He returned home in a daze of recrimination. Exiting the elevator, head down, he found his way to his apart-ment, unlocked his door and stepped inside.

And halted.

Coming from the den he heard Christmas music. Had he left the TV or stereo on? No, he was sure he hadn't. Was this his housekeeper's day to come? No, he'd given her the holidays off. What the hell was going on? The building was secure. No one could get in or up the elevator without a key, let alone into his apartment.

Wait, Mallory had a key to his place. Shrugging out of his coat and gloves, he left the scarf around his neck to remind him to be kind and headed for the den. All he needed was another confrontation. In the doorway, he geared himself up for it.

But what he heard made him suck in his breath. What he saw deflated him like a balloon losing air.

"On the fourth day of Christmas, my true love gave to me…" played softly from his stereo, and next to the row of windows was a vision. He would have thought he was hallucinating, but the scent of the bubble bath, his second present to her, permeated the room, and her new suede coat was tossed over the leather couch.

Kate stared at him, a mirage come to life. She wore the cashmere dress he'd given her. Her hair was curled and gloriously full around her face, which, though it looked tired, held a small smile. "Hi," she said simply.

His eyes stung and he gulped back the emotion in his throat. Gripping the doorjamb for support, he said, "Hi. I, um, I don't understand. How did you get in here? How did you get to New York?"

"I drove."

"From Riverbend? It had to take you—"

"Fourteen hours and twenty-six minutes. I would have made it sooner, but I got stuck in rush-hour traffic when I hit the city."

"You *drove?* Here?"

"Yes."

"Why?"

"I was afraid I wouldn't be able to get a flight like you did. Your aunts said you waited standby for ten hours. I didn't want to risk it."

"Alone? You drove to New York *alone?*"

"Uh-huh. But don't worry. I had a Travel Safety list from Ruth and Rachel." She smiled and ticked off the directives on her fingers. "Don't pick up strangers. Drink coffee to stay awake. Stop halfway and get a motel room to sleep. Call them every two hours." She gave him a shy smile. "They didn't want me to drive."

He moved farther into the room. "Why did you?"

Shaking back her hair, she met him halfway. "Because I had to see you." She raised her hand and cradled his cheek in her palm. "You're cold."

He leaned into her touch and savored it. "Why are you here?"

"To bring you back to Riverbend."

His heart plummeted. He should have known. She hadn't come to New York for herself. For him. She'd come for his aunts. Stepping back, he went to the bar. "Would you like something to drink?" He poured himself a brandy. After a gulp, he was able to face her again.

"Maybe later. We can celebrate."

"How did you get in here?" He was delaying the inevitable, hearing that she'd come for his aunts, but he wanted to look at her as long as he could. She was so lovely in the outfit… The outfit. Wait a minute. Why would she wear that outfit—his eyes darted to her coat—and why would she wear the coat if she was just here for Ruth and Rachel?

Hope flared and wouldn't be denied this time. Before he could ask her to spell out why she'd come, she was telling him how she'd gotten into the apartment. "I met Mallory coming out of the building. She and I had a little talk. She let me in."

That made him speechless.

"She left her key on the table, but I put it in my purse."

"Wh-why did you do that?"

"Because no other woman's going to have access to you, Jay Lawrence, for a long time."

His eyes closed. "Don't tease me. Please."

He could hear her come near, sense her standing before him. When he opened his eyes, she was looking up at him with an expression he was afraid to decipher. She said, "All right." Looping her arms around his neck, she rose on tiptoe and whispered, "I love you. Come back to Riverbend with me. Celebrate Christmas Eve at the farmhouse. With our family."

Our family. He managed to set his drink down before he crushed her to him. "Do you mean it?"

"Of course I do." Her lips were on his neck, grazing his jaw. Finally, they found his mouth. She kissed him gently, then hungrily.

When he broke the kiss, he buried his face in her hair "I'm so sorry, Katie. For everything I did to you."

"Shh. We're done with that. We both made mistakes, but we're going to put them behind us."

He drew back. "Can you do that?"

"I already have." Her face softened. "I just wish I could take back the awful things I said to you."

"Oh, sweetheart…" He hugged her again.

After a long moment, she pulled away. "You *do* want this, don't you?" she asked, seeming uncertain for some reason.

"Are you kidding? I've been so miserable I thought I'd die."

She didn't look convinced. Then it hit him. She'd said she loved him. And he hadn't said it back. Hadn't said it to anyone in fifteen years.

Cupping her face in his hands, he stared into eyes so green and so warm he wanted to lose himself in them for a lifetime. "I love you, Mary Katherine McMann. More than life itself."

She smiled the biggest smile he'd ever seen and threw herself at him. "Then let's go home."

He held her to him, closed his eyes again and thought, *Yes, love, let's go home. To Riverbend.*

EPILOGUE

FROM THE DOORWAY, Kate watched Hannah gaze long-ingly at the angel on the top of the Christmas tree. The little blond figure resembled her and Hope, and Hannah had begged to play with it since Jay had put it up there Christmas Eve.

Hannah's gaze traveled from the angel to the oak mantel over the fireplace, then to the hassock beside the chair in the corner, outlining a clear route to the top of the tree. Kate was just about to warn her daughter not to try it when Hannah glanced over at Jay, who sat in a chair on the opposite side of the room leafing through a book with Hope. His gaze lifted to Hannah, and studying the situation, he gave her a meaningful look. After a long moment, Hannah sighed, skipped over to Jay and climbed onto his lap with her sister.

Jay smiled broadly at Hannah. Kissing the top of her head, he said, "Good girl."

Kate shook her head. Her wild child had changed since Kate and Jay were married on December 27 at Disney World, with two sets of twins as witnesses. Simon had been right—Hannah needed a father to temper her spunkiness, and Jay had embraced the job. For the past two weeks, since they'd returned from New York City, he had entrenched himself so deeply in the girls' lives that it seemed he'd always been a part of their family. Watching the big man with the linebacker shoulders—wearing the red sweater they'd gotten him for his birthday—cuddle two little girls, daintily dressed in denim jumpers and red-checked blouses, Kate thanked God for the new life she'd been given.

When she crossed into the room, Jay glanced up at her. Undiluted joy and love suffused his face. "Hi, babe."

"Hi." She perched on the edge of the chair, smoothing down the red velour dress he'd bought her. "What do you have there?"

"A new book Jacob brought home from the store today," Hope said as her fingers crept to her mouth; but she pulled them away before they made contact. With Jay's encouragement, little Hope's New Year's resolution had been to stop sucking her fingers, and she'd had six days of success.

Kate rolled her eyes. "What is it this time?"

Hannah giggled, in on the joke. *Susie Wants a Brother.*

Shaking her head, Kate gave Jay a sideways glance. The glint in his eyes made her shiver.

"When we gonna have a brother, Mommy?" Hope asked.

"As soon as we can, sweetheart." She frowned at Jay. "It might make the waiting easier if your stepdaddy would quit bringing these kinds of books home from the store." For several nights running, he'd shown up with titles like *That New Baby* and *Mommy Has a Child.*

"Just gettin' us all ready for when it happens." One eyebrow arched. "Actually, I thought an announcement might be my birthday present."

"You know it's too soon for that." Kate feigned

chagrin, but she, too, was hoping that she might have good news any day now.

"Well, we'll keep workin' on it," he said with a wink.

"What does that mean, Mommy?" Hannah wanted to know. "How you gonna work on it?"

Raising her chin, Kate said, "You tell her, wise guy."

The doorbell chimed, saving Jay from having to explain his teasing remark. "That must be Ruth and Rachel."

To celebrate Jay's thirty-sixth birthday, the six of them had gone out to dinner at Charter's; the aunts had said they'd meet Jay and Kate back here for cake and ice cream. They had something to do first.

Toppling off his lap, the girls raced to the front door. Jay reached over and laid a palm on her stomach. "It *could* have already happened, love."

She grinned. "I hope so."

He held her tightly, as he sometimes did, reminding them both how they'd almost lost each other. "I love you."

"I love you, too. Have you had a nice birthday?"

"The best ever."

From the doorway Kate heard Hannah say, "They're smoochin' again, Aunt Ruth. Jacob says we better get used to it."

Ruth giggled. "Maybe you'll get a baby brother out of it."

Kate sighed, just as the doorbell rang again.

From the hallway, Rachel called out, "I'll get it."

Jay said, "That must be the Baineses and the Mazeriks." Though Aaron and Tom hadn't come along to dinner tonight, they'd promised to be at the farmhouse for dessert.

Jay stood just as Tom and Lynn entered, with Lily and Aaron right behind.

"Happy Birthday, cuz." Tom shook hands with Jay and presented him with a bottle of wine. Kate noted how Tom's dark eyes were untroubled now that he'd been married almost a month.

After helping Lily remove her coat, Aaron crossed to Jay. A little shyly he said, "Happy Birthday, bro," and handed him a large square box. "It's a basketball."

Setting the package down, Jay bypassed Aaron's outstretched hand and gave him a bear hug.

The doorbell sounded again, and Kate watched Ruth and Rachel exchange odd looks. Something was going on.

As Ruth answered it, Jay asked Kate, "You didn't plan anything else for my birthday, did you?"

"No. You said you wanted just the family."

Accompanied by Ruth, the Sterlings entered the room.

"Mitch, Tessa, hi," Kate said. She cooed at the sleeping baby Tessa carried as Caleb, Mitch's father, and Sam, his son, came in behind them.

"Can I hold Laura Marie?" Hannah asked.

Sam edged in around Caleb. "Why does everybody wanna hold her, Grandpa?" He spoke the words and signed them. The twins studied him carefully; he'd been teaching them sign language.

Caleb ruffled Sam's hair. "You should talk, boy. Every time I turn around, you got her out of the crib."

When Charlie and Beth arrived minutes later, Jay felt a sense of well-being so strong it warmed his heart.

"Hey, this looks like a gathering of the old River Rats."

Ruth said, "It sort of is, dear. Now, if you all will take a seat, Rachel has something she wants to share with you."

Jay noticed that Ruth's voice wavered. And Rachel seemed nervous, too. Dressed to kill in navy wool suits, they kept darting glances from him to each other. Kate must have seen it, as well, because she moved closer to him. God, he didn't know what he'd do without this woman. She had quietly become the center of his life.

"Is everything all right, Ruth?" Kate asked.

"Yes, dear. Sit."

They all sat—Beth and Charlie on the floor near the fire, holding hands, knees touching; the Baineses also took the floor with their backs to the couch. Caleb made sure Tessa, holding the baby, had a padded chair, then he and Mitch brought in two hard-back chairs from the kitchen while Sam settled near the television. Aaron and Lily sat on one end of the couch, and Kate and Jay the other, with the twins at their feet.

Rachel faced Jay. "Jacob, I have a birthday present for you."

He cocked his head as she drew a small rectangular package from her purse. "A videotape? It's not of me when I was growing up, is it?" He scanned the room. "Or of the River Rats?"

"No." Her voice was hoarse.

"Rachel?" he asked gently. "What is it?"

"It's a video that Abraham left to me in his will."

A hush fell over the room. No one, not even the twins, spoke a word. Jay felt Kate's arm twine through his.

At last she said, "What's on the tape, Rachel?"

"I'm not exactly sure. The note with it asked me not to play it until Jacob's birthday. If he had come back to stay in Riverbend by then, I was to invite all the people in this room to come together and view it."

Jay looked at his half brother. "Aaron, do you want to do this?"

Lily squeezed her husband's arm. After a long pause, Aaron said, "I'm okay with it."

"Then go ahead, Rachel." Jay sat back, and Hope climbed onto his lap. He held her closely as Rachel placed the video in the cassette and switched on the TV. Before she joined Ruth on the love seat, she gave the remote control to Jay. He stared at it a moment, then pressed "play."

The video began.

Nothing could have prepared Jay for the sight of his father on the screen. Abraham had aged, of course, since Jay had last seen him. His thick head of hair was white, and he was thinner. He wore wire-rim glasses. But his dark eyes were sharp as he looked at the camera from where he was seated in the fancy chintz chair in the living room of his East Poplar Street home.

"I assume, if you're watching this, that I've passed on—" the deep baritone sent a chill through Jay "—and my bequests have been given out." The old man swallowed hard. "I also assume that Jacob has come home, and that Aaron knows who his father is."

Sam Sterling edged closer to the TV, and Hannah said, "That's old Mr. Steele, from the bookstore."

"Yes, honey, it is," Kate told her daughter.

Jay heard some sniffling from the corner. He glanced over and saw his aunts holding hands, tears streaming down their cheeks. He pushed the "pause" button.

"We don't have to do this, Ruth, Rachel. If it's too hard."

"No, we're fine. Go on."

"Aaron?" Jay saw how his brother gripped Lily's hand.

"I want to hear it."

Lynn said, "Jay, if *you* don't feel up to this…"

"No, I'm okay." Taking another deep breath, he pressed "play."

Abraham continued, "You're probably wondering how I had time to determine all these bequests. Well, I just found out from Julian Bennett that I have a weak heart—the arteries to be exact. We're talking about some bypass surgery. Nobody else knows about this, and I want it that way. I'm grateful that it's given me time to put things in order." He paused and seemed to look at everyone. "I'd like to talk to each of you, personally—" he smiled "—well, as personally as this thing can get, and explain a few things. I'll start with Lily Holden."

Lily gave a start.

"I hope you like the paintings. I left them to you as an inspiration. I gave you your first set of paints, and from what I heard, you didn't follow through with your art. You should. You have talent, and I'd like to know my eye didn't deceive me. Go for it, young lady."

Lily smiled at the screen and whispered, "I am, Abraham."

Abraham stared at the camera. "Mitch Sterling, I hope you brought Sam with you, as I asked. And your father." Abraham seemed to give the old man a mocking smile. "Did you ever tell them about the bet we had that day at the river, Caleb?"

Caleb chuckled and nodded.

"Do you remember we bet a quarter that I could make it across the icy river? And I didn't?" He chuckled. "You saved my hide."

Sam laughed. Mitch and Tessa smiled.

Abraham went on, "Well, I never paid off the bet, so I left Sam that amount, with savings, interest and investments taken into consideration. It amounts to twenty-seven thousand dollars and change."

Sam straightened. "That's how much money he left me, right, Grandpa?"

"Sure did."

Abraham said a few words to Sam about the kind of man his grandpa was, then finished, "And that daddy of yours. I hope he finds somebody soon. He needs a good woman."

Mitch leaned over to drop a kiss on Tessa's hair. "I did, Abraham," he said.

Another pause.

"Charlie and Beth Callahan, you there?"

Beth said, "He got my name wrong."

"Not for long," Charlie told her, taking her hand.

"Do you like your houseboat? You both always loved it, and I figured that was where it all started between you two. You were too young to realize it, though, so I'm giving you a second chance, hoping you've grown out of your damned stubbornness and can get together about the boat." His dark eyes glinted with mischief. "You're gonna have to deal with each other now, and maybe those sparks will fly again."

Beth said with feigned indignation, "Why, that old geezer, he planned this all along."

Charlie tugged her close and kissed her. "Looks that way, doll."

Everybody laughed.

"Now. Let's see. My nephew Tom Baines around?"

Tom straightened and, like the others, behaved as if Abraham was actually in the room speaking to him. "Yes, Uncle Abe," he said dutifully.

Abraham's expression was thoughtful. "A man needs roots, boy. A place he can always return to. I know you're some hotshot reporter, but Riverbend, Indiana, is your home, and I wanted you to have a place to come back to when you needed it. So I left you one of the farmhouses."

Jay could tell Tom was choked up.

Now Abraham stared sternly out at the camera. "Ruth and Rachel, I left you all that money, but don't go spending it on just anything. You especially, Ruthie. No more Jack Kerouac books. You know how I felt about that."

"You old coot," Ruth said, tears sparkling in her eyes. "I'll buy whatever I want with it."

"Rachel, you keep her in line." Everyone laughed. Abraham smiled, as though he could see them. "I loved you, sisters. I hope you knew that."

"We knew." Rachel whispered.

"We loved you, too," Ruth told him.

As if on some hidden signal, Hope slid off Jay's lap and Hannah stood up, and they both ran into the aunts' arms.

Jay inched closer to Kate, his throat tight, his eyes glued to the screen.

Abraham leaned over and linked his hands between his knees. "Aaron, I have a few things to say to you. The money I left you was so you could keep your summer basketball program going. But Nick Harrison will soon be telling you that I've also put more in trust for your children." Abraham sighed heavily. "My grandchildren.'' He cleared his throat. ''I have two regrets in life, boy. The first is not telling the truth about you. You turned out well, no thanks to me, and I want you to know I respect the man you became on your own. I was a fool for never claiming you.'' Moisture sparkled in the old man's eyes. ''I'm very proud of you, son.''

Without a word, Aaron stood and quietly walked out of the room. Lily followed him.

Jay gripped Kate's hand tighter. ''Jacob, my last regret is what I did to you.''

Closing his eyes briefly, Jay struggled to remain in control.

''I never should have done what I did and I'm sorry. I hope your being back in town means you came to claim the bookstore, the farmhouse, and Katie and her girls.''

Kate sputtered, *''What?''*

Abraham chuckled. ''Now don't get your back up, Katie girl. I've known for years you were the right one for my boy, and I was hoping my little scheme would show you that.''

''Why, you manipulative old man,'' Jay said softly.

Kate shook her head. ''I don't believe it.''

''However, Jacob, in case you didn't see the wisdom of my plan, I've left Katie plenty of money in a separate account so she can have the life she wanted, anyway.'' He chuckled. ''Harrison had instructions to keep that quiet, too. Until now.''

Sighing, Kate stared at the screen's image. ''Oh, Abraham.''

''I want you to find happiness, Jacob. I want that for Aaron, too.''

From the corner of his eye, Jay saw Aaron had come

back into the room to watch the rest of the tape. "I hope both you boys learn from my mistakes. Take care of those you love and never let them down. I let both of you down and I died regretting it. Missing so much of your lives was my punishment." Again he cleared his throat. "Stay in Riverbend. Be better Steeles for the town than I was. Let that be my legacy to both of you."

Jay's eyes stung. He sensed that Aaron had come back to the couch, and then felt his brother place a comforting hand on his shoulder.

With one last smile that seemed to encompass the whole room, Abraham nodded and the screen went dark.

For a moment, no one spoke. Then Hope and Hannah climbed off the aunts' laps. "Can we have cake and ice cream now?"

Tessa got to her feet with the baby. "I'll get it out. Sam, come with me. You can watch Laura."

Choruses of "I'll help" came from around the room. Soon it was only Jay and Kate, Lily and Aaron and the aunts left in the family room.

Head down, Jay took a few moments to compose himself, then looked over at Aaron. Aaron gave Jay's shoulder a last squeeze.

Ruth and Rachel came to stand before them, and both men rose. They exchanged sad smiles. "We love you boys," Rachel said, first hugging Jay, then Aaron.

Trying to lighten the mood, Ruth put in, "Glad we got two strappin' young men to take care of us when we get old."

"We're never getting old, sister," Rachel quipped, then took her hand, and they, too, went into the kitchen.

Jay and Aaron faced each other.

"Well," Aaron said simply. "That was something."

"Yes, it was." Jay smiled. "Brother."

Aaron smiled back, took Lily's arm and left the room. Jay turned to Kate and put his hands on her waist.

"Matchmaking from the grave," he said, chuckling.

She smiled up at him. "Are you glad?"

"Very." More than he could ever express. More than she'd probably ever know. As he bent his head to kiss her, Jay felt a tug on his shirt. He looked down to see Hannah, her face smeared with chocolate. "After you and Mommy have cake," she asked ingenuously, "are you gonna work on my baby brother?"

"Sounds good to me," he whispered against Kate's mouth.

"Me, too," she whispered back.

After a solid kiss, Jay grasped Hannah's hand and led her and his wife to the kitchen, where his family and friends waited to celebrate his birthday.

On the way, he offered up a silent prayer of thanks.

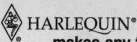